Ten years of hoping, of longing, of wishing . . .

and now he had Shay back in his arms.

Ten years of remembering the rich taste of her, the seductive scent of her. Ten years of struggling against the need for her, of yearning for the touch of her.

Ten years of agony, dissolving in a kiss....

She'd been a girl when he'd first touched her, but the years had ripened her, and her full breasts pressing against his chest had him aching.

Breathing hard, Luke abruptly pulled back, fighting his reaction. Her hold on him was breathtaking. This small woman could make him beg, could bring him to his knees. She was in his blood, in his heart. But how could he ever keep her in his life?

Dear Reader,

Welcome to Silhouette **Special Edition** . . . welcome to romance. Each month Silhouette **Special Edition** publishes six novels with you in mind—stories of love and life, tales that you can identify with—as well as dream about.

This Valentine's Day month has plenty in store for you. THAT SPECIAL WOMAN!, Silhouette **Special Edition**'s new series that salutes women, features a warm, wonderful story about Clare Gilroy and bad-boy hero Reed Tonasket. Don't miss their romance in *Hasty Wedding* by Debbie Macomber.

THAT SPECIAL WOMAN! is a selection each month that pays tribute to women—to us. The heroine is a friend, a wife, a mother—a striver, a nurturer, a pursuer of goals—she's the best in every woman. And it takes a very special man to win that special woman!

Also in store for you this month is the first book in the series FAMILY FOUND by Gina Ferris. This book, *Full of Grace,* brings together Michelle Trent and Tony D'Allessandro in a search for a family lost . . . and now found.

Rounding out this month are books from other favorite writers: Christine Rimmer, Maggi Charles, Pat Warren and Terry Essig (with her first Silhouette Special Edition).

I hope that you enjoy this book and all the stories to come. Happy St. Valentine's Day!

Sincerely,

Tara Gavin
Senior Editor

PAT WARREN
SIMPLY UNFORGETTABLE

SPECIAL EDITION®

Published by Silhouette Books New York

America's Publisher of Contemporary Romance

To Aline Moore, my Montana connection,
with gratitude and affection.

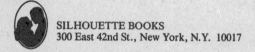

SILHOUETTE BOOKS
300 East 42nd St., New York, N.Y. 10017

SIMPLY UNFORGETTABLE

Copyright © 1993 by Pat Warren

ISBN: 0-373-09797-2

First Silhouette Books printing February 1993

Printed in the U.S.A.

Books by Pat Warren

PAT WARREN

is a mother of four who lives in Arizona with her travel-agent husband and a lazy white cat. She's a former newspaper columnist whose lifetime dream was to become a novelist. A strong romantic streak, a sense of humor and a keen interest in developing relationships led her to try writing romance novels, with which she feels very much at home.

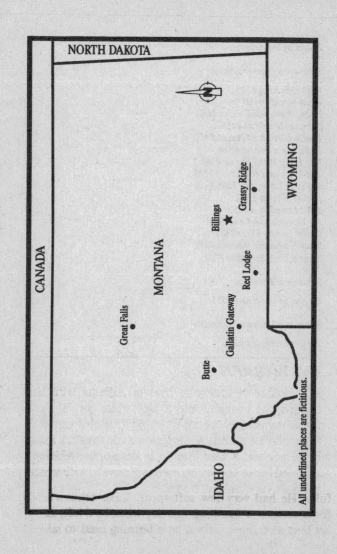

NORTH DAKOTA

CANADA

MONTANA

WYOMING

IDAHO

Great Falls

Butte

Gallatin Gateway

Red Lodge

Billings

Grassy Ridge

All underlined places are fictitious.

Prologue

Luke Turner sat down at the kitchen table and studied the return address on the envelope he held. Liz McKenzie, a woman from his past. Ten years and he hadn't heard a word from her, and now this. He ripped open the envelope and removed the single sheet of pale blue paper.

Dear Luke
This must come as a real shock to you. I learned of your address from Hollis. I realize you may not be able to help me, but I have to try. I need you, Luke. Please come home.

Love, Liz

He read the brief message twice, then sat back thoughtfully. He had very few soft spots, Luke acknowledged, fewer now than that long-ago day when he'd left, nursing his hurt and anger, driven by a burning need to succeed.

Ten years knocking around, first on the rodeo circuit, then working on three different cattle ranches in Oklahoma, Wyoming and Texas, had toughened the green twenty-four-year-old he'd been and made him harder and more cynical. Except when it came to Liz McKenzie, the woman who'd been the only mother he'd known.

She needed him, she said. Liz, who rarely asked anyone for anything, was asking him to go back. She was one of the few people he couldn't refuse. Yet the thought of returning to the Circle M Ranch had his stomach tightening with nerves.

His visit was bound to be rough. Memories lingered in every corner of the place, some good and some bad. Luke wasn't a man who dwelled on the past, but back there, it would be difficult to ignore. He would have to face Jacob McKenzie, Liz's husband and the driving force of the family, while she was the heart of it. Then there'd be their son, Gil, the man Luke had once so badly wanted to think of as a brother. And Rhea, the pesky kid sister who'd tagged after them everywhere.

And he would probably have to face Shay.

He'd been in love with Shay McKenzie since he'd been fourteen years old, since the first day he'd arrived at the Circle M Ranch, reluctantly dragged along by the drifter who'd been his father. Gavin Turner had been thin and worn-out before he'd turned forty, ill-equipped to care for himself, much less the motherless boy he'd been left to raise when his wife had died in childbirth. Liz and Jacob had taken one look at the long-legged boy with the hungry eyes and given his father a job.

Luke remembered Gavin's fondness for the bottle during his free hours, but he'd been a hard worker. Yet one day, Gavin had gotten careless and been gored by a bull. They'd buried him as a dry-eyed Luke had stood stoically watching. That evening, Liz had moved him into the big house, giving him his own room, the first he'd ever had, not just a place to sleep in a bunkhouse shared by numerous transient cowboys.

The McKenzies had taught him so much, but Shay had taught him to love. Yet he'd had to leave her, and she'd married another man.

Luke stood and looked around the kitchen, then strolled through the rest of the small house. It was like so many others he'd lived in, a rough-hewn cabin, really. This one was on the Royce Ranch in Texas where he'd managed the cattle operation for the past two years. He'd quit that position yesterday and had just finished packing all his belongings into the two suitcases standing by the door. The rest of his stuff was in the back of his pickup parked out front, along with the horse trailer that would house his stallion on the long drive. The drive he'd been intending to begin this afternoon to his newly purchased ranch in Wyoming.

Until he'd received Liz's letter just now.

Frowning, he stared at the words she'd written in her neat, feminine handwriting. So she'd learned of his whereabouts from Hollis. The grizzly old trail boss had to be somewhere in his seventies by now, having worked for the Circle M when it had been run by Jacob's father. Hollis had been the only one Luke had kept in touch with through the years, mostly because Hollis had taken him under his wing back then. He'd taught Luke how to whittle and how to roll his own cigarettes, and he'd helped him recover from his first beer binge when Luke had been about sixteen. Liz had known of his affection for Hollis and had apparently guessed that if anyone would know where to reach Luke, the old cowhand would.

Yet her note left so much unsaid. Most important, she hadn't given him a clue as to why she needed him. He could call, of course. But her request had been very explicit: *Please come home.*

Luke had been on the move a lot of years working for others. Finally he'd saved enough and decided it was time to work on his own dream. His own place, run his way. The ranch house in Wyoming was bigger than this cabin, though not much, but it was in good repair. Later he could build on. The barns and outbuildings were sturdy and well kept, the pasturelands green and fertile, the water plentiful. He would start slowly, with a few head of purebred cattle and one young, healthy bull.

Like with the house, he could build from there until he had a herd to be proud of. He'd never been afraid of hard work. The best thing his ranch had going for it was that it would be his alone. Finally he would have to answer to no man.

Luke sighed. Now he would have to put his dream on hold. He was a man who'd always paid his own way. Yet some debts you couldn't pay in money alone. And he owed Liz McKenzie.

Luke picked up his bags and walked outside. Wyoming would have to wait. He would drive instead to Montana and the Circle M Ranch.

Whatever Liz McKenzie needed him for, he hoped he'd be in time to help her.

Chapter One

Some things never change, Luke thought, as he slowed his pickup and stopped outside the arched gate of the Circle M Ranch. A wave of nostalgia washed over him as he looked around. The fencing on both sides stretched as far as the eye could see. As boy and man, he'd done his share of repairing those weathered posts and taut barbed wire.

The manager's cabin was the first building on the right and directly across from that sat the guest bungalow. Straight ahead, gleaming white in the noonday sun, was the big house with its slanted green roof and wraparound porch. Beyond that were the barns, the corrals, the bunkhouse, the tenant cabins and acres of fenced pastureland. On the range, he knew, roamed thousands of head of cattle, the life's blood of the Circle M.

Everything looked much as it had when he'd ridden away ten years ago. Yet it seemed different somehow.

Who was it who'd said you can't go home again? Luke wondered. Probably a true statement, yet he had come back to the only place that had ever seemed like home. Back to Grassy Ridge, Montana and the McKenzies.

Luke popped a lemon drop into his mouth, then shifted into gear and drove through the gate. He drew the truck to a halt near the big house and climbed out, then walked around to the horse trailer hitched to his truck to check on his stallion. They'd been on the road several days, and Maverick was restless and anxious to be free. Early on, Luke had learned that a man took care of his horse before he took care of himself, or he'd regret it soon enough.

Murmuring reassuringly to Maverick, Luke took the lead rope and led him down the ramp, walking toward the closest grassy area. The stallion shook his large black head and sniffed the air restively. "Relax, boy, we're finally here," he told Maverick as he tethered him to the wooden post.

His steps slow, Luke strolled to the large side corral, wiping his damp brow with the back of his hand. Damn, but it was hot—and only mid-June. Or was he experiencing a case of nerves, he wondered as he leaned on the top board of the fence. At the sound of horses' hooves approaching, he trained his eyes on the distant pasture. He could see fat summer flies dashing about in the late-morning air and smell the earthy animal scent from the barns.

Then he saw her.

She was on a sleek chestnut mare, riding bareback, her hands buried in the horse's thick mane, heading home. Leaning forward, as one with the animal, Shay's slender legs gripped the mare's thick sides. Her long auburn hair rippled behind her like silken streamers. As she neared, Luke could see her mouth moving, murmuring to her mount, heading for the open corral gate. The horse slowed in response, though obviously reluctant to end the exhilarating run.

Over and over, Shay's father had told her not to ride bareback, Luke remembered, and she'd listened respectfully and nodded as he'd outlined the dangers. Yet she was still doing it years later. She wasn't so much rebellious as stubborn.

He watched Shay slide off gracefully, her booted feet hitting the grass. Faded jeans molded lovingly to her slim frame and she'd rolled up the sleeves of her checkered shirt high on her tan arms. Tossing back her flyaway hair, she began walking along the fence line to cool down the mare, thinking herself unobserved. As she rounded the near turn, she glanced up, then stopped abruptly, nearly stumbling as she recognized him. On her face was a look of stunned disbelief.

Involuntarily Shay raised a hand to her chest in an effort to slow her suddenly racing heart. *Luke Turner. Dear God, after all these years.* Her fingers closed around a silver key that hung on a chain around her neck and she automatically tucked it inside the front opening of her shirt. For long seconds, she didn't move, frozen to the spot, staring at Luke as a myriad of questions slammed into her sluggish brain.

Was it really him? What was he doing here after silently slipping away in the middle of the night without a word, without an explanation? Where had he been all these years and why, now, had he returned?

Swallowing around a lump in her throat, Shay released Dancer to prowl the corral on her own and walked through the gate, closing it behind her.

Wordlessly Luke watched her approach, studying her face with the intensity of a thirsty man who'd been searching too long for water and couldn't quite believe he'd found it at last. She'd been nineteen when he'd last seen her and she'd changed, of course. He'd walked away from a girl, but he now faced a woman.

Seeing her again was like taking a fast kick from a newborn colt in the solar plexus. She was just as slender as she'd been, yet her body had rounded out, fulfilling its early promise. Her hair shimmered with red highlights, hanging loose instead of twisted into a thick braid the way he'd remembered she'd preferred years ago. The freckles she'd hated had faded and her high cheekbones were golden from the sun and slightly flushed now as she returned his gaze.

But it was her eyes that had changed the most. They'd always been warm and guileless, but no more. The shock at seeing him diminished and was replaced by a cool wariness. He saw a new maturity in their brown depths and a loss of innocence that had Luke wanting to reach out, to touch and reassure her.

Instead, he broke the uncomfortable silence. "How have you been, Shay?"

She had prayed for this moment almost as much as she'd dreaded it. Why couldn't she control the furious pace of her pulse that merely looking at him caused? Squaring her shoulders, she tipped up her chin. She would *not* let him know how deeply he'd hurt her. "Fine. I've been fine, Luke."

Luke leaned an elbow on the top of the fence. "You look wonderful."

She didn't acknowledge the compliment, just crossed her arms over her chest in a defensive posture a five-year-old couldn't have misinterpreted. Luke felt a quick flash of old anger. All right, so he'd walked away and left her. But she could have called him back. Instead, she'd turned around and married another man. What right did she have to harbor a grudge, still, after all these years?

Shay kept her gaze on his eyes, those eyes so startlingly blue in his tan face. Yet, as always, she couldn't tell what he was thinking. Luke had always been guarded, always in control. Except maybe that one time.

If he had to come back, why couldn't he have developed a beer belly, bowed legs and a scruffy appearance? she thought. Why did he look even better than he had in her restless dreams? His thick hair was streaked blond from the sun, and the shaggy length that on others looked unkempt, looked natural on Luke. His blue denim shirt stretched over a muscular chest and arms that looked hard as steel. He looked comfortable in his clothes, like an animal does in his skin, with none of the affectations or vanity of some cowboys.

And he looked dangerous.

"What are you doing here?" Shay asked, pleased that her voice wasn't the least bit shaky, while inside, she felt herself slowly shattering.

He meet her eyes. "Your mother asked me to come."

"What?" Shay shook her head. "That can't be."

"But it is. She wrote asking me to return." Did Shay know what was bothering Liz? Would she tell him if she did?

Shay brushed back her hair with a hand that barely trembled. "I can't imagine why."

Luke released a frustrated breath. "I sense that you're angry with me."

How astute of him. Angry? He didn't know the half of it. "Should I be?" she asked testily.

Luke felt as if he were in a play and he'd lost his script. This was a different Shay than he remembered. She'd never been evasive or challenging, but rather open and up-front. As he preferred to be. "No, I don't think you should be."

"You don't?" She'd had enough of his games. "How about the way you ran out on us all?" *Especially me. You ran away and left me aching for you.*

Luke held on to his temper, but just barely. "I didn't run away. I left what I felt was an impossible situation. I'd done everything I could to fit in, to belong. But when the chips were down, I was still the maverick kid with no mother and a drunken father. And no money of my own. Blue blood won and I lost." Pointedly, he looked at her hands and found them ringless. "And how is your dear husband?"

"*Ex*-husband. We're divorced."

He hadn't known that, hadn't heard. Though he'd written sporadic letters to Hollis, mostly during his lonely bouts, the old man had sent him only an occasional brief note, rarely referring to any of the McKenzies. And Luke had never asked.

He took a step closer to her. "Shay, I . . ."

"Luke!" A soft voice from the direction of the porch steps called out.

He turned to see Liz McKenzie hurry down, her footsteps quiet on the lush grass. Shay's mother, he knew, was in her mid-fifties by now, yet she was as slim as a young boy, wearing the plaid shirt and western jeans she'd always favored. Her hair was cut shorter and had acquired a few gray strands, but otherwise was thick and reddish brown like her daughter's.

Reaching him, Liz hugged Luke to her with arms that trembled only slightly as she blinked back a sudden rush of moisture. He smelled of the outdoors with a hint of lemon, and he felt strong and solid. She hadn't given birth to Luke Turner, but he'd been a child of her heart since she'd first laid eyes on him.

Easing back, Liz smiled up at him. "Thank you for coming," she said quietly.

She'd been the one constant in his life, the only person who'd always been in his corner. "You had only to ask," Luke answered as he kissed her soft cheek.

Shay watched the tender scene, growing more agitated. Why had her mother asked Luke back here when she knew he would disrupt them all?

Sensing her daughter's discomfort, Liz reached out a hand to include her. "I felt Luke should be here," she explained to Shay as she met her questioning gaze. "He's family."

Shay stiffened her spine. "Is he? Is that why he turned his back on us all?"

Luke heard lingering fury in her voice, aware she wasn't even bothering to disguise her bitterness.

Her hand on Luke's arm, Liz felt Luke's muscles tense up. She squeezed Shay's fingers before answering. "That all happened many years ago, Shay."

Shay watched Luke's eyes frost over, but he didn't bother to explain further. Her gaze dropped to his lips and she saw them flatten into a thin, angry line. That same mouth that had been the first to touch hers, to kiss her breathless. "Some of us have a long memory," she said, then turned. "Please excuse me. I think Cora needs me in the kitchen."

Liz sighed as she stepped back, running a slender hand through her hair. "I'm sorry, Luke. Shay's a bit on edge." That wasn't all of it, of course, but her explanation would have to do for now. Though she'd never stopped loving Luke and had pardoned his abrupt departure, believing he'd had his reasons, Liz also had a family to protect. She would go slowly, confiding more details only after reacquainting herself with the man Luke had become.

"She's never forgiven me for leaving," he commented, almost to himself.

Sadly Liz shook her head. "No."

Luke shifted his attention to Shay's mother, noticing how much thinner she was, her skin so pale with dark shadows under her expressive eyes. "Something's wrong. What is it?"

She took hold of his hands. "Jacob's had a heart attack."

His fingers on hers tightened. "When? How bad?"

"Nearly a month ago, but he's better now." She took his arm and started walking to the house.

"Where is he?"

On the porch, Liz pulled open the screen and waited until they were in the vestibule before answering. "Upstairs in his own bed. He was released from the hospital two days ago. He's weak, but he'll be all right. *If* he follows the doctor's orders."

Luke shook his head as he glanced toward the stairs. "Hard to believe." A big man, easily six feet four inches, Jacob McKenzie had always had the constitution of a lion, as Luke remembered. Luke couldn't recall Jacob ever being sidelined by a cold, despite doing the work of two men even during the rugged Montana winters. "He's like a rock."

Her eyes softening, Liz nodded. "But a sixty-year-old rock whose love for his own beefsteaks and those smelly cigars have all but ruined his arteries."

"Does he know you sent for me?"

Liz shook her head. "No one knows. I wasn't certain you'd come."

He saw the concern in her eyes for the man upstairs in their bed, saw the love she dispensed so generously, and the lingering doubt that obviously centered around himself. "I've always found it hard to turn you down."

"Hard, perhaps, but not impossible."

He, too, remembered that last conversation they'd had shortly before he'd left. "I made a mistake, leaving like that ten years ago. I've paid for it, Liz."

Luke had always had so much pride and a sensitivity he'd hidden under a facade of arrogance, Liz thought. Just like Jacob. Perhaps that was why she cared so much for both of them. She knew how hard it was for either man to admit to a mistake. She reached to touch his face. "I know."

He nodded in the direction of the kitchen. "Shay hates me."

"No. She...she's had some difficult years." Liz linked arms with him and turned them both toward the stairs. "We have a lot to catch up on. But first, let's go see Jacob. I just left him and he's awake."

He climbed with her. "Will seeing me shock him? I don't want to trigger another attack."

Liz shook her head and smiled. "Good news is never hard on the heart, Luke."

Outside Jacob's bedroom door, he turned to face her. "*Is* my returning to the Circle M good news, Liz?" He'd had his doubts on the long drive here, wondering if he shouldn't have called, instead, if his arrival would do more harm than good.

"Yes, very good news. But be patient with us, Luke. Ten years is a long time."

He'd learned patience a long time ago, because he'd had no choice. He gave Liz a nod, then followed her into the dim room.

"Someone to see you, Jacob," Liz said.

The furniture was dark pine, the bed a huge four-poster that Jacob had had specially made to accommodate his long frame. In his youth, Luke had often been in this room, talking with the big man as he'd sat propped up in bed, pillows stuffed behind his back, going over the endless paperwork involved in running a ranch. Now, as Luke stepped closer, he tried to keep his expression even as he noticed that Jacob appeared smaller under the sheet and light blanket that covered his frailer frame, and paler beneath his perpetual tan.

"Hello, Jacob," Luke said, his hand on the cane-back chair alongside the bed. But he didn't pull it over, didn't sit down.

Jacob's gray eyes were clear as he glanced at his wife, then back to Luke. Thirty-five years he'd lived with Liz—so he wasn't at all surprised that she'd found Luke and had him come back. And, though he'd been angry with Luke for some time for the way he'd left, he no longer was. There was something about a heart attack that made a man come face-to-face with his own mortality and realize how stupid it was to nurture grudges.

Especially against Luke Turner, who as man and boy had had a special place in his heart. Jacob had never been good at sharing his feelings, except maybe with Liz. But he was learning lately, perhaps because he wasn't certain how much longer he'd be around. Just as he'd guessed that Liz might hunt down Luke, he'd also been certain that Luke would come if she found him.

Jacob reached out a hand. "You're looking good, son."

The last word he heard shattered Luke's tenuous control. He set the chair aside, moved to the bed and leaned down to hug the man who'd been more of a father to him than his own. Closing his eyes, he swallowed around a lump of emotion. After a moment, he straightened. "I owe you an apology. I shouldn't have left...."

Jacob waved his hand, dismissing that. "You owe me nothing. You must have had good reasons. A man has to do what he has to do." His eyes shifted to Liz as she moved to sit beside him and take his hand. "And so does a woman. Thank you, darlin'," he said, knowing she'd understand what he meant.

It still moved him, the wordless communication between these two, Luke thought. How he'd envied that in years past. He'd wanted that same sort of connection for himself and Shay once and had thought they'd almost had it. But things hadn't worked out.

The emotional moment passed and Jacob could see Luke withdrawing behind that careful facade he wore. "You *are* planning to stay, aren't you?"

"For a while," Luke answered carefully. He hadn't thought beyond his arrival, beyond helping Liz with her problem. Had she asked him here as moral support during Jacob's recovery? Or was Jacob more seriously ill than she'd said?

"I've fixed up your old room," Liz told him.

That would probably be more than he could handle. He was too used to being on his own. "I'd prefer staying in the guest cabin, if it's not being used. And I'll need a stall for my stallion."

Liz didn't let her disappointment show. "Of course. I'll have Cora make sure the cabin's ready, and Hollis will see to your horse."

Luke smiled, the first since his arrival. "It'll be good seeing Hollis again."

"I'm sure. Hollis is as much a part of this ranch as we are." Leaning down, she kissed Jacob's forehead. "You rest now, and I'll take Luke down for something to eat. The two of you can talk later."

He hated the weakness that tired him so quickly, but Jacob nodded. Again he held up his hand and Luke took it, holding on for a long moment. By the time they were in the hallway, Jacob's eyes had closed.

"That was terrific, Cora," Luke told the energetic little housekeeper who'd welcomed him home with a fierce hug and damp eyes a short time ago. "I've been all over, but nobody makes chicken-fried steak like you."

Cora beamed her thanks as she cleared the table. "More coffee?" She refilled his cup and then Liz's without waiting for an answer. Turning to the kitchen counter, she walked over to where Shay was icing a chocolate cake with pale pink frosting. "Would you like a cup of coffee, Shay?"

"No, thanks. It's too hot." She dipped the knife into the frosting and carefully lathered it on.

Cora set down the coffeepot. "We're having chicken and dumplings and birthday cake for supper, so you be sure you're here, Lucas Turner. Six sharp." She bent to the cupboard for the silver polish. "And we're eating in the dining room tonight. A double celebration." Stepping through the swinging doors, she left the kitchen.

While Liz sipped her coffee, Luke studied Shay's somewhat stiff back. She hadn't said a word to him since Liz had brought him in, letting Cora fuss over feeding him, the housekeeper's chatter filling the silence. Maybe he could loosen her a little. "Whose birthday is it?" he asked, aiming his words at Shay.

Liz waited for Shay to answer, but when she didn't, she let out an exasperated sigh and turned to Luke. "Beth, Shay's daughter. She's seven today."

"Seven." Luke frowned at her silence, then swung his gaze back to Liz. All right, if that's the way Shay wanted it, he'd talk around her. "I'd heard you had a granddaughter, but I thought she was older. Eight or nine."

"No." Liz toyed with her teaspoon as she spoke, obviously annoyed with Shay, but her pride in Beth won out. "She's in the calving barn just now, but wait until you see her. She's simply beautiful. Looks just like her mother."

Shay set the second layer on top of the first. "No, Mom, she looks like you."

"Then I'd say she's doubly blessed," Luke said, placing his hand atop Liz's.

Liz looked at his fingers, strong and tan and ringless. "What about you, Luke? Did you marry?"

Luke shook his head.

She *would* ask him personal questions, because as the woman who'd all but raised him, she had a need to know, Liz thought. And because she knew that Shay was listening hard despite her cold shoulder. "Why not?"

Luke was very aware of the woman behind him trying so desperately to ignore him. He shrugged, feigning an indifference he was far from feeling. "The rodeo circuit is no life for a wife, nor is following a cowboy from ranch to ranch." There had been women. He'd forgotten most of their names. "My father never had anything of his own, never should have married and had me. I didn't want to wind up like he did."

Liz remembered that Luke had never felt close to his father. He'd also struggled against her mothering, though no one she'd known had ever needed nurturing more. She'd recognized that he'd wanted to fit in so badly, to belong. Studying his unreadable expression now, she wondered if he ever felt he had.

She could tell that Gavin's shiftless ways still haunted him. "You're not your father, Luke," Liz reminded him.

He wrapped his fingers around her fragile hand, amazed at how well she was able to read him after all these years. "I hope not. And speaking of fathers and sons, how's Gil?" Another McKenzie who would undoubtedly not be pleased to see him back.

Concern darkened Liz's brown eyes. "Better now, I think. He left us, too. About the same time Luke went away, wasn't it, Shay?"

She should have known her mother would find a way to draw her into this conversation. She couldn't be rude and not answer again. "Yes," Shay said.

Liz nodded. "I thought so. He went back to school in Billings. What was it he studied, Shay?"

Shay gave up. Finished with the cake, she put the knife into the sink and turned to face them. "A general business course," she answered.

"Yes, that's right. Then he tried a variety of jobs, but nothing seemed to catch his fancy." As always, Liz felt a stab of guilt over her only son. Gil had had asthma as a child, had been small and sickly. While she'd hovered over him protectively, Jacob had demanded more of the boy, hoping Gil would fight to overcome his infirmity and be strong. Perhaps they'd both been wrong. "I think Gil got homesick for the ranch, don't you, Shay?"

She kept her eyes on her mother. "The Circle M has a way of getting in your blood, of drawing you back even if you leave. At least for most of us."

Luke caught her not-so-subtle message. "It's the people who draw you back more than the ranch itself," he said quietly.

Feeling the tension between the two, Liz rushed on. "Gil came home when Jacob had his first heart attack."

Luke's head jerked around. "He's had others?"

"Two years ago, but that one was quite mild. A warning, Dr. Emmett told him. But Jacob still thought he was infallible."

The man he'd visited upstairs earlier looked as if he no longer believed that. "So Gil is back living here, too?"

Liz nodded. "Apparently Gil thought his father would automatically put him in charge when he returned, since he's our son. But while he'd been gone, Jacob had made Zeke Crawford manager."

Luke frowned. "I don't think I know him."

"Probably not. He hired on after you'd been gone awhile. Zeke's worked all over, like you. And he really knows cows. Naturally, that didn't set too well with Gil, especially when Jacob had Gil work every job on the ranch, making him earn his way back up." She'd given in to Jacob on that, knowing that if she started coddling her son again, she'd only weaken him.

Shay rinsed her hands, then reached for a towel. "Gil and Zeke co-manage now and they get along just fine. Gil was Zeke's best man when he married Rhea three years ago."

Surprised, Luke smiled. "Little Rhea, married? She was only seventeen when I left."

"We're all older, Luke," Shay went on, "and we've all changed. Rhea's happy and so is Gil." She wanted him to know all was basically well on the Circle M, that the McKenzies hadn't fallen apart after he'd left, if that was what he was thinking. Perhaps it wasn't exactly the truth, but close enough.

Why was she so defensive? Luke wondered. "I'm glad to hear it." He'd been brought up-to-date on most everyone, and still Liz hadn't revealed the reason she'd sent for him. "Is there anything else you haven't told me, Liz? Is

Jacob more ill than he realizes? Is that why you wrote me?''

Liz glanced at Shay before shaking her head. ''I've told you the truth about Jacob's condition. I did think you'd be good for him, that your being here might hasten his recovery. But there is something else I'd like your help with, something Jacob doesn't know about.'' She folded her hands on the table. ''I only found out about two weeks ago. Gil told me, not wanting to worry Jacob. We have cows missing, eighty to a hundred head last count, some of them pregnant.''

He raised curious eyebrows. That was one he hadn't been expecting. Cattle rustling was hardly new to Montana ranches, even in the nineties, but he'd somehow thought the Circle M inviolate. ''You're sure?'' When she nodded, Luke looked at Shay and saw her frowning.

''I thought Gil and Zeke were looking into that, Mom.''

''They're both quite busy. I feel they can use some help before the problem gets out of hand.'' She appealed to Luke. ''I don't want Jacob to know, at least not until he's stronger. You know how he feels about this ranch.''

He'd once felt very strongly about the Circle M, too. Leaving it and the people here had been the hardest thing he'd ever done. But returning wasn't easy, either, and now Liz wanted him to stay long enough to get to the bottom of a rustling. That would take weeks, months. Luke stood and began to pace the length of the large kitchen. ''How do you think Gil will feel about my being asked to help him? Or Zeke, for that matter?'' Both of them were related to the family, whereas he was still the outsider, despite the warm welcome from Liz and Jacob.

''Not thrilled, that's how,'' Shay commented.

''They'll do as I ask,'' Liz said with quiet authority. Zeke, because he was the newest member of the family and unfailingly polite around her. And Gil, because he wouldn't want to go against her wishes, knowing how upset she'd been over his father's illness. Emotional blackmail, her conscience warned. Perhaps, but she would use it without a second thought, if she could save Jacob from further worry, from more stress. And perhaps unite this family again in the bargain.

Luke stopped pacing to study Liz. She looked fragile, but he knew she had a backbone of steel. He also knew he could no sooner refuse her than he could walk on water. After all these years of waiting to realize his dream, what could the delay of a few weeks matter? He sat back down. "I'll give you a month and not a day more."

Liz's slow smile spread and she put her hand on his. "Thank you." A month. It would do, for openers.

Tight-lipped, Shay tossed down the towel and left the kitchen, not trusting herself to speak.

Staring at the swinging doors, Luke sighed. "It's not going to be easy, Liz."

"Give her time, Luke."

Suddenly the back door opened and Rhea came in, her light brown hair ruffled from a breeze, her smile widening as she recognized the man seated alongside her mother. "Luke! I wondered who that truck out front belonged to, and that gorgeous stallion." She hurried over as he rose, moving into his embrace for a long hug, then leaning back to look at him. "I can't believe it's you."

He grinned down at her. At five foot three, Rhea had often joked about being the runt of the litter. She'd never been as pretty as Shay, and still carried a good twenty excess pounds, but Luke thought she had a great smile and a terrific sense of humor. "And I can't believe it's little Rhea, all grown up and married."

"Well, I couldn't wait forever for you to come back and marry me. Have you met Zeke?"

"Not yet."

"You'll like him." She stepped back and caught Liz's eye. "Right, Mom? Everyone likes Zeke."

"Yes, he's very personable." Liz stood and walked over to put an arm around both of them. It was beginning, and she'd been the catalyst. If only all went well, she prayed.

"How's Daddy today?" Rhea asked.

Liz smiled. "Feeling good, I think."

The back door swung open again, and they all looked toward it as Gil McKenzie strolled in with his usual jaunty gait. But suddenly, seeing Luke, he stopped in his tracks.

Her arm around Luke's waist, Rhea smiled. "Look who's here, Gil," she called out. "The prodigal son returns."

Gil's expression hardened. "Luke's not a son, not a McKenzie," he said. "His name's Turner, remember?"

Chapter Two

"Gil's not a bad sort, you know," Hollis said, before he slipped a plug of chewing tobacco into the left side of his mouth. "Just a man having a hard time growing up."

Sitting next to his old friend on the front stoop of the bunkhouse, Luke raised a questioning eyebrow. "He's thirty-two, Hollis. Just two years younger than me."

The seasoned cowhand slipped the tobacco pouch into the pocket of his flannel shirt. Despite the summer heat, Hollis preferred flannel year-round, and most months wore red long johns underneath. "Takes some longer than others." He angled his body around and looked Luke over with pale blue eyes that had seen a lot of men come and go on the Circle M. Luke Turner had been one of his favorites. "I was hoping you wouldn't be mad 'cause I gave Liz your address." When he saw Luke shake his head, Hollis smiled. "Good, 'cause you're a sight for sore eyes, boy."

Luke heard the warmth in the old man's voice and smiled. Hollis had always called him *boy,* but he'd done so with affection. "Thanks. I'm not sure too many folks around here are glad to see me."

Hollis settled his wad more comfortably in his cheek before answering. "Don't go by Gil. He had trouble accepting you years ago. What made you think he'd changed?"

Luke shrugged. "Time, maturity, and the fact that I've never given him a reason to dislike me."

Yet dislike him Gil did. Earlier, when he'd come into the kitchen and found Luke there with Liz and Rhea, Gil had not only pointed out that Luke wasn't a McKenzie, he'd rudely demanded to know why Luke had come back to the Circle M. Liz had quickly stepped forward, her disappointment in her son evident in her stormy gaze, explaining that *she* had invited Luke back. Gil had calmed then, but his eyes had remained distrustful, much as Shay's had been.

Luke still wasn't sure why Gil carried such a long-term grudge against him. As boys, they'd gotten along. As men, they'd worked well together. Then, suddenly, Gil had revealed a hidden animosity, and the last conversation they'd had—the one that had convinced Luke he had overstayed his welcome—had been tense and wounding.

He hadn't gone up to the big house for supper, despite Liz's repeated invitation to help celebrate Shay's daughter's birthday, explaining that he wanted to get settled in at the guest cabin. The truth was he felt drained after the long drive and didn't want to eat under the hostile gaze of both Shay and Gil. So he'd eaten in the mess hall with the hands who worked the ranch, reacquainting himself with several who'd been with the McKenzies for years and meeting a handful of new cowboys. Then he'd wandered back to sit with Hollis and see if maybe the wizened old man could update him on the past ten years.

Hollis removed his summer straw hat and ran a gnarled hand over his sparse gray hair. "Dislike ain't the same as distrust. Gil liked you well enough when you were both teenagers growing up on the ranch. But when he got older, he figured he should be favored, being his daddy's only blood son. And he got to worrying that Jacob was beginning to grow overly fond of you."

"Yeah, I came to the same conclusion after I'd been gone a while." Luke stretched out his long legs and looked up into the early-evening sky. A nearly full moon was already visible in the west, hanging above the distant mountain range. Two men he didn't recognize left the huge white milking barn and leisurely strolled off in the direction of the tenant houses where the married hands lived. From inside the bunkhouse drifted the plaintive sounds of a harmonica singing out a lonely man's song. The pungent aroma of animals and oiled leather hung in the dry summer air, mingling with the smoke from somebody's pipe. Luke longed for a cigarette, but instead searched his pockets for his roll of lemon drops.

"Why didn't you come back then, and explain things?" Hollis didn't blame Luke for leaving, had never asked him why, knowing instinctively that the young man hadn't done so impulsively. He thought he knew Luke's reason, but he wanted to hear him say it out loud.

Luke fiddled with the candy wrappings. "By then, there didn't seem to be any reason to come back."

Hollis narrowed his eyes, studying the younger man's face. "Because Shay'd left to marry that Whitney fella?"

Luke swung around, not in the least surprised. "You always did see more than most folks would guess."

Hollis grinned at the compliment. "Hell, boy, even the one-eyed bull we got in that corral over there couldn't have missed seeing how you felt about that girl."

"She's not a girl anymore, and she hates me."

The old man made a grunting sound. "Love and hate. Mighty strong stuff. The way I figure it is if a woman finds herself hating a man, it's usually 'cause she loves him. Otherwise, she'd have let it go awhile back."

Luke found himself smiling. "You an expert on women, Hollis?"

"I've known my share. Even married one once. That don't mean I understand 'em."

The back screen door of the big house slammed shut and Luke glanced over. In the dim shadows of twilight, he recognized Shay's long-legged stride, her wild hair confined to a thick braid that bounced along as she made her way toward the first corral. She passed about three hundred feet from them, but she didn't turn her head to look over, keeping her eyes straight ahead. She held herself ramrod straight, and he had the feeling she knew he was watching her.

Luke felt a rush of defensive outrage, and he didn't much like the feeling. He'd agreed to help Liz out, but he'd be damned if he'd stay without learning why Shay was so filled with anger at him. It was bad enough putting up with Gil's resentment without Shay treating him like a leper, as well. He wouldn't rush it, but before too long, he'd get some answers out of Shay one way or the other.

He brought his attention back to his conversation with Hollis. "I know what you mean. I don't understand women either." A sudden flash in the sky had them both looking up.

"Heat lightning," Hollis commented. "Sure wish it was the real thing, a summer storm and a nightlong downpour." He nodded in the direction of the outlying pastures. "We keep it watered around here, but out there, it's so dry it'd take twenty acres to rust a nail."

Luke saw a man walking toward them, lean and rangy, coming from the direction of the manager's cabin. "Is that Zeke Crawford?"

Hollis squinted. "Sure is. You met him yet?"

"No, but I think it's time I did." He'd been thinking about this rustling matter. It didn't seem as if Gil was going to be much help, so he'd better see if Rhea's husband was any friendlier.

With deference to his arthritis, Hollis got to his feet slowly. "Come on then, and let me introduce you."

The chestnut mare bobbed her head in thanks for her nightly apple treat, chewing contentedly. "Did you think I wasn't coming, girl? I know I'm a little late tonight. Couldn't be helped." Standing just inside the corral fence, Shay stroked Dancer's sleek neck.

Someone in the adjacent barn flipped on the outside lights, bathing the area in front of the bunkhouse in a soft glow. Shay moved to the other side of Dancer so she could watch without being seen.

Walking over, she'd felt eyes on her back and had sensed they were deep blue and belonged to Luke Turner. She'd been right, she thought, as she saw him rise from the stoop and saunter over with Hollis to speak to Zeke. The two younger men shook hands, talking in low tones.

Zeke was tall, but Luke was taller, his shoulders considerably wider, his stance as always alert and watchful. She'd managed to avoid him since leaving the kitchen, and she'd been grateful he hadn't joined them for supper. His presence would have spoiled Shay's enjoyment of Beth's birthday celebration.

Yet she knew she couldn't dodge him forever, since he was apparently intending to stay for a month.

Shay ran slender fingers through Dancer's thick mane and sighed deeply. Feelings she'd thought forever buried were suddenly churning inside her. Memories were dragging her back into a past that held its share of pain. Why couldn't her mother have let things be? Why couldn't Luke Turner have turned down Liz's request to return?

She'd been nine years old when Luke, a thin, silent boy of fourteen, had shown up on the Circle M with his father. At her mother's insistence, Dad had hired Gavin Turner to work in the barns mostly, so he could keep an eye on his son. After school, Luke had cleaned stalls, curried cows, handled hay, helped with the milking—anything and everything, wanting to pay his own way, even at that young age.

She and Gil and Rhea had tried to interest him in their games or in riding, but he'd rarely joined them, always working or studying. When Gavin had gotten killed and her mother had moved Luke into the big house, Liz had asked them to look upon Luke as a brother.

Shay stepped to the fence and swung up to sit on the top board. Dancer moved closer, nuzzling up to her. Absently she patted the mare's smooth coat. Gil seemed glad to have another male in the house as they moved into their teens. He tried to coax Luke to go fishing, riding with the herd or sleeping outdoors with the hands on the range. Then Gil had developed asthma, curtailing his activities, and he'd become jealous watching Luke fill out, grow stronger and learn more about ranching than he could with his limitations.

Rhea had regarded Luke as another big brother, following him everywhere. Shay had been amazed at how tolerant he'd been of her younger sister.

But Shay had never thought of Luke as a brother. She wasn't sure when it had happened, when she'd first become aware of it. She only knew that it seemed as if she'd loved Luke Turner all her life.

She'd been sixteen when she'd discovered he cared for her, too. She'd been invited to a school dance by an upperclassman and her mom had made her a beautiful dress, floor-length white chiffon. Shay smiled, remembering. The boy, Mel Clayton, had come to pick her up in his red convertible, wearing a tuxedo and a big smile. Luke had watched them leave, sullen and unfriendly. Then he'd shocked her by following them to the school gym and hanging around, his cool blue eyes watching her every move.

As it turned out, it was a good thing he had. Unknown to her, Mel had hidden a flask of liquor in his glove compartment and kept visiting it all evening. By ten, he'd become bleary-eyed and suddenly amorous. When Luke had made his presence known, telling Mel he'd drive him home to sleep it off, the young man had taken a swing at Shay's protector.

That had been a big mistake. Luke had cuffed Mel on the chin, easily knocking him out. His mouth a grim line, Luke had settled them both in his truck, taken Mel home, then pulled off into a quiet, dead-end road with Shay. He'd told her then—not asked but *told*—that she wasn't ever to go out with anyone but him.

That was the same evening he'd taught her to kiss.

Dancer sniffed the air and whinnied, moving to the middle of the corral, probably picking up an unfamiliar scent. Shay straddled the fence and gazed up at a rounded moon. How had it happened, two people perfect for each other, so much in love, and it had all turned to ashes? For years, she'd asked herself that question, wondering what

she'd done to cause Luke to leave the night of her nineteenth birthday, right after he'd given her a lovely gift.

Shay fingered the silver key she still wore on a chain
around her neck. She'd been so thrilled at his thoughtful
gift. But the next morning, she'd awakened to find him
gone.

She lifted her heavy braid off the back of her neck,
wishing for a cool breeze. It was hot and sticky, trying to
rain but not quite making it. Grassy Ridge was in a valley,
surrounded by high mountains on all sides, mountains that
broke up the rain clouds before they got a chance to reach
them and drop their revitalizing contents on the parched
land. Thunder rumbled in the distance, adding to the rest-
lessness of the night.

Glancing behind her, Shay saw Luke and Zeke part
company, Zeke entering the bunkhouse with Hollis while
Luke headed for his cabin. For an instant, she considered
following him, confronting him, demanding that long-
overdue explanation. But she quickly dismissed the
thought, certain she wouldn't like his answer.

Her mother had said she'd asked Luke back to help get
to the bottom of the rustling. With luck, he would be kept
busy with that. She had her bookkeeping, her need to
spend more time with Beth now that she was out of school
for the summer, and her writing. She would steer clear of
Luke and pray that he would soon be gone. On the occa-
sions she would have to be with him, she'd be cool and indifferent.

It seemed like a good plan, Shay thought. If only she
could stick to it.

A cricket was serenading him vigorously as Luke stepped
onto the porch of the guest cabin. An old-fashioned glider
beckoned invitingly by the back wall. Wearily he sat down.

A long day, he thought, and an unsettling one. He'd brushed shoulders with all the McKenzies again, and the jury was still out on how the majority of them felt about his return.

Luke ran a hand through his hair and rolled his tired shoulders. It was too nice an evening and still too early to turn in. Besides, he was too keyed up to sleep.

Zeke seemed to be a nice enough fellow, though he obviously hadn't been thrilled that Liz had asked Luke to help with the rustling problem, as Shay had predicted. But he'd bowed to his mother-in-law's wishes and pretended to be pleased to have Luke's input. Tomorrow they planned to take the Jeep out onto the range so Zeke could show Luke where the loss had first been discovered. Zeke had said he'd talk to Gil to see if he wanted to join them. Luke was pretty sure that Gil would refuse.

Just then, a sleek black Labrador scurried onto the porch and right up to Luke, sniffing him curiously. Luke leaned forward to scratch his big head. "Hey, boy, where'd you come from?"

"He's mine." The young lady with the long pigtails stepped out of the shadows and came onto the porch. She wore shorts, a striped shirt and a shy expression.

Of course, the only member of the family he hadn't met. Luke smiled. "Hi. My name's Luke. You must be Beth."

Nodding, she moved into a splash of moonlight and gave him a gap-toothed grin. "My grandma said it was okay if I came over." She held out a covered dish. "You didn't get to have a piece of my birthday cake, so I brought you one."

"Thanks. It looks great." Carefully he placed the dish on the small table next to the swing. "What's your dog's name?"

"Beechie, short for Beechnut. You want to know why?"

"Yeah, why?"

"'Cause he likes to chew gum." She giggled, charming him.

The child was seven today, Liz had told him. Two years younger than when he'd first met her mother, yet the resemblance was eerie. The same hair and eyes, the sprinkling of freckles, the promise of beauty to come. The child who should have been his, Luke thought, with a pang of jealousy.

"No! Does he really chew gum?" he asked her solemnly.

"If you've got some I'll show you."

Luke shook his head. "Never touch the stuff." He reached into his pocket. "I've got lemon drops if you'd like one."

"Okay." She moved to sit beside him, took the candy and slipped it into her mouth. "Grandma says you used to live here and play with my mom when she was a little girl."

He stretched his arm along the back of the swing, keeping them in motion with one foot. "I sure did."

"Did she used to eat all her vegetables? I hate vegetables."

Luke smiled. "Your mom wasn't too crazy about them, either, but your grandma made us all eat them anyhow."

Beth nodded knowingly. "She's still like that." She watched Beechnut amble over and lie down across from them. "I'm going to get my own horse in just three years, when I'm ten. Grandpa promised."

"You're pretty lucky. He didn't give me my own horse until I turned sixteen." Luke still remembered how special owning that stallion had made him feel. He'd named him Baron and no matter how tired he'd been, he'd never gone to bed without checking on his horse. But he'd left Baron behind when he'd moved out, unable to justify taking him. "Do you like to ride, Beth?"

"Better than most anything. Mom takes me nearly every day." She twisted around, her long pigtails flying back. "Maybe you can come with us sometime."

"Maybe." If he could get Shay alone long enough to talk things out. "We'll have to ask your mom."

They both heard the banging of a screen door, then the porch light at the big house went on and Liz stepped out. She moved to the railing and peered across the grass. "Beth," she called out. "Time to come home and get ready for bed."

Beth sighed somewhat dramatically, and Luke was reminded of how Shay used to do the same thing. "I'm coming, Grandma," she answered, then turned to Luke. "I have to go."

Luke stood. "I'll walk you over." They started across, Beechnut leisurely strolling alongside.

"I'll get some gum tomorrow," Beth promised, "so Beechie can show you his best tricks."

"Does he blow bubbles, too?"

"Not yet, but I'm trying to teach him." They reached the steps where Liz was waiting for her, but Beth seemed reluctant to go in. "You like dogs, Luke?"

He gave in to the urge and touched the ends of her hair lightly. "I like dogs a lot. I'll see you tomorrow, Beth."

"Run along inside, sweetie," Liz said. "Start your bath and I'll be up in a minute." She watched Beth wave to Luke, then she turned and saw him staring after the child somewhat wistfully.

"She's a cute kid," Luke said. "Another charmer like her grandmother and her mother."

Liz smiled at the compliment. "So, are you getting settled in and acquainted?"

Luke nodded. "Not too much has changed around here." Except maybe a few attitudes. He glanced through the screen door. "Is Shay around?"

Liz leaned forward to peer around the porch post. "She's over there, talking to her horse, a nightly ritual."

He'd thought she'd gone inside, but he could just make out a shadowy form by the fence. All day, he'd been piecing together bits of information in an effort to learn why Shay had been drawn to Max after he'd left. "Well, at least Shay finished college before she married Max, right?"

"I'm afraid not. She went back that fall for her second year, but she hated every minute of it. One day, she came home and announced that she simply wasn't going back, that she wanted to work on the ranch. Jacob wasn't happy, but you know how strong willed Shay can be."

Luke remembered going head-to-head with Shay often. "She could sell ice cubes to the Eskimos if she put her mind to it."

But she hadn't been able to keep you from breaking her heart, Liz thought. Shay had just turned nineteen, such a vulnerable age, and in love for the first time. She'd seen it coming and had asked Luke to keep a level head since he was older, telling him that love, if it was real, would last and grow. She'd been trying to protect her daughter, but her warning had only provoked Luke into a desperate course of action. For years, Liz had berated herself for interfering, for having forgotten the intensity of youthful passion. Watching Luke now as he spoke of her daughter, she wondered if perhaps it wasn't too late to right a wrong.

"So she dropped out of college, came back here and married Max Whitney." Why did it still hurt saying the words aloud?

"Yes, about a year later. We didn't approve, but again, Shay wouldn't listen. Neither Jacob nor I had ever had much to do with the Whitneys, even though they're our nearest neighbors.''

Luke remembered Morgan Whitney as a gentleman rancher who'd never worked his spread as Jacob had. He'd hired men to do everything from managing on down, never getting his hands dirty. And his wife Cybil was known as a terrible snob. Yet Luke had been led to believe back then that Jacob had approved of Max. ''I thought Jacob wanted Shay to marry Max?''

Liz looked puzzled. ''I don't know where you got that. The Whitneys weren't our kind of people. Still aren't. But Max could be charming. Suddenly he started coming around, asking Shay out, romancing her.''

Luke felt his stomach muscles tighten at the thought. He remembered Maxwell Whitney as a teenage bully and later as a lazy, spoiled only son who'd stop at nothing to get his way. When Luke had heard that Shay had married without even attempting to contact him through Hollis, he'd been devastated. ''I can't believe Shay fell for Max's romancing.''

Liz raised eyes so much like her daughter's to meet his troubled gaze. ''You've forgotten that Shay grew up quite sheltered on this ranch. Even away at college, she was shy and didn't date. Jacob and I tried to discourage her relationship with Max from the beginning, but she ignored us. She was young and inexperienced, no match for a persistent charmer who had a hidden agenda.''

He'd figured there had to be more. ''What was that?''

''This is only a guess, of course. I believe Morgan Whitney prodded Max to go after Shay, to marry her.''

Luke frowned. ''Why?''

Liz's sigh was ragged. ''For several reasons. It was a very hot summer and we were experiencing a drought, much like this year. As you know, we have water rights to

a rich streambed and the Whitney property does not. I
don't have to tell a cattleman like you what happens to
cows when there's not enough water."

Luke felt a rush of impotent anger. "You mean to tell
me that Max married Shay so his father's cows wouldn't
die?"

"Partly, and it worked. After they married, Jacob allowed Morgan's herd to share our water supply. The
Whitney spread was already in financial difficulty. Without our water, they'd have been wiped out."

Disgusted, Luke kicked at a stone in the grass. "So they
used Shay."

"Yes." There was more, a lot more, but she'd said
enough for the time being.

Now he knew what had put that new maturity into
Shay's eyes, Luke thought. Nothing like disillusionment to
make a person grow up fast. It would seem Shay hadn't
been any happier than he had these past years. "I hadn't
heard she'd left him, or that she'd moved back here."
Fleetingly he wondered why Hollis had never mentioned
that to him, though he thought he knew the reason. "The
truth is, once I heard she'd married, I didn't want to know
any more."

Again he glanced toward the corral and saw Shay's
slender figure slip off the fence. The mare moved closer to
nuzzle her. Luke looked up at Liz. "Thanks for the cake."

But Liz's mind wasn't on cake as she held his gaze. "Be
kind, Luke. She's more fragile than she realizes."

He reached up, squeezed her hand, then set out for the
corral. He walked slowly, uncertain what to say, how to
begin. He only knew he couldn't live this close to Shay
without attempting to clear the air.

She heard him coming, he knew, yet she didn't move.
Inside the fence, she was leaning against the weathered

boards in a shaft of moonlight. Her mare hovered nearby, the only horse in the corral. Luke closed the gate after himself and moved to within six feet of her, then stopped.

"We have to talk, Shay," he said quietly.

She kept her eyes on the ridge of mountains, barely visible in the distance. "About what?" Keep cool, she reminded herself. She'd seen him heading her way and had guessed he'd want to talk. He'd always been one for the direct approach. Indifferent, that was the approach she'd take.

"The situation between us."

What an interesting way of wording things, Shay thought. "There *is* no situation between us, Luke."

"I was hoping we could be friends." It wasn't exactly what he was hoping for, but it was a start.

The day pigs fly, she thought, but she forced a small smile. "Friends. Well, why not? We grew up together."

Her words were friendly, yet they were spoken with little warmth. Had he misjudged her years ago, perhaps even been remembering her all wrong? "Yes. We share a lot of good memories." The clouds had drifted, allowing the moon to play across her face. She was so lovely, but her eyes were colder than a Montana winter sky.

And a few bad memories, Shay recalled. She searched for a topic that wouldn't drag them into the past. "So, you think you can catch our cattle rustlers?"

He edged closer, then leaned back against the fence. Her scent drifted to him on the warm night air, wildflowers and some fragrant soap. A rush of recollections flooded him— Shay in her first party dress, Shay reaching for him and sharing her first kiss, Shay in his arms that last night, moaning low in her throat as his hands had closed over her breasts. Luke swallowed hard before answering. "I'm going to give it a shot. Zeke and I plan to drive out tomorrow, have a look around.''

But not Gil. Her brother seemed even angrier at Luke's return than she. Shay knew her reasons but wondered about her brother's. Did Gil still feel threatened in Luke's presence, afraid their parents would choose him over their own son? Surely not.

Shay unclenched the fists she'd hidden behind her back, and felt the tension shift elsewhere. It was time to end this chatty session. ''The whole thing has upset Mom. I hope you and Zeke get to the bottom of it.'' *So you can leave and I can breathe again.*

He would try another tactic, appeal to her soft heart. ''I could use a little help. Gil doesn't seem cooperative and...''

''I'm pretty busy these days. Since Dad's been sick, I've taken over the books. Very time-consuming.''

''I see.'' She moved past him, but he stepped in front of her. ''I met your daughter, and Liz was right. She's lovely, almost as lovely as her mother.''

For the first time, her features softened. ''More, much more, but thank you.''

''She doesn't resemble Max at all, as I remember him.''

A fact for which she was grateful. She had enough unpleasant reminders of her ex-husband. ''No, she's all McKenzie.''

So the marriage had been bad enough that Shay wanted no traces of Max in their child. While he was sorry she'd been hurt, he was glad she wasn't pining away for Beth's father. ''Beth reminds me so much of you when you were young. Her love of animals, her charming ways, her dramatic streak.''

Shay frowned. ''I wasn't dramatic.''

''Really? Do you recall the time I found you screaming in the hayloft over a little brown spider? You told me he was going to eat you alive." He smiled and reached to touch her hair as earlier he'd touched Beth's, finding both silky soft and fragrant. "Do you remember, Shay?"

No, he was not going to force her to walk down memory lane. "I remember a lot of things." She stepped back out of reach. Sensing her owner's tension, Dancer came over to nuzzle Shay's shoulder. She turned to the horse, grateful for the diversion.

"Beautiful mare," Luke said, raising his hand.

"Be careful. Dancer's skittish around men."

Like her owner? he wondered. Ignoring her warning, he caressed the mare's neck, then reached to stroke along her head. Sensing a friend, Dancer shifted, allowing him to pet her more freely. "It seems she likes my touch."

"She's young, easily impressed."

"Not wordly-wise like you."

"That's right."

Luke nudged the horse aside and stepped closer, causing Shay to back up against the fence. "I remember when you wanted my touch badly." His fingers closed around her wrist and he had the pleasure of feeling her pulse escalate. Then he trailed the backs of his fingers along her satin cheek and watched her eyes darken. The need to taste her again after ten long years nearly overwhelmed him. One long, greedy kiss to wipe out all the accumulated loneliness. "Do you remember?" he asked for the second time that evening.

She saw it then, the hint of danger that danced in his eyes when he grew angry or annoyed or felt challenged. Many a Circle M cowboy who'd ignored ranch rules had seen the same warning and disregarded it, only to find himself on the receiving end of Luke's powerful fists. From age seventeen on, after a few such bouts, he'd never had to fight for loyalty or respect among the hands again.

Shay had never understood why that look in Luke's eyes both frightened and fascinated her. She only knew that it did.

His hand cupped her chin as his gaze locked with hers. She was stunned by a quick stab of awareness and felt an instant response deep inside. His touch had her trapped, just as it had years ago. This was what she'd instinctively known would happen the moment she'd set eyes on him this morning. This was why she'd avoided him all day. This was what her treacherous body craved, even as she knew she must deny it.

With a quick movement, she shook off his hand. "Let's not play turn-back-the-clock. Yes, there was a time when I ached for your touch, and I thought you wanted mine. But no more. You gave up that right when you left." So much for cool and indifferent, Shay thought. "Don't touch me again without my permission, Luke."

He watched her walk away with her head held high, then slip through the gate and hurry to the big house. Leaning against the fence, Luke gazed up at the moon. Shay could deny her feelings all night long. He'd seen her eyes, felt her response and now he knew.

She may not want to admit it, but she'd never stopped wanting him.

Zeke Crawford rolled his own cigarettes, and he was good at it. Luke watched him lick the glue strip, pat the paper firmly in place, then light up. Crunching down on a lemon drop, he turned away, wondering when this damnable nicotine craving would end.

"Roll you one, buddy?" Zeke asked.

"No, thanks. I gave them up awhile back." He walked alongside Zeke to behind the horse barn to where the Jeep was parked, inhaling the sweet scent of hay and grain. It was early morning, almost daylight. The stock had been fed and turned into the corrals. Work on a ranch started before the sun came up.

Zeke climbed behind the wheel as Luke swung in beside him. "I should quit, too, but a man's got to have a few pleasures. Most of the guys chew these days. I can't stand the thought of sticking a wad in my mouth and chomping on it like some damn cow with a cud."

That form of tobacco had never appealed to Luke, either. "Did you ask Gil to come with us?"

Zeke started the Jeep. "He had plans to go into town today to get some supplies. He's ordered himself some new boots, made out of lizard, I hear. Mighty fine stuff." He maneuvered the Jeep toward the first pastureland, aiming for the fence line that separated the grazing area from the acres of grain undulating in the soft morning air.

Luke heard a hint of envy in the man's voice. Zeke was dressed pretty much as most cowhands were—western-cut shirt, denim jeans, cowhide boots scruffed and a bit worn. His only vanity seemed to be his wide leather belt sporting a silver rodeo trophy buckle that Luke recognized as similar to several he had tucked away in his drawer, preferring a plain solid-brass buckle. He'd have thought that Zeke, as a son-in-law and co-manager of the Circle M, would have been well paid. None of his business, Luke decided, returning to his original question.

"Then you didn't mention to Gil that we were going out?"

"I thought it best we go alone for now." Zeke downshifted as they bounced over a small hill. "I take it there's bad blood between you two?"

Luke rearranged his hat as he tamped down on a rush of annoyance. It would seem Zeke liked to do things his way. He should have spoken to Gil himself. Luke would be cautious with Zeke, uncertain whether he was just nosy or a troublemaker. "We've had our ups and downs," he answered.

"So Rhea tells me." The land leveled off as Zeke drove through the first pastureland. Off to their far left, McKenzie cattle grazed while cowboys on horseback kept watch.

Luke shifted in his seat so he could see Zeke's profile. Hatless, the man's thinning sandy hair blew about his lean face. "What exactly did Rhea tell you?"

Zeke shrugged. "That you all grew up together here on the Circle M. That Gil resented you stealing his parents' affection. That you led Shay on until she was crazy in love with you, then dumped her so you could hit the rodeo circuit. You broke her heart so she married Maxwell Whitney on the rebound. Then he messed her up real good." Squinting into the rising sun, he shot Luke a glance. "That about right?"

Luke struggled with his temper, his hand gripping the Jeep's crossbar. "Not even close." It would seem he would have to have a little talk with Rhea at his first opportunity.

"Then what is the real story?" Zeke persisted.

With effort, Luke unclenched his teeth. "When I want you to know, I'll be sure to tell you."

"Hey, no hard feelings, buddy. You asked me, remember?"

It was time for a change of subject. Luke brought his mind back to ranch business. "How long ago did Jacob get the plane?"

Zeke blew smoke out the side of his mouth. "About two years. Gil talked him into it when he came home and we began to manage together. You know how to fly?"

"Yeah. We had a little Cessna on the last ranch I managed. They make a rancher's life easier."

The Jeep bumped down another hill as they headed into the second pastureland. "Sure do. I take her up nearly every day. When you've got this many acres, it's damn near impossible for the men to find every stray, especially the cows that drop their calves in remote areas."

A man on horseback passed and called to Zeke. He waved back. They came to the stream and turned to follow it.

"I see you've got ditch riders. A good move." Many ranchers had a cowboy or two patroling the water route, monitoring the levels, making sure no nearby neighbor's cows were poaching their water. In a dry season, it was the best protection.

"One of Gil's better ideas."

Luke studied the depth as they rode along. "Looks like water shouldn't be a problem, even if this heat continues."

"Not for us, it won't." Zeke snuffed out his cigarette in the ashtray. "But a lot of ranches will be hurting, including old man Whitney next over." He eased the Jeep to a stop. "This is the pasture where the count came up short."

"How short is it now?" Luke climbed out and walked toward the fence line that ended at a primitive road just up ahead.

"About a hundred," Zeke said, following him.

"About? Don't you think we should get another head count so we know exactly?"

Zeke swallowed his irritation. "I'll order one as soon as we get back."

Luke let his eyes roam over the herd grazing nearby. He remembered how Jacob used to bring him out as a boy and be able to tell if the count was off by even one just by sitting astride his horse and looking. Luke had never quite managed that.

Turning, he strode along the fence for several yards, examining it with his practiced gaze. This would have been the logical place to round up the cows, cut the wire fence, walk them through the stream and have a cattle truck waiting on the bordering dirt road. He bent closer to check out a support post. "If they cut fence anywhere along here, they did a professional job of repairing it," he commented.

Zeke stood back, his hands in his back pockets. "So I thought. I've gone over every bit of fence along here. Nothing looks suspicious."

Luke straightened. "Then again, most cowhands know how to rewire fence, don't they?"

"I suppose. But all that takes time, to get the cows across, to board them onto trailers, then come back and rewire the fence. The rustlers took a hell of a chance that one of our men wouldn't come along and see such a long operation."

He had a point. "Are all the cattle branded?"

"Sure. And we try to get to the calves soon after we find them. But if they're taking them to be slaughtered, that wouldn't count for much."

"But if they're taking them to start up their own ranch, it might. The Circle M is a rather distinctive marking."

"If a new ranch sprang up around here, we'd know it. Word travels."

Luke started back to the Jeep. "What if the rustlers were taking them some distance, maybe over the border into Wyoming?"

Zeke slid behind the heel. "Possible, I suppose. My gut tells me they're going to a slaughterhouse. There're a couple of less reputable owners of small houses who aren't too fussy as to who owns the cattle they buy."

"I'm going to talk to Liz, see if she'd be in favor of bringing Jacob in on this. He knows a lot of people, ranchers, slaughterhouse owners, cattlemen who move around. He could give us a starting place."

Smoothing back his hair, Zeke shook his head. "I don't think that's a good idea. Jacob's been awfully sick."

"But he's on the mend. Working on this problem from his bed might make him feel he's a part of things again."

Zeke turned the Jeep around. "You want to see anything else or head back?"

"I've seen enough for now. Let's go back. Tomorrow, I think I'll take the plane up and cover the whole area."

"I can go with you."

"Thanks, but I know you've got other things to do." And he had someone else in mind to ask along.

"Maybe Shay'll go with you, then."

Taken aback at the accuracy of Zeke's guess, Luke turned to look at him. "What makes you think so?"

"I saw you with her in the corral last night." Zeke shot him a knowing smile. "Guess you haven't got her out of your system."

It was time he set Zeke straight. "Whatever's between Shay and me is between the two of us and no one else. I'd appreciate it if you'd remember that."

"Sure, sure, buddy," Zeke said, as if to humor him.

Luke slouched back in his seat, deciding that the ride back would be a silent one.

Chapter Three

Shay leaned back in her father's desk chair and stretched. Morning sunshine drifted in through the window as she glanced out. Another hot day, she thought as she closed the last ledger. She'd been working on the books since seven, enjoying the peace of the quiet house in Jacob's comfortable den.

Most ranchers had their managers do the bookkeeping, but Jacob McKenzie hadn't wanted to let the control slip out of his hands, so he'd always done it himself. But with his second heart attack, he'd had little choice. Honoring her husband's wishes to keep the accounting in the family, Liz had asked Shay to take over since Gil already had a great deal to do. Though she'd told Luke that the paperwork was very time-consuming, Shay actually enjoyed this end of ranching.

She'd come into Jacob's office most mornings, appreciating the masculine room, the huge fieldstone fireplace, the book-lined shelves along two walls, the supple feel of the leather furniture. And she enjoyed keeping track of ordering the supplies, updating the cattle records, balancing the profit-and-loss statements that would then go to their CPA. There was comfort in working with numbers, in making them come out right.

And most mornings, when she finished her bookkeeping, she'd put away the ledgers and bring out her own work. She would lose herself in words, in stories she wrote about the West, about ranching. And about love.

At first, writing had been her only outlet for creative dreaming, a way to channel her imagination, an escape from some of life's harsher realities. She wrote in longhand on yellow legal pads, mostly in the den, but sometimes out under a shady tree or in the hayloft where it was quiet, then later typed a revised copy. She'd told no one about her attempts at producing a salable book. If she failed, she wanted no sympathetic looks. If she succeeded . . . well, she would handle that when it happened.

Opening the bottom desk drawer, she pulled out her latest effort, a story set on a ranch much like the Circle M. A story of a stubborn man and an independent woman, each grappling for control of a cattle dynasty, and struggling against the passion that drew them together. She'd sent it off to a publishing company several months ago and received an encouraging letter from one of their editors. If she would be willing to make the outlined changes, they would be willing to take another look at her book. She'd had several submissions rejected outright, and though she knew that this editor's directive was hardly a sure thing, Shay couldn't help being excited.

She'd nearly completed the changes and would be sending off the revised manuscript in another week or so. With it would go her hopes for not only creative recognition but eventual financial independence. Shay sighed and slipped the pages back into the drawer. She would come back later to work on it, after completing her ranching chores.

She was close this time, really close. She could feel it. The sale of a first book didn't necessarily mean a lot of money, but it would be a foot in the door of publishing. They would then look at her next submission with more interest. And she'd be on her way.

Not that her parents were asking her to pay for her and Beth's keep, other than the work Shay did on the ranch. Nor would they ever. The two of them would have a home on the Circle M forever if they wanted it, Shay knew. But *she* needed to be independent, to be free of relying on anyone. She needed to know that the choice to go or stay would be hers, that her fate would be in her hands, not someone else's.

All her life she'd relied on others, Shay thought, as she cleared off the top of the desk. First her mother and father, then Max. She badly wanted to control her own destiny, to be able to make decisions for her daughter without the need to consult others. She loved the ranch, loved living and working here. But having other options, as well, had become her primary goal.

Which was another reason she mustn't let Luke reawaken all the hungers she'd once felt for him, to stir up things best left alone. She must fight against the needs that raged through her the moment he touched her. Because if she didn't, she'd find herself giving in to him, and she'd no longer be her own woman.

She'd been free of Max's influence for five years now, and she'd vowed after she'd left the Whitney spread to never again let a man control her destiny. Luke was the only man she'd ever had a weakness for, a craving so strong that she knew he could easily bend her to his will.

But she must not let that happen, must not fall for him a second time.

She would have to be alert with Luke hovering around, to be polite and friendly, but not warm and inviting. She would get through this and protect her emotions so that when he left this time, she would feel nothing but relief.

And leave he would, for it would seem Luke had more of his father's wanderlust in him than she'd thought. Her mother had told her he'd traveled a great deal over the past ten years, with the rodeo, then working on ranches in three different states. That was surely another reason to stay uninvolved. The last thing she'd want to do would be to drag Beth from place to place, following a man and his nebulous dream.

Rising, Shay picked up her coffee cup and walked to the kitchen for a refill. The aroma of baking bread filled the big room as she entered, causing her to inhale hungrily. "Mmm, that smells good," she commented to her mother as she poured coffee from the seemingly always-full pot. She topped off her mother's mug as Liz sat at the table going over a grocery list.

"Thanks, dear," Liz said without looking up. "I think this is everything, Cora." She handed the list to her housekeeper. "Who's driving you into town?"

"Charley's offered," Cora answered, putting the sheet of paper into her purse. "You won't forget to take out the loaves when the oven bell rings?"

Liz smiled. "I'll remember. Take your time." She watched the efficient little woman hurry out the back door, then turned to study her daughter.

She'd heard Shay rise early and go to Jacob's den as was her daily habit. Liz had almost followed, almost asked what Luke had said to her last night to make her look noticeably tense and shaken when she'd returned from

Dancer's corral. Keeping out of a grown child's personal problems was one of the hardest acts of discipline a parent faced.

She still looked edgy, Liz thought. Shay sipped her coffee as she stood gazing out the kitchen window, her expression bordering on anxious. She would bet her best china bowl she could guess the reason for her daughter's mood, Liz decided, as she quietly walked over to peek around Shay's shoulder.

There was Luke in the rear paddock grooming his stallion. He'd removed his shirt in the heat of mid-morning, and the sun glistened on his damp back, the well-defined muscles rippling as he brushed Maverick down. Liz turned and saw such a look of longing on her daughter's face as to bring tears to her eyes before Shay became aware of her mother's scrutiny and quickly masked her expression.

"It's good having him back with us, isn't it?" Liz asked.

"Is it, Mother?"

"I think so. He spent an hour this morning upstairs talking with your father. Jacob seemed more alert when I went in later than he has in days. Luke has a way with people."

"Doesn't he just."

"You're still in love with him," Liz said softly. It was not a question.

Shay took a final swallow of her coffee, then placed the cup in the sink. "I'll get over him. Just as I did before."

Had she been wrong to call Luke back? Liz wondered. "Why must you? You're free, and so is Luke. If there are strong feelings between you, why not pursue them?"

Shay patted the back of her damp neck, wishing it wasn't so damn hot. "Because Luke has the power to hurt me. He did it before and he could do it again, worse than

Max ever could. I'm tired of being hurt, Mom. No man's going to get the chance again."

Liz hated the bitterness she heard in her daughter's voice, yet knew there was truth in what she said. "That sort of thing is a two-way street, Shay. You have the power to hurt Luke, too."

Shay released a ragged breath. "I don't want to hurt him. I just want him to leave before there's more pain, so I can get on with my life."

How simplistic a solution. "Sometimes we have to face things from our past before we can go on with our lives."

"I'm stronger this time," she said, and prayed she was right. She watched Luke straighten, then run his hands down the stallion's front flank, checking him over. Those strong, tan hands that could be so gentle, that could bring such pleasure. But pleasure always had a price tag.

She narrowed her eyes, considering her mother's words that she, too, held some power over Luke. "Maybe it's time that Luke Turner had a taste of his own medicine."

Liz frowned. "I'd be careful if I were you. People who set traps often get caught in them."

Shay shifted her gaze and met her mother's troubled eyes. "If he stays away from me, there won't be a problem. No one will be hurt."

"And if he doesn't? If he comes after you?"

Unexpectedly Shay smiled. "Mom, you worry too much. Luke's a big boy, and I'm sure he can take care of himself." She pushed off from the counter. "I'll be in the big barn if you need me."

Liz returned to her chair, worry lines on her forehead deepening. Despite her warnings to her daughter, she believed Luke could take care of himself.

But could Shay? she asked herself.

* * *

"Nice of you to let me know you went riding fence yesterday, Luke."

Luke straightened from bending over cleaning Maverick's front foot with a hoof pick. Stepping clear of the stallion, he turned to face Gil. "I told Zeke to ask if you wanted to come along. He said you already had plans to go into town."

Gil removed his hat and ran a hand through his short brown hair. "Plans can be changed."

"Why don't you check with Zeke? You'll find I'm telling the truth. Why wouldn't I want you along?"

"My question exactly." Gil slapped his hat back on and spread his feet, his stance challenging. A head shorter and much slighter than Luke, he still had to let him know he wasn't afraid of him.

Luke was hot, sweaty and damn tired of having to defend himself again. He tossed his tool into the box on the ground and stepped closer to Gil. "Look, what is it with you? You're the one who wanted me out of here years ago, my so-called brother who told me a drifter's son wasn't good enough to marry a McKenzie."

Gil's hands formed tight fists at his side. "You're still not. And don't call me your brother."

"Is that right? Well, I don't see as how that blue blood Whitney made Shay happy, now did he?"

"That's not the issue here. Why did you *really* come back? Have you run out of money and decided to take another stab at marrying a McKenzie, getting a share of the Circle M?"

Wearily Luke wiped his brow. Some time ago, he'd come to the conclusion that that's how Gil regarded him, and obviously the man hadn't changed his mind. Banking his rising temper, Luke promised himself he wouldn't start a

fight with Gil on his father's land. "I came back because
your mother asked me to. I promised to help find the rustlers. Why don't you try cooperating with me so we can get
the job done? Then I'll be out of here again."

Gil considered that a moment. "You really are going to
leave once we find those guys?"

"Yeah, I really am. I told Liz I'd give her a month and
no more."

Gil relaxed a fraction, wondering if he dared to believe
Luke. He'd never known him to lie in the past, but ten
years away could change a man. "What about Shay?" he
asked.

"What about her?"

"She's had it rough. I don't want you making moves on
her again."

Luke had had enough. "We can talk about the rustling,
the ranch, Jacob's health and most anything else, you and
I. But not Shay. What's between Shay and me is private.
She doesn't need you to protect her from me. Are we
straight on this?"

That dangerous look Gil well remembered blazed from
Luke's eyes. He would take him at his word, that he would
leave as soon as the rustling problem was solved. Which
meant it would be in his own best interest if he cooperated
and worked with Luke. "All right."

Luke nodded. Gil was stubborn, but he wasn't stupid.
"How about later on you and I go over the ranch records
and find out if any cowboys left under a cloud recently,
unhappy over something and maybe wanting to get even?
Or some newcomer with a shady past who might be working with someone on the outside. Unless you and Zeke
have already checked out those possibilities?"

"No, we haven't. That's a good idea." The truth was he
hadn't had time to do much about solving the rustling.

One of his foremen had broken a leg and couldn't ride, and another of his best range cowboys had reconciled with his wife and left for Texas. Gil was shorthanded and feeling the strain. He'd pretty much decided the rustlers had taken only a handful of cows on a one-shot, quick-money scheme, so he hadn't spent much thought on catching them. Now it would seem he'd have to.

"I'll finish here and meet you in Jacob's study in about an hour, okay?"

"Yeah, an hour." Gil turned and left the paddock.

Luke picked up the hoof pick. Maybe, just maybe, there was a chance he could get through to Gil and learn the real reason the man considered him a threat.

Something didn't add up here. He didn't know what it was, but he meant to find out—and soon. Luke picked up the stallion's foot and bent to his task.

It was one of her favorite times on the ranch, early evening. Leisurely Shay strolled toward the cattle barn. The heavy work of the long day was done—the milking, the animals fed and settled, the cook house deserted except for a few lingering hands drinking coffee. The heat of the day had cooled to almost bearable and the night sounds were taking over. Men sat around whittling, working in leather, listening to music, exchanging stories on the stoop.

Shay slid open the heavy door and walked down the cement aisle to check on the calves. Since the daytime temperature had climbed past ninety-five, several newborns had been brought in from the pastures with their mothers, out of the sun and the humidity until they were stronger. The barn was cooler, and the piped-in music was soothing. She strolled past several stalls, murmuring a word here and there.

Past the saddle room, she spotted Charley Brice, one of the newer hands, leaning over a stall, and walked over to him.

"Hi. What brings you here, Shay?" he asked, removing his hat.

"Come to visit the babies," she said with a smile. Charley was not the typical working cowboy, and she'd wondered about him more than once. He looked like the Marlboro man, with clothes straight out of the L.L. Bean catalog. Still, he was always polite to her.

She peered into the stall and saw the long-legged calf in the corner. "What's wrong with this one?"

"He's an orphan," Charley explained. "Breech birth. We had to do away with the mother. He's going to follow her 'cause he refuses to nurse from any of the other cows we put him to. And he won't take the bottle. Stubborn little cuss." Charley's silver spurs jingled as he stepped back.

"Did you try force-feeding him?" Shay asked, as she opened the stall door and walked in.

"Yeah, but he got sick right after. I think we're going to have to call this one a loss."

But Shay wasn't one to give up so easily. Moving slowly, she reached a hand out toward the calf. "Hey, there, aren't you hungry?" She spoke over her shoulder to Charley. "Would you get me a bottle of warm milk, please?"

Charley grunted as if to say that she was wasting her time, but he went to do as she asked. By the time he returned, she was sitting cross-legged on the hay-covered floor, stroking the calf's thin face while his big eyes watched her. Charley handed her the bottle, then left them alone.

Shay dribbled a bit of milk onto her palm and held it up to the calf's nose so he could smell it. He sniffed tentatively, then his rough tongue snaked out and curved around. After a moment, he licked the milk off. As his tongue darted out, looking for more, Shay quickly inserted the nipple into his mouth. The small head tilted up and he wiggled and stretched, fighting the unfamiliar invasion. Finally he began to suck.

"There, that's a good boy." She leaned her back against the stall wall and settled the calf more comfortably across her lap. Catching on, he attacked his dinner vigorously, his sad eyes on her. "You miss your momma, I know. And no daddy around to take up the slack. Life's not fair, is it, fella?"

Only the night lamps were burning, leaving the stalls in dim light, but Shay didn't mind. She'd grown up among all these familiar scents and sounds—the bawling of another calf down the way, a restless cow making snuffling noises across the aisle, the smell of oiled leather drifting from the saddle room. There was a kind of contentment here that she'd found nowhere else. Perhaps it was the trust the animals gave so freely to the people who cared for them.

The calf twisted around, draining the last drop from the bottle as Shay smiled. "You were hungry, weren't you?" She pulled the empty bottle from him, and he gave her a startled look. "That's all you can have for now, or you'll be sick." He stood uncertainly, but his wobbly legs spread wide and he slid down, then rolled over to place his head in her lap. "More tomorrow morning, little guy."

"He's not so little," Beth said, coming through the stall door to join her mother.

"Hi, sweetie." She didn't have to coax Beth to pet the calf for she, too, had grown up around animals and was always drawn to the newborns.

Beth went down on her knees and stroked the calf's soft hide. He lifted his head and burped, and they both laughed out loud. "Maybe we should call him Mr. Piggy."

"It certainly fits," Shay agreed.

Beth sat for a moment, her face sobering. "I feel sorry for him, Mom. He's got no one."

"He's got us, sweetie. In no time, he'll be big and strong, and we'll put him out to pasture where he can eat grass and be with the others."

"But his mother died, and his father doesn't care about him." The freckles on her solemn little face stood out in the muted lighting as she pondered that.

Shay studied her daughter, wondering where this conversation was coming from. Beth knew that Maxwell Whitney on the adjacent ranch was her father, but Max seldom visited, and paid child support even less frequently. He was like a stranger who dropped in occasionally, usually upsetting Beth, who didn't know what to make of this man who drifted in and out of her life. Was she, at seven, comparing her situation with that of this orphaned calf?

"Animals aren't like people, honey," Shay said, reaching to touch Beth's face.

"Yes, they are," Beth persisted. "The bulls never care about the calves, but the mother cows always do, unless they die." Dark, worried eyes raised to meet Shay's. "Just like with me. You love me, but Daddy doesn't care at all."

Shay stiffened, instantly alert. "Did he come by after I came out here? Is that why you're upset?"

"He called. Grandma wouldn't let him talk to me. She said he'd have to ask you. Mom, I don't want to talk to him."

Shay reached to pull her daughter close, shifting the drowsy calf against her other side. "You won't have to. I'll talk to your father." Damn Max, she thought. Beth was right in that he had absolutely no interest in developing a relationship with his daughter. Why, then, did he come around at all, unless to irritate Shay?

Gritting her teeth, she made up her mind to tell Max to back off and stay away. A man who didn't bother to support his child, whose parents had never once come over to see Beth or ask her over there since they'd left, didn't deserve a beautiful girl like Beth.

Beth's head was on her mother's shoulder. "I don't know why he doesn't want me."

"Oh, honey, it's not you. It's nothing you did or didn't do. It's just the way he is. But not all men are like your father. Look at Grandpa. He adores you."

"I guess so." Her voice was small.

Shay tilted her daughter's face up so she could look at her. "You *know* he does. And Uncle Gil and Uncle Zeke care."

"Mom, how come you never mentioned Luke to me before?"

Taken aback that Beth changed subjects abruptly, as children are apt to do, Shay took a moment to answer. "He left here a long time ago, way before you were born."

"Don't you like him? I do. He took me for a ride today on his horse. We rode double. It was fun."

Shay struggled with a flash of temper. What right did Luke have, taking her daughter without her permission? "He shouldn't have done that without asking me. I'll talk with him and..."

"You were busy in Grandpa's den. He asked Grandma, and she said it'd be okay. He showed me this rock down by the stream where he said you used to like to go sit and daydream. Did you, Mom?"

The rock. Yes, she'd spent many an hour there when she had something to mull over, some problem to work out. Often as not, she'd gone there trying to come to grips with her growing feelings for Luke back in those teen years. He'd discovered her favorite spot and afterward had occasionally joined her there. They'd talked and shared so much, sitting there on that big, smooth rock in the shade of a huge pine tree alongside the rushing stream.

But that had been then, and this was now. "Where else did Luke take you?" Shay asked.

"Nowhere. I took him into the henhouse, and we gathered eggs. He told me a funny story about a chicken named One Foot that used to live here."

Despite her annoyance, Shay smiled. "I remember. She lost her foot to an infection and Luke whittled a peg leg for her and taped it onto her stump. Silly chicken used to strut around, proud as you please, with that wooden leg. I'd forgotten all about One Foot."

Beth pulled back. "See, you do like him. I knew it." In still another mood shift, she scrambled to her feet. "I've got to find Beechie. We're practicing chewing gum so we can show Luke. See you later, Mom."

"Stay close to the house, Beth," Shay said automatically.

"I always do." Beth skipped down the cement walkway.

Sagging back against the wooden wall, Shay sighed, absently petting the calf as it dozed, contentedly curled against her side, its belly full. The big question, from her mother and now from her daughter: did she like, perhaps even love, Luke Turner? Not a new question, certainly. One she'd asked herself a trillion times. She knew the answer even as she fought against the knowledge.

Yes, she did. It seemed she always had. However, she'd become very adept at burying the feeling. Until recently.

Hold on, she told herself. Just a few more weeks and he'll be gone. She tipped her head back and closed her eyes.

"Have you taken to sleeping out here with the animals?"

Her eyes flew open as she looked up into the amused blue eyes of the man in question. How long had he been in the barn? she wondered, as wordlessly she watched him come into the stall and stoop down to stroke the sleeping calf.

"Are you his adopted mother?" he asked with a slow grin.

"It wouldn't be the first time," she answered. His scent reached out to her, that intoxicating combination of the outdoors and maleness and sex all rolled into an irresistible pull on her senses.

"You were always a soft touch for young, motherless things." Like the boy he'd been when he'd first arrived.

Shay tried to harden her heart against him, but found his comment weakening her resolve. She had been deeply sympathetic to the orphan boy he'd been. But he was a boy no more, as she was increasingly aware.

Luke found himself drawn in by the velvet softness of her eyes, huge and vulnerable. They were a warm brown, but he remembered how they darkened to the color of bittersweet chocolate when she was aroused. He hadn't meant to eavesdrop on her conversation with Beth. He'd been in the saddle room using neat's-foot oil on his tack, something that needed frequent application since leather dried out quickly in the heat of summer. Finishing, he'd heard low voices and come over.

He'd stood in the shadows, listening to Shay try to explain Max's obviously painful negligence of his daughter to Beth. And then he'd heard their discussion of him, picking up on Shay's annoyance, as well as her unspoken admission of buried feelings for him. It had been an enlightening few minutes, and when Beth had run off, he hadn't been able to resist joining Shay.

Luke sat down beside her, admiring her long hair, the way he preferred it, hanging loose about her shoulders. Her cheeks looked warm and flushed. It was all he could do not to reach up and touch her skin.

"I took your daughter riding today," he said, knowing that Beth had already told her.

"Don't you think you should have checked with me first?"

"Don't you think you can trust me with her, Shay?"

Yes, she did think him trustworthy. She wasn't exactly sure why his taking Beth irritated her. She shifted her gaze to the calf. "I like to know where she is at all times."

"I asked Liz, just as Beth told you." He saw her head swivel around, watched the realization that he'd heard them settle in her eyes. "Yes, I was listening, and I won't apologize. It seems to be the only way I'm going to learn what you're thinking."

"Is that why you took Beth riding, to pump her for information about me?" The instant the words were out, she regretted saying them as she saw the temper flare in his eyes.

"I think you know me better than that."

"I thought I knew you well once, but it turned out I didn't know you at all."

He frowned. "What do you mean by that?"

"Nothing. Forget it." Shay shifted the sleeping calf onto its side away from her and made as if to rise.

His hand on her arm stopped her. "No, I won't. Talk to me. What did you mean?"

Hadn't she known they'd come to this? All right, she'd talk to him, but he wasn't going to like it. Her pulse was shaky as she met his eyes. "Do you remember that last night we were together, the night before you left?"

"Your nineteenth birthday. Yes, I remember."

She felt the heat spread, felt a throbbing in her temples. "Do you remember what we did, what we almost did?"

Luke knew exactly what she meant.

It had been a hot summer evening, much as tonight was. They'd had the usual birthday dinner at the big house, then cake and candles and presents. Only he hadn't given her his present until much later, when he'd asked her to go for a walk down by the stream and they'd stopped by her favorite rock.

A pale moon had dribbled leafy shadows across her face as he handed her the small package. His heart pounded along with the rushing water gliding over the rocks as she opened the box, her dark eyes wide with anticipation. Carefully she removed the fine chain and studied the silver key that dangled from it.

"It's for all the doors you've yet to open," Luke told her.

"It's beautiful," Shay whispered, then turned so he could fasten it around her neck. When she was facing him again, she smiled up into his eyes. "We'll open those doors together." Rising on tiptoe, she reached for his kiss.

As always, with the touch of her mouth on his, Luke felt totally consumed. He'd been the first man to kiss her when she was sixteen, the only man in the three years since, and yet she overwhelmed him each time. In seconds, she was as involved as he, as transported as he, as filled with raw passion as he.

With Shay in his arms, Luke forgot everything. Forgot that his beginning years had been raw and painful and lonely as hell. Forgot that though he lived on the Circle M, he wasn't a McKenzie and never would be. Forgot that he had no right to love Shay McKenzie, though he knew he would till the day he died.

His head spinning, he wound his arms around her and felt her hands slide into the thickness of his hair. The kiss went on and on, demand meeting demand, until they were both breathless with need. That was when he moved her to the soft grass beneath a nearby tree.

Night birds skittered in the treetops, and a distant coyote called out as Luke lay with her on the warm ground. With a sigh of desperation, he dragged her mouth back to his, certain he would never get enough of her.

She stretched within his arms and made a soft sound as his lips moved to nibble at the sweet line of her throat. When his hands pulled her shirttail free from her jeans and slid inside to touch warm flesh, he heard her moan close to his ear. He'd never touched her like this, never wanted her so badly. And he knew she wanted him with the same unbridled passion.

But he was the older one, supposedly the wiser one. He would be the one answering to Jacob if he dared spoil his little girl. So he settled for loosening her bra and touching her breasts while rivers of fire had him hard and hurting.

Her hands on his head maneuvered him lower as she arched and offered her breasts to his mouth. No man could have resisted and he didn't, tasting her for the first time as his body strained against hers. He felt her heartbeat pound under his lips and nearly lost control.

"I love you, Luke," Shay whispered, her hands clutching him closer.

"I love you, too," he told her, and knew he always had.

"Make love to me, please. I want you so much."

And God, he wanted to. No one had ever wanted him like this. No one had whispered words of love to him, not ever. He was totally hers in a way he'd never dreamed he would be. But loving her fully now could ruin everything.

"I can't," he said, struggling for breath. "You're a virgin and your father... no, we can't." He hadn't brought protection, hadn't thought they'd get this far.

"I don't care about my father," she said, pressing herself against him. "I need you, Luke."

He heard an owl hooting in the distance and took a moment to come to his senses. One of them had to and he was the experienced one, the one who would shoulder the blame if things went wrong.

Shifting her in his arms, he laid her across his lap, then buried his face in her hair. "There's another way. Trust me."

Her lips were on his throat, her restless body moving as she grappled with her first serious arousal. "I do."

He touched his mouth to hers, kissing her already swollen lips, his tongue dueling with hers. Slowly he inched his hand down to the waistband of her jeans, then paused a moment before pushing down her zipper. He felt her skin jump as he slid his fingers inside the silky material that covered her moist secret. He deepened the kiss, swallowing the sweet sounds she made.

She moved against him with an abandon that was as wild and beautiful as she herself was. He drove her up and watched her climb, then held her as she rode with her first frantic taste of desire set in motion. He badly wanted to ease the swelling that already had him shaking with need, but this night was for Shay and Shay alone. There would be other nights when he would be able to do every delicious thing he'd ever dreamed of with her. After Jacob and

Liz gave their permission, after Shay was really his. Until then, he would protect her, for he loved her too much not to.

At last, she crested and cried out as he held her close to his shuddering heart. She was everything he'd always known she would be, the passionate lover who would walk by his side all the rest of their lives. Luke brushed back her hair from her damp face as she quieted.

When she opened her eyes, he saw a tear trail down her cheeks and he experienced a moment of fear. Then she smiled.

"Oh, Luke," she whispered, her voice ragged. "I didn't know."

"There's more, Shay," he said, hugging her to him. "So much more. One day soon, I'll show you everything."

"I'm counting on that," she said, then closed her eyes and curled up on his lap.

No, they hadn't made love, conventionally speaking. But they'd made love all the same. And no, he'd never forgotten that night, Luke thought now, as he stared into her huge eyes. "I remember what we did, and it wasn't almost. We made love that night."

Her face felt heated, but she went on. "Yes, that's how I think of it, too. So how could you leave me without a word and just disappear? Did all that mean so little to you, words of love, an act of love?"

Luke was honestly surprised. "Wait a minute. What do you mean, without a word? I left you a note, right on the vestibule table where we always left notes to each other."

She regarded him with suspicion. She'd never known Luke to hide behind an untruth, yet this seemed like a convenient answer out of the blue. She shook her head. "There was no note."

He grabbed her arm, growing angry. "Shay, I left a note for you, and one for Liz. I don't lie."

Shay studied his eyes a long moment. "I don't, either. My mother didn't find a note. I know, because I asked her that next morning, over and over."

Luke believed her and felt the fury rise inside him. Turning aside, he propped his arm on his bent knee. "I'd sure as hell like to know what happened to those notes." Or who took them, he thought.

She was thinking along the same lines. "Why would someone take your notes?"

"A good question. I put each one in an envelope, wrote your names on them and placed them in plain view because I wanted you to spot them first thing in the morning." Luke rubbed a weary hand across his day's growth of beard.

Getting to his feet, Luke felt a rush of impotent rage he'd often experienced growing up. Unfair happenings that he'd been helpless to change. Only he was no longer a youngster under someone else's control.

He thought he had a pretty good idea what probably happened to those notes. He also knew that proving it or even revealing his suspicions would upset this family more than his return already had. He regretted that, but there were times when pain couldn't be avoided. He'd left once in the dark of night, guiltily, like he was walking away from an unpaid debt. This time, he would get to the bottom of things, clear his name and leave with his head held high.

Luke stretched out a hand to help Shay up. Maybe the others would judge him, but he badly wanted this woman to believe him. He took her hands and waited until she faced him. "Shay, that night meant a great deal to me." He couldn't tell her all of it, couldn't say that it was the first time he'd ever been told that he was loved, unwilling to invite her sympathy. "We made love and . . ."

"No, not we." She saw that his eyes had turned deep blue and troubled. She felt her heart opening to him despite her best efforts. "You made love to me, protected me. It wasn't until later, when I was a bit older, that I realized how what we did couldn't have been very good for you."

He stepped closer and raised his hand to touch her face. "It was wonderful, and I meant every word I said that night. I wouldn't have left without an explanation."

She badly wanted to believe him. "What did you say in the note?"

"That I knew your parents wanted you to finish college. That I needed to go, needed to make something of myself so you would be proud of me, so Jacob would accept me."

"I *was* proud of you, and my father *always* accepted you."

"Jacob accepted a young kid he'd taken in. But I wanted to ask him for his daughter's hand in marriage, and I had nothing to offer you."

She felt her heart twist at hearing the words. "You should have asked me. I'd have gone with you in a minute."

Luke shook his head. "I wanted to do it right. I came from nothing, Shay, and I was damn tired of being the orphan kid everyone felt sorry for, not as good as that blue blood Whitney." Especially after someone had cruelly pointed that out to him.

She shook her head. "That wasn't ever how I looked at you. And you were twice the man even then that Max is."

"But you married him."

She let out a huff of air and walked to the other side of the stall, her face in shadow. "Yes, I married him. After I thought you'd left without a word even though you'd said you loved me. After I cried until I couldn't cry anymore. After I went back to college and found I was lonely and lost. And after... after I saw your picture in the paper, appearing in some rodeo, your arm around a woman. You were both smiling.''

He moved to her, wishing he could turn back the clock. ''I don't even remember her name. We'd probably both won in some event that day and some photographer snapped our pictures. I went on the rodeo circuit thinking I could make some quick money, buy myself a spread and come back for you. I told you in the note to wait for me if you cared, to wait and I'd come back when I could give you all you deserved.''

She raised anguished eyes to his. ''All I deserved? What about what I wanted? I didn't want *things*. I wanted *you*.'' Her voice was low and filled with remembered pain.

Luke took a deep breath. ''I also wrote that if you found you didn't care enough to wait, that I would understand, that I wanted you to be happy, to make a life for yourself. Later I heard that you married Max.''

Shay blinked back the tears. ''I was young and impatient and hurt. I've paid for my mistakes.''

''So have I, Shay. And I'm still paying. Now I know why Jacob and Liz have been looking at me with a question in their eyes, with that hint of accusation. No one is ever going to really believe I left those notes until I find out just what did happen and prove it. And I will. If I have to turn this family upside down, I will.'' He turned and shoved open the stall door.

Her need to protect her family had her going after him. ''No, don't. I believe you.''

Luke looked back over his shoulder. She was saying the right words, but did she mean them? He wouldn't live under a suspicious cloud. "I have to do this my way." He walked away and left the barn.

Shay slouched against the wall, her heart heavy. She'd known the moment Luke had shown up that they were in for turmoil. She didn't know how much her father would hear of it, and who Luke would hurt with his probing questions. Even as a boy, he'd always needed to get to the bottom of things.

Perhaps some things were best left alone, Shay thought. Yet she couldn't help but wonder. Who had wanted to keep Luke and her apart back then? And why?

Chapter Four

Dr. Silas Emmett was a short man with a pleasant smile and a graying beard, who was seldom seen without the beige felt hat that hid his balding head. He leaned toward suits with vests, white shirts and bolo ties, dressing more formally than most around Grassy Ridge. Born and raised in Montana, he'd practiced medicine in and around the town for well over thirty years, knew nearly everyone in the county by name and medical history and had delivered all three of the McKenzie children. Luke sat at Liz's kitchen table and watched the doctor accept her offer of a cup of coffee after his lengthy visit with Jacob.

"You honestly feel he's improving, Doctor?" Liz asked as she set a cup in front of Luke, then refilled her own.

Dr. Emmett took a cautious sip before answering. "Yes, Elizabeth, I do," he said. "There's a lot of good years left for Jacob McKenzie, provided he follows directions this time. He's getting stronger every day."

Liz slipped onto a chair and leaned forward, placing her crossed arms on the table. "We're all trying to make sure he does."

"That's the ticket." Dr. Emmett shifted his pale blue eyes to Luke. "So, Lucas, are you back to stay?"

"For a while," Luke answered. "Tell me, Doctor, do you feel Jacob's up to hearing some troubling news?"

Silas set down his cup, his pinkie ring sparkling in a shaft of sunlight. "How troubling?"

Luke glanced at Liz and saw her curious frown. "May I speak confidentially?"

"Certainly," Silas answered.

"We have some cows missing and—"

"Rustling, I take it you mean, not strays?"

"We believe so."

"Have you called the sheriff?"

"We're handling it ourselves for now." He felt Liz's hand touch his arm. "Hear me out, Liz. Frankly, we could use Jacob's input. No one knows the hands, the neighbors, the men in charge of the slaughterhouses, the way Jacob does. As you're probably aware, Doctor, many a ranch has had cattle stolen, often by insiders. A man as active as he's always been gets to feeling left out lying around in bed all day."

Dr. Emmett sat back thoughtfully. "You mean to involve him to the extent of advice mostly?"

"Yes, that's right. I spend time with him every day, and I can sense his annoyance at not being told what's going on on his ranch, which has been, along with his family, his major concern all his life. I believe he needs to feel needed." Luke glanced at Liz to see how his idea was sitting with her.

Reluctantly she nodded. "You have a point, Luke. Sometimes my tendency to protect leads me in the wrong direction."

He put his hand over hers. "It was the right approach when he was in danger. But, if Dr. Emmett says drawing him back in gradually won't harm him, then I think we should move in that direction now. Jacob will feel more inclined to strive to get well if he knows we need him."

Liz smiled. Funny how no one else had seen what Luke had noticed in one short week. She'd been right to ask him to return. Luke had always seen through to the heart of the matter. She squeezed his hand and turned to Dr. Emmett. "Do you agree?"

The doctor nodded. "We all need to feel as though our contribution matters. I think he can handle a minor problem if it doesn't work into major stress. How many cows are missing?"

"We're getting an updated head count now," Luke answered, and made a note to check with Zeke and get him moving on that. "Around a hundred, maybe more."

Silas knew that the Circle M counted their stock in the thousands. "It would seem you've discovered the loss before it's gotten out of hand. Yes, go ahead and draw Jacob in on the problem. Naturally, you can't minimize the situation, but don't make it sound alarming, either. He's a worrier, which is one reason he's in that bed right now."

"I'm sure Luke can tell him in a way that won't upset him too much," Liz said.

The doctor finished his coffee, checked his watch and rose. "Got to be on my way. Call me if there's any change."

Liz stood to see him to the door. "I will."

"I'll be back next week, then." He picked up his case. "Good to see you, Lucas."

"You, too, Doctor." Luke followed them out and waited until the man was gone and Liz had turned to him, before asking, "Do you want to tell him, or maybe Gil should be the one?"

Liz shook her head. "No, you explain things to Jacob. After I talked with him last night about the missing notes, he'll be more inclined to listen to you."

He would love to have been in on that conversation. Perhaps in time Liz would say more. "If you're sure . . ."

"I am. Go on up. I know he's awake."

Gathering his thoughts, Luke climbed the stairs.

It was two days since he'd had that disturbing conversation with Shay in the barn when he'd learned his notes had never gotten to either of them. When he'd approached Liz, she'd been as adamant as Shay that she'd found nothing from him the morning after he'd left. He almost believed that both Shay and Liz felt he was telling the truth or at least wanted to believe him. But he'd have to prove himself to everyone else.

Only one person really knew what happened, the one who somehow saw him put the notes on the table and leave, the person who then read them and tore them up, for whatever reason. Or someone who happened across them on an early visit to the big house. He had a few possible suspects in mind.

Jacob had wanted Shay to finish college and to marry well, Luke had been aware. He might have destroyed the notes in the hope that his daughter would get over Luke and move on. Luke felt Jacob was an honest man, yet his instincts would lead him to protect his daughter as he saw fit, and he could be hiding the truth even now.

Gil had had every reason to want to discredit Luke in his parents' eyes, and tearing up the notes would have been a golden opportunity. Was that why Gil felt so threatened now that Luke was back?

Rhea had been a mischievous seventeen, yet she'd had a crush on him back then that had had her cornering him in the barn one evening and drawing him into a surprisingly passionate kiss. When he'd politely but firmly disentangled himself from her and made it clear he wasn't interested, she could have been embarrassed and angry enough to want to get even. Though it seemed unlikely, for Rhea was always laughing and joking, the possibility still existed. People weren't always what they seemed, Luke knew.

And there was one other suspect. Aaron Huxley had been a foreman on the ranch back then, a tall, muscular cowboy, handsome and somewhat arrogant. He'd been after Shay since she'd turned sixteen and her body had matured, but she'd never given him a second glance, to Luke's knowledge. All the managers and foremen had access to the big house, so Aaron could have dropped by and spotted the notes, read them and seized the opportunity to remove the competition.

Again, not likely, but not to be discounted, either. Aaron had quit his job and moved on the very week Shay had married Max, Luke had learned. Quietly he'd been trying to track Aaron's whereabouts, but so far, he'd had no luck. Cowboys moved around a lot, but he would locate the man sooner or later. Luke knew himself to be both patient and persistent.

At Jacob's door, Luke hesitated. He had no doubt that the older man would be able to handle hearing about the rustling. He'd heard stories about such occurrences on the Circle M when Jacob had been a boy and his father had been in charge. It was a happening that nearly every rancher had to deal with at one time or another.

But if Jacob hadn't taken the notes, how would he react to Luke suspiciously investigating members of his family who had tried to manipulate Shay and discredit Luke? A horse of another color, Luke thought, as he opened the door.

Shay set the glass of milk on her father's tray alongside his plate of broiled fish and salad. "I'll just take this up to Dad and be right back," she said to her mother.

"Thanks, dear," Liz said as she served Beth a grilled cheese sandwich. "Can I make you one of these in the meantime?"

"I don't think so, Mom. It's too hot to be hungry." She hefted the tray and went to the doorway, bumping the swinging door open with her hip.

"Shay, you've got to eat. You're too thin as it is."

"Don't worry, Grandma," Beth interjected. "Aunt Rhea will eat Mom's share."

Putting sugar into her iced tea, Rhea sent her niece a mock scowl. "Hey, shrimp, are you calling me fat?"

"Not fat. Just sort of plump." As Rhea rose above her in her best monster imitation, Beth pretended fright. "Only kidding, honest."

"Shay," Liz went on, "I'm fixing you a plate and that's that."

Shay smiled at this familiar discussion. "Mom, you can't be too rich or too thin." She swung through the door before Liz could think of a comeback.

Her father's bedroom door was ajar and she went in. Luke was seated in a chair he'd pulled up close to the bed, and it appeared as if the two of them had been having a serious discussion. "Am I interrupting?"

"Shay, darlin'" Jacob greeted her, "come in."

"I've got a great dinner here," she told him as Luke leaned forward to prop Jacob's pillows behind his back. When her father was sitting upright and comfortable, she placed the tray on the bed, anchoring the support legs.

"Wonderful," Jacob commented dryly, looking over the food with disdain. "Fish again." He turned to Luke. "Have you noticed? I'm growing scales."

"Now, Dad," Shay said, seating herself at the foot of his big bed on the opposite side from Luke, "you know red meat's not good for you."

"My father ate it every day of his life and he lived to his mid-eighties."

"But he didn't smoke," Luke reminded him.

"And he didn't drink," Shay tossed in.

"You two ganging up on me?" Oddly Jacob looked pleased. "Like old times." He took a sip and made a face at the glass of skim milk. Damn stuff tasted like water. "So, Shay, do you know about the rustling, too?"

Shay's eyes slid over to Luke for verification. She saw him nod.

Jacob caught the look. "Yes, Luke finally told me. Why does everyone think I'm so fragile? The missing cows are a problem, but I've been handling problems on this ranch for more years than most of you have been alive." He took a bite of the tasteless fish and longed for a steak, rare, with Cora's wonderful béarnaise sauce.

Shay finally found her voice as she wondered if Luke had decided to tell her father on his own or if he'd checked it out with her mother. Luke was headstrong, true, but she knew he cared about Jacob. "We don't think you're fragile, Dad. There just seemed to be no point in bothering you with that particular problem when there was little you could do about it from your hospital bed. And it's being handled."

Jacob stabbed at his salad, toying with the greens. He'd have preferred French fries. "Handled, eh? Maybe, maybe not."

"Let me tell you what's been done so far, Jacob," Luke went on. "Gil and I went through the payroll, and we've come up with a couple of sudden departures that we're looking into. And there're a few hands who've come on board during the last six months who have a questionable background, and we're checking them out. Often as not, these are inside jobs."

"That sounds like a good start to me," Shay said, a bit surprised Luke and her brother were working together.

"We'll have a better idea after we get an exact head count and know our losses," Jacob insisted. "You'll have to get after Zeke on that, Luke. He's a good man but works at his own speed."

"I will," Luke assured him. Twice, he'd checked with Zeke and each time, the man had put him off. He was getting annoyed.

"Of course, I know Zeke and Gil have a lot to do." Jacob set down his fork and looked at Luke, his eyes lively. "Did you get a chance to look over our new plane? Fine piece of machinery. I don't know why we didn't get one years ago. Cuts down on a lot of work around here."

Luke hid a smile. They hadn't gotten a plane years ago because Jacob had wanted to cling to the old ways of the cowboy, fighting modernization. Since changing his mind, he'd evidently decided to take credit for the idea. "Yeah, I saw it. We had one down on Royce. Big time-saver."

Jacob swallowed a mouthful of lettuce and stabbed the air with his fork to make his point. "That's right, and it may help us in this situation. I'd like you to take it up, Luke, and fly low over the whole ranch. You haven't seen the spread in a long time. With fresh eyes, you may spot something Zeke's missed.''

"Sure, if you want me to."

Jacob nodded, satisfied. "Good. Shay, you go with him. That way, you can point out the changes we've made since Luke left and answer any questions he may have."

She sent her father a leery look. What was he up to? "I'm sure Luke can find his way around the Circle M without my help."

"Actually, I'd appreciate your coming along," Luke said evenly. "Four eyes are better than two."

"Right you are," Jacob agreed, pushing aside his tray. "In the meantime, bring me the records of those men you mentioned. Maybe if I look through them, something will ring a bell."

Shay rose to pick up the tray. "You didn't eat very much, Dad."

"A man doesn't get very hungry when he spends day and night flat on his back."

He was getting feisty again, which was probably a good sign. He also had a brightness to his eyes in talking about the rustling, an alert look that hadn't been there in a while. Still, it wouldn't do to rush his recovery. "Why don't you take a nap, and Luke can bring up those records later?"

He waved an impatient hand at her. "Now, Shay, quit this babying. I know when I'm tired and when I'm not. Luke, you bring me those files, then you and Shay take that plane up right now and let me know this evening what you saw, will you?"

There was no arguing with Jacob when he got in one of his moods. Luke rose and took the tray from Shay. "Sure thing. See you later."

In the hallway, Shay closed the door, then spoke in quiet tones. "Was bringing him in on things your idea?"

He'd seen the fire dance in her eyes and knew she'd question him. "Now, hold on, tiger. I checked it out with Dr. Emmett this morning and he was all for your dad knowing. And so was Liz."

"I'm not sure I am. Look at him. He's ready to jump out of that bed and take charge."

"Simmer down. He is not. He's feeling involved again, needed, alive. Isn't that what you want for him?"

"Yes, but..."

"No buts. Jacob's recently learned a very hard lesson, that life can be a whole lot shorter than he'd hoped. He wants to live, but not as a useless man chained to his bed. Helping solve this will get his juices flowing again. There's more to recovering from a heart attack than rest and the right food, Shay. A man has to know there's something worth recovering for, that he's not going to be shunted aside."

She thrust her hands into her pants pockets. Her father *had* looked good today. "Okay, so you're probably right. Just go easy, will you? We... we almost lost him."

It had been her fear talking, not a desire to argue. Luke could understand that. "I will. Now let me take this down to the kitchen, and I'll get him the papers he wants. Then we can take off." He started down the stairs.

"You don't need me. You know this ranch as well as I do, probably better."

He stopped two steps down and looked up at her. "You heard your father."

Shay disliked going against her father's wishes, but she had a valid reason. She'd been up in the plane before. It was a quiet, peaceful and very private world up there. And a fairly intimate one. She'd be all alone with Luke and his unnerving nearness. Chances were that he'd get to her.

It was a chance she was reluctant to take. "I really do have work to do."

But Luke was determined. "If you had only one wish, Shay, what would it be?"

Shay closed her eyes briefly, recalling how frequently he'd posed that question to her in the past, trying to nudge her into a decision. It had inevitably worked.

"Mine would be to spend the day with you," Luke went on. "Come on, Shay. Come fly with me. No funny stuff, honest."

He really did know the right buttons to push. Shay sighed in defeat. "All right. I'll meet you at the hangar." She skipped past him so she wouldn't see his victory grin.

In the kitchen, Luke set down the tray just as Beth finished lunch and hurried out to where Beechie was waiting for her. Liz excused herself to go up to Jacob. Luke sent Rhea a smile as she sat finishing her iced tea, then looked around and found Cora in the pantry, eyeing a bag of flour on the top shelf. "I'll get it," he told her, and easily reached up and brought it down.

"Thank you, Luke," Cora said with a smile.

"I need a favor, Cora," he said, following her to the counter.

"Certainly. What can I get you? Are you hungry? There's some cold chicken in the fridge and noodle salad."

"Anything would be fine, but I'd like it packed in a picnic basket. Enough for two people. And maybe some fruit and something to drink. Would that be too much trouble?" He gave her his winning smile.

"Not at all. I'll have it ready in a couple of minutes."

He guessed that Shay hadn't eaten, either. Perhaps a shared picnic would relax them both. "You're wonderful." He gave her a quick hug. "I've got to get something for Jacob, then I'll be back for the basket." He turned toward the door.

"Sounds like a romantic tête-à-tête," Rhea said, her voice stopping him. "Who's the lucky woman?"

"It's just lunch, Rhea, nothing fancy. And it's business."

"Sure it is," she said, chuckling out loud.

Her laughter followed him out into the hall as he hurried to get the records Jacob wanted. There were too damn many people around this house, he decided. The lack of privacy was hard to live with.

It was pretty much as she'd remembered, the small two-engine plane a bit noisy, but Luke held her steady. Shay sat buckled in beside him and watched the ground speed by under them as they rose.

He took them up over the fields of grain, looking like a beige blanket blowing in a lazy breeze. The pastures were squares of pale green with stretches of brown strips, and then they came upon the stream weaving through the land like a bright blue ribbon. The cows were small dots below, reddish brown, black and white. The men on horseback looked up at them and several waved. Feeling foolish, she waved back, then laughed.

Plain and simply, it filled her with awe, the vastness, the splendor. Distant mountains ringed the valley on three sides, standing guard like aged sentinels. Hardly a cloud could be seen in the pale sky as the sun bathed the whole area in warmth. Shay leaned her head against the window and sighed.

"It leaves you speechless, doesn't it?" Luke asked. He'd been watching her and saw how the beauty of the land affected her. This valley was in her blood, as it was in his.

"Yes, it does. It makes you wish you could paint."

"Or write. I envy people who can describe how they feel."

She glanced over at him curiously. Surely he hadn't discovered her attempts at writing. No, she was just jumpy. She gazed back out the window. "Isn't that the area where the count is off?" she asked, pointing to the western slope.

"So Zeke told me. That pasture's nearest to the road." Luke dipped the plane so she could see where the fence line hit. "It wouldn't be too difficult for a couple of men to cut the wire, walk the cattle across the stream and up into a couple of those long gooseneck trailer rigs. Then go back, fix the fence and drive off down that dirt road."

"Is that how you think it happened?"

"It's one way." Straightening, Luke took the plane higher. "I want to check out the section just past the farthest border of the Circle M. See if maybe there's room there to land a cargo plane."

"You're thinking they may have taken the rigs there and loaded the cattle onto a plane? If they were setting up a ranch elsewhere, that would be logical. It wouldn't take much to skip across the border. Canada's pretty far, but Idaho or Wyoming would be the perfect distance away."

He liked the logical way her mind worked. "Too many mountains to fly over into Idaho, but Wyoming would be easy."

Shay kept her eyes on the ground. "See that flat plain area over there? Would that be large enough to accommodate a cargo plane?"

"A smaller one, I suppose. But that would mean several trips."

She turned to him with another thought. "We should check some of the neighboring ranchers. Maybe they've got cows missing, too. If this rustling crew is clever, they could be taking a couple of hundred from several ranches, which probably wouldn't be noticed very quickly, instead of hitting one real heavy.''

''That's a possibility.'' Luke maneuvered the plane into a low canyon area, a rough section where the crude road wound and twisted through jagged, jutting rocks.

''What are you looking for?''

''Signs of a slaughtering. It occurred to me that several men could drive the cows someplace, slaughter them, then transport them packaged for quick sale miles from here.''

''They'd have to have a refrigerated truck in this heat.''

Luke nodded. ''Not that hard to get a hold of.'' Carefully he dipped the plane in and out of the clumps of a low mountain range, his eyes searching. ''I can't spot any remains, can you?''

Shay's nose was all but pressed to the window. ''No. And wouldn't there be vultures hovering?''

''Unless it happened several weeks ago. Then you'd see only dried bones.'' Suddenly he took her back up and turned. ''I don't think that's it, but at least we checked it out.'' Without hesitation, he angled back in the direction they'd come from but at a more northerly tilt.

Shay watched the checkerboard squares beneath them become less familiar. ''Aren't we over the Whitney spread now?''

''Yeah. I want to see how their cows are doing in this near-drought. Your mother told me that one other time, they had a lot of trouble because of the lack of water.''

Shay stiffened and sat back in the seat. It had happened nine years ago, yet the memory could still jolt her.

He'd been watching her face. ''I'm sorry. I didn't mean to remind you of something painful.''

So he knew. She'd rather thought so. If her mother hadn't told him, he'd surely have heard the story from Hollis or one of the other old-timers. ''Don't apologize.

It's common knowledge that I was traded for water rights. It's a distinction not too many women have.''

Luke bit back an oath. "Maxwell Whitney's a fool, Shay. He was then, and he is now."

She made a small sound in her throat. "I'm the fool, Luke. I thought . . . oh, never mind what I thought. It was a long time ago."

He thought it best to drop the subject for the present. They were over the stream now that flowed from the mountain runoff and then forked in two directions. The narrow one trailed onto the Whitney ranch and was weak, the water shallow. The larger fork angled onto the Circle M land and was wide and deep. "I can see why they're hurting again this year."

Good, Shay thought nastily, then closed her eyes with a sigh. How very uncharitable of her, she thought, wishing the Whitneys' cows would die so their owners would suffer. She should be over her hurt, her anger, by now.

"Look at those cows," Luke commented as they dipped low over the sparse herd gathered near a salt lick. "Downright scrawny." He pulled the nose up and headed back. "I'd say Whitney's in trouble again."

Shay gazed out as he'd suggested but didn't comment. Up ahead, she could see the large gray ranch house where she'd spent several years of her life as Mrs. Maxwell Whitney. She fought a shiver as she turned from the reminder.

Luke glanced over at her profile. She was silent and pale, obviously lost in her own disturbing thoughts. He'd wanted to check out the neighboring spread, but he hadn't guessed her feelings were still so raw after all this time. He'd have to make it up to her.

Executing a turn, he swung the plane out toward a spot he remembered would be perfect for a picnic.

With the change in direction, Shay sat up straighter, determined to shake off her melancholy mood. "Where now, Captain?"

"You'll see, in a minute." It took about five before he spotted the meadowlike stretch where aspen and cottonwood trees grew, their shade ideal for a picnic. Wildflowers in colorful profusion looked as if they'd been dropped by a careless hand. He set the plane down easily and taxied closer, then turned off the engine.

"I remember this place," Shay said, unbuckling her seat belt. "We used to come here often."

Luke climbed out and helped her step down. "I thought you might." He grabbed the plaid blanket and picnic basket and led the way to the shadiest spot. The sun was still high in the sky, but it was cooler here.

Luke spread the blanket and sat down, opening the basket to peer inside as Shay sank down and leaned against the rough bark of a tree. "Well, well, look at this. Cora gave us a thermos of her special lemonade." Luke removed two plastic glasses.

"It's lovely here," Shay commented, relaxing by inches.

He handed her drink over and scooted closer. He touched the rim of his glass to hers in a silent toast, then took a sip. Cool and tart, the liquid slid down his dry throat. Turning to her, he realized once again that she hadn't quite been able to remain unaffected at seeing the Whitney ranch again. He was reasonably certain she no longer cared for Max. Perhaps observing the place where she'd been unhappy had put the sadness back in her eyes.

"I shouldn't have taken you over the Whitneys' place, Shay. I didn't mean to upset you."

"You didn't." It hadn't been him, but the tug of memories.

"Tell me what it was like, living there."

It surprised her that she wanted to, and worried her a bit. "It was formal, cold, humorless, lonely. We had *discussions,* not arguments, though both father and son tend to get very loud. Morgan likes to pound the table to emphasize his point. And Max *always* sides with his father."

"Max is pretty much out of your life now, isn't he?"

"I wish." Shay slowly twirled the glass between her fingers. She rarely talked with anyone about Max, but there were times when she longed to. She'd confided some of the problems in her marriage to Liz after she'd come home, but no one else. Yet lately, with reminders of those awful years all but choking her, her nerves felt raw. Luke had once been a dear friend and always a good listener. "He thinks he can use Beth the way he used me, but he's got another think coming."

"How do you mean?"

Shay tasted her lemonade, then set the glass down. "He ignores his daughter most of the time and owes me thousands in unpaid child support. I could let that go, because I don't want his money. Beth's mine, and I'd just as soon he disappeared."

Luke disagreed. "You shouldn't let him get away with that. You could take him to court and . . ."

"I tried several times. He has attorney friends who manage to delay things time after time, then he has excuses that somehow the judge believes. It's simply not worth it. But that isn't the worst of it."

He shifted to sit cross-legged, facing her. "Tell me."

Why not? Maybe sharing the problem would somehow lighten her load. "Max is running for the state senate. He's been calling lately, wanting to take Beth to Billings where they would go sight-seeing and have a fun day, with a reporter and a photographer trailing them, of course. So he would look like a concerned parent, a loving father." She gave a harsh laugh. "Over my dead body, I told him last night. He'll not use my daughter to get himself elected."

"What did he say to that?"

"That he'd find a way."

"Beat him to the punch. Call a news conference yourself, tell the press that he's a deadbeat father. That would end his political ambitions in a hurry."

"And what about Beth?" She shook her head. "I couldn't do that without hurting her."

He was unused to thinking as a parent. "You're right. If you'd like me to go talk to Max, to set him straight, I'd be more than happy to."

She almost smiled at that. She'd struggled alone with this, because it was *her* problem, admonishing even her parents not to interfere. But she couldn't help being pleased at his offer. "Still the knight in shining armor out to rescue maidens in distress? Still climbing trees to free a kitten and a young girl?"

He smiled at the reminder. The incident had taken place shortly after he'd come to live at the Circle M. Shay had had a calico kitten who'd gone up into the huge old apple tree in back of the big house. Without a thought of her own safety, and being a tomboy at heart, Shay had scurried up after her pet, only to get stuck herself. He'd heard her call out and had rescued both of them. She'd been both romantic and dramatic, having read stories of King Arthur, and had likened him to Lancelot, much to his embarrassment.

"Yeah, well, I think my armor's a little rusty these days. Most grown-up girls are too independent to want rescuing."

Her chin rose a notch as she studied him. "Do independent women intimidate you?"

"Intimidate?" He shook his head, setting down his empty glass. "No. I find them fascinating, tempting and very attractive." In a swift movement, he tugged her away from the tree and eased her onto her back on the blanket, then followed her down. "And they challenge me." He saw the surprise in her dark eyes along with a hint of temper.

Shay felt his warm breath on her face and the shock of his long, hard body pressing against hers. "You said there'd be no funny stuff."

"There's nothing funny about the way I feel about you, Shay." Before she could turn her head, his mouth closed over hers.

The one thing she'd dreaded most was happening, Shay thought, as she squirmed to push him off her. The one thing she'd wanted the most was happening, she admitted. Like an injection that spread through the veins with rapid precision, the taste of him exploded on her tongue, and, instantly, her blood began to heat and her head began to swim.

Her movements beneath him caused her body to rub against his, and the flame growing inside her flickered more brightly, more insistently. Without her giving them permission, her hands stopped pushing and crept upward, curling around his shoulders. And her mouth opened under his as she heard a soft moan, uncertain whether it came from her or him.

She was alive again, sensually aware again. How long had it been since she'd wanted like this? Too long. Only Luke had ever been able to make her feel such joy at simply being alive.

Ten years of hoping, of longing, of wishing, and he had her back in his arms, Luke thought, as he molded her pliant body to his. Ten years of fantasizing, of daydreams and night schemes, of remembering the rich taste of her, the seductive scent of her. Ten years of struggling against the need for her, of waking with thoughts of her, of yearning for the touch of her. Ten years of agony dissolving in the force of a kiss that had been as inevitable as the sunrise each morning.

She was slender and delicate, yet fit beautifully to him as no other woman ever could. She'd been a girl back when he'd first touched her, but the years and bearing a child had ripened her woman's body despite her slim frame. The weight of her fuller breasts pressing against his chest had him tightening, had him aching.

She'd striven to forget this drugging sensation, Shay knew, though she'd never quite managed it completely. But her traitorous body remembered. Oh, how it remembered the simmering seduction of this man's kisses, the rising need that turned her thoughts incoherent, the relentless sensation of inhaling his heady male scent. Despite her best intentions, she was lost, lost inside of him.

Breathing hard, Luke abruptly pulled back, fighting his own reaction, staring into her eyes filled with hazy passion and a hundred questions. He'd wanted this, had prayed for it, yet knew that the power of her hold on him was breathtaking. He knew instinctively that this small woman could make him beg, could bring him to his knees, a sobering thought. She was in his blood, in his heart, but could he ever find a way to keep her in his life?

Shay's eyes searched his, wanting desperately to find a reason to back away from this . . . this incredible passion. She could see desire there, which she knew must be reflected in her own, but that alone would never have held her. It was something else, something so fleeting that she'd almost missed seeing it. Raw need. Not a physical need, but a need for love.

Just as he had when she'd first known him, Luke Turner needed love more than anyone she'd ever known. He would deny it, he would try to hide it, but she saw, she knew. And her woman's heart responded to that need as her girl's heart had years ago. With her pulse pounding, she pulled his mouth back to hers.

She no longer struggled, no longer squirmed to free herself of him. Instead she reached out, enfolded him and gave to him. She wouldn't think just now, or worry about later. There would be time for that, but for now, she would just act on her instincts and give to this man who'd owned her heart from the beginning. And in giving, she would receive.

Luke felt the change in her and wondered at it, but only for a moment. She was softer now, her hands gentler, her body straining nearer rather than striving to be free. It wasn't surrender, but rather a joyous sharing of a mutual need. He was too wrapped up in her to question this wondrous response. It felt too good to hold her, to kiss and touch her, to let all worries slip away and allow himself to just feel.

Glorious. Shay felt glorious as Luke's tongue toyed with hers, as his clever hands crept under her blouse and set her skin humming. He was doing it again, making her want to relinquish control of her body and turn herself over to his command. How could she ever have deluded herself into thinking she could settle for less?

He was doing wonderful things to her mouth while his hands had her breasts aching for his special touch. She wondered how she'd lived these ten years without it. And she wondered how she'd get through the next ten when he'd leave.

That thought had her sobering, had her realizing she was getting in over her head again. If she didn't quit now, she'd have too many empty years to regret giving in to needs she would have to learn to do without again. With trembling hands, she held him away, then struggled to sit up and straighten her clothes.

Dazed and more shaken then he wanted to admit, Luke took a moment to catch his breath. While it was true that he wanted her, he knew that a lot of problems separated them. He also knew he couldn't overcome a ten-year absence in a couple of weeks.

Her hold on him was unmistakable, probably irrevocable. Perhaps he'd been fooling himself that he wanted to pursue his dream alone, that he'd be better off without anyone. With Shay at his side, he could be so much more than he could be without her.

But his dream was just that yet. It would take much hard work to make his ranch a success, with no guarantees. He would rather not take her along than fail in her eyes.

"I...I didn't mean to lead you on," Shay began, unable to look at him.

"You didn't. We're neither one to blame. I hope you know I didn't bring you out here to seduce you."

She turned to him then and found she could be honest. "You never had to work very hard to seduce me. I've wanted you as far back as I can remember. God help me, I still do. But I don't think it's in the cards for us right now. Maybe it never will be."

Luke stood, then took her hand and pulled her up. "Never's a long time."

Shay felt in control again, and with it came the return of her good sense. She had set herself goals, financial independence, the ability to come or go as she pleased, to take her daughter far away from Max's influence and be free. She couldn't do any of that if she let herself start depending on Luke emotionally or physically. He was too strong.

He would weaken her determination and all but destroy her self-reliance. He was the only man she knew who could, and she must not let that happen.

"I don't want to feel all the things you make me feel, Luke. I was content with my life before you returned. I want to be that way again."

"Content, but were you happy?" he challenged.

She sent him a questioning look. "Do you still believe in happy?"

"I'm not sure."

"I'll settle for contented." She stepped off the blanket and grabbed it up. "I'm not very hungry. Could we go back, please?"

Chapter Five

Luke walked into the barn, his stride purposeful. He spotted Gil at the far end, overseeing the men handling the huge hay blocks, and made straight for him. It was showdown time.

He was angry, bone angry. It would seem whoever had been trying to get rid of him ten years ago was still unhappy and anxious for him to leave again.

They'd been branding calves yesterday and he'd joined in to help, knowing the ranch was shorthanded. He also had thought it would be an opportunity to mingle with the men and perhaps hear something that could be useful regarding the missing cattle. Branding was hot, dirty work and by the time he'd made his way back to his house, all he'd been thinking of was a shower and some dinner. Maybe that was why he'd almost walked past the white sheet of paper on the kitchen table.

He'd picked it up and the simple message had shocked his sluggish brain. "You're not wanted here. Go back where you came from."

He hadn't locked his doors, so anyone could have put it there, for he hadn't been back inside since early morning. He badly wanted to get his hands on the person who had left it, obviously a coward afraid to talk to his face.

He was about to find out if that coward was Gil McKenzie.

Gil's shirt was soaked with sweat, and he had on heavy haying chaps to protect his legs as he sank the metal tongs into a big cube of hay. Luke stopped in front of him. "Have you been avoiding me?"

Gil shifted the mound into place, then turned and wiped his damp forehead with his shirtsleeve. "Now, why would I be doing that?"

Luke glanced up at the half a dozen men working in the loft. "I'd like to talk with you, in private."

Pulling off his thick gloves, Gil walked toward the door. Outside, he swung around and narrowed his gaze at Luke. "Something wrong?" They'd been getting along lately, burying whatever animosity one may have felt for the other. He hadn't talked with Luke during the past day or so, but the last time they had, they'd been in agreement on how to check into the rustling. He hadn't a clue as to why the man seemed suddenly upset.

Luke's eyes were watchful. "Do you remember the night I left ten years ago, the conversation we had back then?"

Gil removed his hat, buying a little time. What had brought this on? he wondered. "Yeah. What about it?"

"After our little talk, I decided it would be best if I left. I packed my things and went to Jacob's study and wrote two notes, one to Shay and one to your mother, explaining why I was going. I put the notes in envelopes marked with their names, and placed them on the vestibule table where we all used to leave messages. Then I left around two in the morning.''

Gil nodded. "So?"

"So they never got those notes. Do you know anything about that?"

"No, I don't."

Luke did a half turn as he stuck his hands into his back pockets. "Funny, isn't it? You wanted me gone, even told me I should leave. Far as I know, you were the only one who did. Yet you didn't do anything or see anything."

Gil's eyes turned angry. "Look, I don't care if you believe me or not. I admit I wanted you gone. I told you so. I even heard you leaving, and I sure as hell didn't get up and beg you to stay. Why would I bother with those notes when all I wanted was for you to go and you did?"

"You heard me leave?"

"Yeah. I'm a light sleeper."

Luke studied Gil's face, wondering if he should believe him. Growing up with him, he'd heard Gil many times invent extremely plausible excuses for not finishing his chores on the ranch, often as not, fooling his mother or father. He was a man who could think fast on his feet. Was he now telling the truth or fabricating an alibi? Was he playing it cool and cowardly, leaving a warning in the house, then lying to his face? Luke wished he knew.

"Then what happened to them?" Luke said, almost to himself.

Gil shrugged, replacing his hat. "Maybe Cora moved them when she was dusting and forgot to put them back."

Luke scowled. "Dusting that early in the morning, before anyone was up?"

"Hell, I don't know. All I do know is, I never saw any notes. What's so important about them, anyhow?"

Here he was, explaining himself again. "They prove that I didn't just walk out like some ungrateful creep after this family had been damn good to me." Luke felt frustrated. He'd been pretty sure in his mind that Gil had been the culprit, his strongest suspect. Now he'd have to alter his thinking and confront the others.

"That's all you said? You didn't mention the talk we had?"

Luke shook his head.

Gil was relieved to hear that. "Then why don't you just tell everyone what was in the notes, and that'll be that?"

Luke cocked his head. "Because I don't think they'll believe that I left the notes. Do you?"

Again Gil shrugged. "Why not? You wouldn't be so upset if it wasn't true."

That, at least, was something. Luke sighed and removed a folded sheet from his pocket. He'd taken to carrying some things with him, not certain if there were others on the ranch who had keys to his cabin. "Then I don't suppose you left this on my kitchen table?"

Gil took the note and read the warning, then scowled. "Hell no, I didn't. Who do you suppose did?"

"Damned if I know." Luke took back the sheet and stuffed it into his pocket. "But I mean to find out." He searched his pockets for his lemon drops, wondering if he'd just been masterfully conned or if Gil McKenzie was on the up-and-up. "Have you seen Zeke? He still hasn't given me that head count. Did he tell you the latest number missing?"

"Nope. I think he's in the back barn. They're collecting a specimen from Bullseye this morning."

"Thanks." Luke headed for the farthest barn. As soon as he walked through the big double doors, he could smell the heavy musk of the animals. Walking down the concrete aisle, he saw four husky hands with lead ropes pull Bullseye off the mock cow frame. The huge bull was breathing hard, his hide damp. Another man disengaged the collection cup and walked it over to where Zeke waited by the worktable. Luke strolled over.

A slight breeze drifted in from the open window above the chest freezer, too weak to make a difference in the heated interior. Luke stood for a moment, watching Zeke pour the bull's semen into containers called straws, which were then put into a large cylinder for freezing. Hollis had told Luke that Jacob had acquired Bullseye only two years ago after a bidding war with another rancher. The consensus of opinion was that the big bull had been worth every cent, for his offspring were strong and healthy despite the fact that Bullseye was blind in one eye.

Trying to appear casual, though inside he was doing a slow burn, Luke stepped closer. Zeke had appeared chatty and friendly that first day they'd inspected the fencing in the Jeep. Luke had asked for an updated head count then and had mentioned it several times since. In his amiable way, Zeke had put him off each time, saying he'd get to it right away. Luke had about run out of patience. He was an invited guest here, true, but he also had been asked to do a job.

"Hey, Zeke," he said, greeting the man as he fastened the lid on the breeding cylinder.

Zeke glanced up, then looked chagrined. "I know, you want the head count." He moved to the freezer and deposited the cylinder inside, closed the lid, then stepped back and removed his gloves.

"Yeah. What's the holdup?"

"I've been busy."

Reaching for patience, Luke stuffed his hands into his jeans pockets. Zeke's arrogance was getting to him. "I'll give you until tonight. If you don't have some figures for me then, tomorrow I'm taking some men out, and I'll do it myself."

Zeke's face lost its congenial look as he reassessed Luke. "The men take their orders from me. Or Gil."

In his present mood, Luke welcomed a challenge. "Is that right? Well, I'm in charge of the rustling problem. You can check with Liz or Jacob on that."

Zeke's eyes narrowed. "Jacob knows?"

"That's right. Just so you understand, I'm getting that count, with or without your cooperation." Luke turned and walked back the way he'd come.

Zeke evidently figured he'd pushed too far. He went after Luke, his smile back. "Hey, buddy, no hard feelings. I've been damn busy is all. You'll have it. Four o'clock for sure."

"Fine." Luke kept walking. The man may know his cows as Liz had told him, but he sure was short on ranch procedure.

"No, thanks," Luke said. "I gave up playing poker."

Charley Brice stood in front of Luke's front stoop where Luke sat whittling. The cowhand had stopped by, trying to interest Luke in a game.

It was Sunday, the only semileisurely day on a ranch. Of course, the animals had to be seen to, but the afternoons were free for most of the men. Some had driven into town, a couple had gone fishing, a few were hand-tooling designs in leather, and still others were working in the corrals with the young horses or their own mounts.

But Charley felt lucky. "Come on, Turner. Just a friendly game."

Luke brushed aside the accumulated wood shavings as he shook his head. "I've lost one too many times."

Glancing up, he wondered if perhaps he shouldn't spend a little time with Charley. He was one of the men whose background was vague and a little disturbing. "Where'd you say you're from again?"

Charley adjusted his suede vest more comfortably. "Texas way," he answered.

Luke eyed the man's boots, appreciating the fine gray sharkskin. Several of the men had nice dress boots, but Charley's looked to be special-order and expensive. The hands on the ranch were fairly well paid, as well as any in the area. Of course, some had put money aside when they'd come to the Circle M.

Was Charley making a little extra by siphoning off some of Jacob's cows? Or was he working with the person who wanted him gone, the person who'd left a threatening note in his cabin? "Nice boots," Luke commented casually. "Get 'em in town?"

"Can't recall." Charley nodded toward the big house. "I hear you used to live there. Why'd you leave?"

Luke returned his gaze to his knife and the piece of wood. "It was time to move on. I spent some time at the Royce Ranch in Texas recently. Did you ever work near there?" Everyone had heard of Royce. Perhaps he could loosen Charley's tongue.

"Nope. I also hear you used to be friendly-like with Shay. How'd you do it? She looks through everyone around here like they were invisible." His voice indicated he couldn't imagine why anyone would rebuff him.

Luke found himself examining Charley's smooth good looks more closely. He was tall, rugged looking, yet he smelled like he'd splashed on too much after-shave for an all-male poker game. He also seemed pretty fond of himself. "Maybe she's just plain not interested." Maybe her taste didn't run to slick cowboys who dressed fancy.

Charley chuckled. "Hey, man, they're *all* interested. You just got to catch them at the right moment." Gazing toward the bunkhouse, he spotted a couple of cowboys outside. "Guess I'll see if I can interest anyone else in a game. See you later."

Luke watched him saunter off, his spurs jingling. Now why would the man be wearing spurs unless he was planning to go riding? For effect? Because he thought he made a handsome picture, all duded up? He returned to his whittling.

Charley Brice was careful in answering questions, revealing nothing much. Luke had known a lot of cowhands through the years, and few had been talkative. Was Charley reticent or evasive? Did he have something to hide and if so, was it worth knowing or something that didn't concern anyone but Charley? Many a man had something in his past he wasn't fond of discussing.

At the sound of loud voices, Luke glanced up and determined they were coming from the manager's cabin across from his. Suddenly the door flew open angrily and Zeke came out on the porch, then down the stairs. He pulled his hat down low over his face and walked toward the bunkhouse, either not noticing Luke sitting there or choosing not to.

Zeke had gotten him the count yesterday by four, finally. Luke had whistled low at the number—two hundred twenty cows missing. Luke had looked at him measuringly, wondering how accurate the man was, but Zeke had just shrugged and walked away.

He'd revised his original opinion of Zeke Crawford. He was friendly enough, "one of the boys" with his men, yet there was something about him that gave Luke an uneasy feeling. He smiled a lot, but his eyes remained watchful under their heavy lids.

And now, it would seem that he fought rather noisily with his wife, as well. Luke glanced over again and saw that Rhea had come out on her porch and was sitting listening to a small table radio. He couldn't help wondering what kind of marriage she and Zeke had.

As much as he'd been able to determine, Rhea seemed to spend most of her day in the manager's cabin, sometimes lunching with Liz at the big house, occasionally riding with Beth or fooling with the newborn calves and colts. She'd never really loved the ranch the way Shay seemed to. Luke had to admit he scarcely knew the person Rhea had become and made a note to talk with her real soon.

Luke shifted his attention to the front of the bunkhouse where Charley stood talking with two men as Zeke joined them. After a minute, the men went inside while Zeke and Charley strolled off in the direction of the barn. Was Zeke a poker man? Luke wondered. Maybe he should have sat in on the game, just to observe those two.

Nah, he wasn't in the mood. He set down the knife and wood, then dusted off his hands. What was he in the mood for? he asked himself as he leaned his back against the porch post and looked over at the big house. Unerringly his gaze drifted to the bedroom window he remembered as being Shay's, even though he guessed she wouldn't be in it at this time of day.

He'd seen her leave with Beth in the white pickup earlier, but he hadn't stopped to inquire where they were heading. After their last conversation at the site of the botched picnic, he noticed she'd been avoiding him. As he'd been avoiding her.

He'd been on the Circle M a week, a week of watching Shay and wanting her. He'd never gone the distance with a woman, never spoken words of love or about sharing his tomorrows—except that last evening ten years ago with

Shay. Shortly after that, he'd thought of her as married and forever out of his life. Coming back, knowing she was free, being with her again, had resurrected all those buried feelings, feelings he was unused to coping with. And this insatiable need for her.

It was enough to make a man cross.

Enough, Luke thought, rising. What he needed was some physical exertion, just man and his horse. He started for the barn where Maverick was housed. As he walked, he heard Rhea singing along with the radio, a sad tune. Not his problem, Luke decided.

The sun was hanging low in the afternoon sky as Shay glanced up, then rolled her shoulders to relieve the kinks. Placing her yellow pad and pen on the soft grass, she gave in to a yawn. Tethered to a small branch of the next tree over from where she sat, Dancer pawed the ground and sniffed the air.

They'd been out here about two hours at one of Shay's favorite spots by the old watering hole where the four of them used to swim as kids. Off the west pasture, it was a spring-fed pond, clear and cool, bordered by tall aspen and a few cottonwood trees. It was a peaceful and private place, which was why she liked to work on her manuscript here.

She hadn't slept well last night, a not-uncommon happening. She'd risen early and gone into Jacob's study, deciding to go through the placement book, to see how many cows were positioned in each of the half-dozen grazing pastures. When she'd finished, she'd gone to the kitchen for coffee and found Gil there. He'd told her what Zeke had come up with as a head count, and her eyes had widened with disbelief. Two hundred twenty cows didn't just wander off somewhere.

She'd sat with her brother and talked awhile, about the cattle, the rustling, Jacob's health. And finally, Gil had asked just how she felt about Luke's return.

It seemed to be the question on everyone's mind. Even Hollis had asked her in his slow, roundabout way. Mostly she answered with something vague or lightly sarcastic. But Gil had seemed genuinely interested.

So she told him the truth, that the sooner Luke left, the better off she'd be. Gil had stared at her a long moment, then said, "Amen." Shay found that odd since she'd thought they'd been getting along better, but Gil had left then and she hadn't asked him anything further.

The pond looked inviting and Shay was tempted to jump in, but she really should get back.

She and Beth had had breakfast on trays with Jacob and Liz in their big bedroom, her father sitting up in a chair. The talk had been inconsequential, and Jacob had been in a good humor. She'd decided not to mention the number of missing cows, concerned she'd spoil the day for her parents. They would find out soon enough.

Then she'd spent an hour reading with Beth, a Sunday ritual they both looked forward to. Afterward she'd helped her daughter clean up and driven her to a neighboring ranch for a birthday party given by the parents of one of her schoolmates. Liz had said she'd pick Beth up before dinner when Shay had told her she'd like to take Dancer for a run.

Hearing a sound, she looked up and spotted a chickadee in the tree overhead, singing its lyrical song, *fee-bee-bee,* and smiled. Feeling lazy, Shay pulled off her boots, then her socks and wiggled her toes in the lush grass that grew along the pond's edge. Across the way, brown-eyed Susans grew in wild profusion, a bright sprinkling of orange and gold. The sun glinted off the sparkling water.

Would another hour matter? Not likely, she decided and quickly stood, stepped out of her jeans and stripped off her shirt. Before easing into the cool water, she removed the rubber band and undid her braid, shoving her fingers through to untangle the thick fall.

Wading in, her feet touching the marshy bottom, she let out a squeal of delight at the welcome coolness. Gingerly she moved farther out and sank in up to her shoulders. Dipping her head back, she immersed her hair and began to float, her arms out at her sides, her eyes closing against the glare of the overhead sun. Lord, but it felt good to relax and let go, to forget her problems for just a little while.

He'd been riding hard, needing to get rid of pent-up energy and frustrations. Maverick had needed the same release. Finally Luke slowed the big horse from a gallop to a smooth canter, then into a slow walk. Squinting into the sun, he spotted Dancer by the tree at the pond's edge. Shay must have returned to the ranch while he'd been inside, then ridden out here. As quietly as possible, horse and rider moved closer. Luke saw Shay's still form lying on top of the water near the center of the pond, her hair shimmering in a reddish gold spill about her head.

Dismounting, he tied his stallion to a distant tree, knowing how restless Maverick would become if he was too near Dancer. About as restless as he himself was with his eyes feasting on Shay.

Luke crept closer, certain she'd be furious if she knew he was there watching her unawares. He knew what a spitfire she could be when she grew angry. He smiled. Some things were worth the risk. Moving behind the tree, he sat down and quickly yanked off his boots. Stripped down to his briefs, he peered around the tree.

She apparently hadn't seen or heard him, still floating with her eyes closed, her arms outspread and her hands gently splashing at her sides. Quietly he slipped into the water, ignoring the quick chill that had his skin jumping after the heated ride over. Even at dead center, the pond wasn't much more than six feet deep, as he remembered. Her head was facing away from him, which gave him a chance to get quite close before she sensed something and turned.

He rose up out of the water, splashing with arms raised high. Startled, Shay jackknifed and dipped under, then paddled away. Moments later, she split the surface and came up sputtering.

"What are you doing here?" She shook back her hair, treading water. "Of all the sneaky things to do!"

Ignoring her tirade, Luke reached out a long arm and shoved her head under again. This time she rose quickly, seeking revenge. In two strokes she was behind him, her hands on his shoulders, pushing him under. Luke kicked out, then came up grinning, his dark blond hair plastered to his head.

Shay couldn't remember the last time she'd horsed around in this pond. It had been a lot of years ago. Oddly, she felt exhilarated, and hadn't yet made him pay enough. "Last one under's a rotten egg," she called out, the warning they'd often hurled at one another those long-ago carefree days.

"Come and get me," Luke taunted, swimming away with powerful strokes.

She did, only to find when she reached his side that he flipped and pulled her under with him. Her legs brushed against his and she found his strong arms pulling her closer as they sank lower in the water. Oh, no, she thought, and let her feet touch bottom, then kicked free to break the surface. As she dipped her head back to smooth out her hair, he rose beside her, his blue eyes filled with amusement.

"I thought I taught you to swim better than that," Luke said, staying near enough to touch her.

He had taught her to swim. And to whistle, to square dance, even to drive the Jeep. He'd also taught her to kiss, and she'd never run across anyone who kissed as well as the teacher. She inched back a bit. "You don't play fair, engaging in sneak attacks."

"All's fair in love and war, didn't you know?" he asked.

"No, it isn't."

"Yes, it is." Again he caught her off guard, his leg moving quickly and catching both of hers behind the knees. Her knees buckled and she sank. When she came up, she was in the circle of his waiting arms. "Say uncle," he demanded.

"Not on your best day." She tried to submerge him, pressing down on his shoulders, but he'd planted his feet and she couldn't budge him. "Okay, so you're stronger. Brawn instead of brains."

His hands slipped to her ribs, tickling the spots he remembered used to put her into near collapse. "Take that back."

Tickling didn't have the same effect under water. She stood her ground and laughed out loud. "That doesn't work anymore."

Suddenly Luke lost interest in the game. "I always liked the way you laugh." He saw her eyes grow darker with a hint of wariness. "And the way your eyes get so serious when you can't quite figure something out." His gaze drifted lower and he noticed a long chain hanging around her neck. He reached to pick up the silver key that dangled between her breasts, recognizing it immediately.

"I see you still have this."

"Yes."

"Do you wear it often?" How would Max have felt about her wearing another man's gift? Or hadn't she told him who'd given it to her?

"Always." Shay found that her hands had drifted down from his shoulders and tangled in the hair of his chest. She felt his heartbeat under her fingertips, felt a ripple of awareness race up her spine as he drew her nearer. "Luke, I..."

"Shh," he whispered as he reached up with both hands to brush back her sleek, wet hair. "I'm not your enemy, Shay. Don't fight me, please. Let me hold you, just hold you."

The simple request was her undoing. She forced herself to relax, to let him draw her close to his solid body, her arms going around him. When her soft breasts, covered only by the thin silk of her bra, flattened against the hard wall of his chest, she closed her eyes in a moment of pure sensual enjoyment. His hands slipped down her back and pressed her lower body into the cove of his thighs, and she stifled a groan.

No, he wasn't her enemy. He was her temptation.

She eased back from him and knew she was trembling. "Why are you doing this, to both of us?"

It was a good question, Luke thought. He felt his entire body teetering on the edge of explosion. No other woman could bring him to this state this quickly, standing immersed in four feet of cool water. He came up with the only answer possible. "Because I can't seem to stop myself."

He waited for her to grow angry or offended or—worst of all possible scenarios—to laugh. Instead she sighed and nodded. "I know. I feel exactly the same."

Luke wondered if he looked as surprised as he felt. "You do?"

"Yes. That's why I've been trying to stay away from you. You make me question my plans, you weaken my resolve."

"Ditto." He took her hand and dipped his head to kiss the inside of her palm, feeling it was the safest spot of his many choices. When her hand lovingly stroked his face, he couldn't help but wonder if this powerful need for each other might mean they had a chance at a future. He shifted to search her eyes. "Does this mean that you don't want me to leave?"

She sighed and shook back her hair. "Since you've come back, I don't seem to know what I want." She turned to head for the shore, thinking it odd that she didn't feel self-conscious in front of Luke, wearing only her underwear. Perhaps it was because the one and only time he'd made love to her on that fateful night had seemed more intimate than anything she'd ever done with Max. But she didn't want to think about her doomed marriage.

Reaching the bank, she sat down in a patch of sunlight and shrugged into her shirt, leaving it open. She squeezed the excess moisture from her hair, threading her fingers through the wet strands, hoping it would dry quickly. Luke followed and dropped to the grass beside her, lying down on his stomach. For long moments they stayed like that, near enough to touch but not touching, alone with their thoughts.

One of the things he'd always liked about Shay was that she knew how to be quiet, that she understood not every second should be filled with conversation. He hadn't met many women he was comfortable with in silence.

After a while, he decided he'd share something with Shay, perhaps the only person on the ranch he could unequivocably trust. "Someone wants me out of here and badly," he began.

Drawing up her knees, she circled them with her arms as she turned to face him. "What do you mean?"

He reached over for the shirt he'd flung to the ground, found the note in his pocket and handed it to her. Watching her face as she read it, he could see the play of emotions: shock, anger, and a hint of fear.

"Where did you find this?"

"On my kitchen table a couple of days ago."

"I can't believe someone would be so bold." She replaced the note in his shirt pocket. "This is no joke. I think we should show it to the sheriff."

Luke shook his head. "Not yet. I want to handle this myself. An investigation would tip our hand, and the guy would pull back."

Shay lay on her side, facing him. "Guy? Do you have an idea who might have written it?"

"I thought I did. Gil and I have had our differences. I'm still not sure, but he seemed genuinely surprised to hear about the letters I'd left and shocked when he read this note. I don't think he's that good an actor that he could have bluffed without giving himself away." He moved his hand to touch the ends of her hair at her shoulders, watching the way the sun turned the strands red.

Shay was frowning in concentration. "Who would want you gone enough to threaten like that?" she wondered aloud. "If it's the same person who took the letters, then..." Her realization made her eyes widen with shock. "It has to be..."

"Someone in the family?" he finished for her. "Yeah, I came to the same conclusion."

Her mind couldn't accept that. "Maybe it's someone's idea of a sick joke. Some of the men have been with the ranch since back when you lived here. Maybe you angered one of them and..." She watched him shake his head slowly and knew she was grasping at straws. But to believe that her parents or Rhea or Gil could have done such a thing was unthinkable. "I don't understand. What motive would any of them have?"

"To protect you perhaps, to get me out of your life and make you hate me." He saw her eyes widen as she stared at him. "Did it work?"

She reached to touch his hand with hers, lacing their fingers together. "What do you think?"

"I'm glad. But someone on the ranch isn't."

She couldn't let it go. "My mother coaxed you back, so she would hardly be likely to warn you away with a stupid, anonymous note. My father hasn't left his room since coming home from the hospital."

He rolled to his side and moved his other hand to her shoulder, almost absently caressing her drying skin, trailing down her arm as it rested on the swell of her hip. "What about Rhea? Do you think her marriage is happy?"

Thoughtfully Shay considered that. "We've never been close. I hear her and Zeke fighting a lot, but they always make up. Rhea's rarely in a bad mood, so it's hard to tell. The only problem I know of is that she badly wants a baby and hasn't been able to conceive yet. But I don't think she's ever had anything against you, has she?"

He'd never told anyone about the time Rhea had cornered him into a kiss. "Not that I can remember."

"Which brings us back to Gil. Did you quarrel with him before you left? I've always thought so."

Luke dropped his gaze so she couldn't read more in his eyes than he wanted her to know. "Not a quarrel exactly, but we had a difference of opinion."

She wasn't about to let him get away with his evasive tactics. She touched his chin until he met her eyes. "About me?"

"About a lot of things." Taking advantage of having her close beside him in this peaceful, private spot, he pulled her down and brushed his lips across hers, then nibbled at the corners of her mouth. He could feel her surprise, then feel her fight her response.

"Luke, you're distracting me," Shay said, putting a hand on his chest to keep him at bay. She'd always loved touching him, the hard muscles he'd developed from years of outdoor work, the smooth, tan skin. He was so big, so solid and comfortable. And she was painfully aware that he wore only skimpy briefs and she wasn't fully dressed. "We were discussing the problem of the note."

"We could discuss it another hour and not solve it," he murmured into her neck. "I can think of better ways to spend that hour."

She could feel herself weakening as his moist mouth trailed along her sun-warmed skin. Of its own accord, her head fell back as he shifted closer to touch his lips to her throat. "This is not going to solve anything," she insisted, then moved out of reach and stood. She bent to get her jeans and pulled them on.

"All right, spoilsport." Reluctantly Luke rose and picked up his pants.

Noticing something, Shay touched his arm as she bent to inspect his right knee. "Good heavens. Where'd you get those scars?"

He touched the longer of the two as he shrugged. "Couple of surgeries. Rodeo souvenirs."

"Is that why you quit the circuit?"

"Partly." He yanked on his jeans. "Rarely hurts anymore." Moving to the tree, he sat down and grabbed his boots. Finishing, he glanced at a yellow pad filled with writing, beside him in the grass. Curious, he picked it up. "Is this yours?" he asked after a moment.

Tucking her shirt in, Shay walked over. "Yes." Quickly she took the pad from him.

But not before he'd read several lines. He watched her stuff the pad into a leather case, then zip it shut. "I didn't know you wrote."

Annoyed that she hadn't put it away sooner, Shay shrugged. "I dabble, that's all."

But Luke wasn't buying her breezy explanation. "I won't tell anyone, if that's what's worrying you."

Shay released a sigh, then sat down and leaned back against the tree trunk. "Thanks, I'd rather you didn't. It's something I want to do, maybe *need* to do, that's mine alone, you know?"

He who had shared nearly everything he'd owned, even his sleeping space, for most of his life, understood perfectly her need for privacy. "Have you ever completed any, maybe tried to sell one?"

She'd never discussed her writing with anyone and felt uneasy now. But Luke seemed more than merely curious. "Yes, there's an editor who's been most encouraging."

He nodded, pleased for her. "That's great. And then what, you move to New York?"

Shay shook her head. "A writer can write anywhere." She wouldn't tell him of her plans to move, to get a place for Beth and herself. The big house was spacious and she loved it, but a grown woman couldn't live with her parents all her life.

Of course she wouldn't leave the Circle M, Luke thought. She loved the ranch and her family too much to ever go. How could he share his dream with her when she was so firmly entrenched here? And how could he, even with the fairly substantial money he'd saved over the years, ever hope to offer her anything close to what she already had? And what if he couldn't make a go of his ranch?

"I wish you luck," he told her, and meant it. Glancing up at the lowering sun, he frowned. "We'd better get back."

Shay watched him walk over to Maverick and wondered what she'd said to bring that shuttered look back to his face.

Chapter Six

A small brown horseshoe hare scurried for cover as Luke paused at the front porch steps of the big house. "Mind if I join you?" he asked Liz. He'd been taking a walk around the outbuildings of the ranch and had been heading for his own cabin when he'd spotted her sitting in her padded maple rocker.

"I'd love the company," she said, indicating the larger bentwood rocker alongside her, the chair usually occupied by Jacob. "Lovely evening, isn't it?"

A full moon hung in the summer night sky, illuminating the area with a pale glow. The insistent buzz of crickets serenaded from nearby as Luke sat down. "Yes, it is." He looked up as a white truck pulled in through the gate, one of the cowboys returning from his Sunday in town. The man sent them a wave as he drove on back toward the parking area behind the garage.

"I was hoping you'd come over for supper tonight," Liz began. "Beth's quite taken with you and keeps asking where you are."

Luke smiled as he stretched out his long legs. After the afternoon at the pond, he didn't think he could sit across the table from Shay and make small talk. "She's quite a charmer. I haven't been around kids much. Are they all so quick these days, so bright?"

Liz had raised three, perhaps four counting Luke, and knew all children were vastly different, even those born in the same family. Still, it pleased her to have him compliment her only grandchild. "Shay spends a lot of time with Beth. She does very well in school."

"As I remember, Shay used to get all A's while the rest of us were thrilled with a B."

So his mind was on Shay, Liz gathered. She'd been out back earlier and seen the two of them returning on horseback from the direction of the west pasture. And she'd been in the kitchen shortly after when Shay had come in, her hair damp and her cheeks flushed. Swimming together, Liz had guessed, and couldn't help wondering what else had gone on out at the old watering hole. "Yes, Shay's always been quick and intelligent. Occasionally, her judgment's been off, of course. Like all of us."

He'd come over to chat because he honestly liked Liz. But he also hoped she could clear up some of his questions. "Tell me about Shay's marriage, Liz."

She took a moment to answer. "Shouldn't that be up to her?"

"I'm not asking you to reveal confidences. Just your impressions, your observations. Why did she leave Max after only two years?" The reasons she'd turned to Maxwell Whitney after he'd left nagged at him even more.

"Shay hasn't shared much with us about her brief marriage. I can only surmise that she left because she was unhappy. Max insisted that they live in the Whitney house and, from the beginning, Shay didn't care for his parents. Morgan Whitney likes giving orders, ruling his ranch from his oak-paneled office. Yet he's never had the good sense God gave a billy goat."

Luke chuckled. "A good description, from what I remember of him. He used to wear these silk shirts he had specially made for him with his initials on the cuffs. Silk, out on the range, can you imagine?"

Liz nodded. "Yes, but of course, he doesn't spend much time on the range. He's run his inheritance practically into the ground, more's the pity. His father's probably whirling in his grave."

"Morgan and Shay didn't get along, I gather," Luke prompted.

"You could say that. As I told you, I feel Morgan urged his son to marry Shay because they wanted to share our water rights. But that didn't mean he had to be nice to her. He deeply resented needing Shay and us."

Luke waited for her to go on, feeling empathy for the sensitive girl he remembered.

"And Cybil Whitney was unbearable, I gather from the little Shay has said. She was born in England and acts as though everyone here is a country bumpkin."

"Sounds like Cybil feels she married beneath her station."

"Probably. Truth is she's not a terribly attractive woman, nor has she bothered to develop likable traits. I'd guess that when Morgan met her on one of his overseas trips as a young man, she jumped at the chance to marry a man she thought was wealthy and living on a huge estate. Turned out to be a big spread all right, but out in the middle of nowhere and populated with smelly cows and rough cowboys. Shay mentioned that Cybil rarely left the house unless to go into Billings and never spoke to the hands. She concentrated on genteel pursuits like needlework and ordering the servants around."

Luke watched a shooting star spiral toward earth, trying to picture Shay in that unfriendly environment. *It was formal, cold, humorless, lonely.* "How did Max react to his wife being unhappy?"

"Pretty much ignored her, I believe. Having gotten his water, Morgan next started grooming his son for the political arena, thinking that would give the family clout and privileges."

"Yes, Shay told me he's running for the state senate."

Liz made a face. "This is his second attempt, and he hasn't managed to get elected yet. I heard he recently became engaged to a Billings socialite, so perhaps her connections will do the trick. It never hurts a rising politician to have a lovely woman on his arm. He used to drag Shay to these political dinners and fund-raising parties, and she hated all of it. Then, she became pregnant and refused to go anymore. I think the problems between them escalated after Beth was born. Then, when she lost the second baby..."

"I didn't know about a second child."

Liz nodded. "She was six months along and the loss devastated her. She couldn't seem to get over it, physically or mentally. She was so thin, so sad every time we saw her."

Luke's fingers gripped the rocker arms angrily. Damn Maxwell Whitney for taking that beautiful woman and using her. If he ever got his hands on the man...

"I brought her and Beth home with us for a while, hoping she'd rally better around those of us who loved her. But after a few weeks, she insisted on returning. She seemed determined to make her marriage work. Then, something went wrong."

"What was it?"

Liz shook her head. "I don't know. To this day, Shay has never said. Late one evening, she appeared on the doorstep with Beth and their things, pale and silent. She called our attorney and filed for divorce. I think it was a full year before I heard her genuinely laugh after that." Liz turned to Luke, studying his face, seeing the outrage. "Now do you see why I asked you to be kind to her? Shay's recovered from all that, but underneath she's still quite fragile. And she's always had a weakness for you. I don't want to see her hurt again."

"Neither do I. I've loved two women in my life, Liz. You were the first, and then Shay. Or perhaps it was the other way around, I don't know."

She couldn't help but be warmed by his admission.

"Have you told her?"

"Not since I left." He thought of their talk at the pond, their separate goals. "It isn't simple. There are problems."

She'd guessed as much. "Such as? Is it Beth, your accepting another man's child?"

Luke frowned thoughtfully. He'd not thought much about being a father, substitute or otherwise. However, he knew that Shay and Beth came as a package deal. "It's not that." He waved his hand, indicating the Circle M. "It's all this. I can't give Shay anything close to this."

Liz leaned forward. "A woman falls in love with the rancher, not the ranch. What makes you think all this matters to Shay?"

"It matters to me that I can't give her all she deserves."

Men could be so obtuse, Liz thought. "She deserves a man who loves her above all else, one who will stand by her always, one who cares for her because of *who* she is, not what she has. That's what we all deserve, including you."

Luke felt a muscle in his jaw twitch. "No man wants the woman he loves to see him as a failure. It's a matter of pride."

She sat back wearily. "You always had a bit too much pride, Luke."

"I came from nothing, Liz. Pride was all I had." It was time to go back to his cabin. He stood, thinking he'd probably said too much already.

"You might find pride makes a lonely bedfellow."

"I already know that, but as Jacob often says, a man has to do what he has to do." He left the porch. "Good night."

Liz watched him go, her heart heavy. She knew that the course of love seldom ran smoothly. But Shay and Luke had been struggling for over ten years. Perhaps if she hadn't interfered back then . . .

Hindsight, she thought with a weary sigh, was wonderfully accurate. Slowly Liz rose and went inside.

"Two hundred twenty cows!" Jacob's voice was loud and angry. "How the hell did this happen without anyone seeing anything?"

Seated on a chair at her father's bedside, Shay touched his hand. "Dad, remember your blood pressure."

"Never mind my blood pressure. Let's concentrate on finding out who's stealing us blind." His brow furrowed as he looked at each of the three men standing at the foot of his bed in turn, the kind of look that over the years had made many a strong man squirm. Zeke shuffled his feet uncomfortably, and Gil looked out the window. Only Luke met his eyes straight on. "Anyone have any ideas?"

Zeke was the first to answer. "We've checked out the backgrounds of all the newer hands and come up empty."

"That foreman, Chet Rollins, who left in such a hurry," Gil said next, "we learned he's married and working a sheep ranch up in Gallatin Gateway." Always nervous being called on the carpet by his father, Gil twirled his hat in sweaty hands. "And Luke's been inquiring all over about Aaron Huxley, but we can't find him."

Hearing Aaron's name—a name from the past, a man who'd been very nice to her after Luke had left—Shay looked at Luke.

"What about Huxley?" Jacob asked Luke. "He's been gone for eight or nine years, hasn't he?"

Luke wondered how Gil had discovered he'd been asking around about Huxley, not regarding the rustling but because the cowboy had been interested in Shay. "Never hurts to check out a man who leaves in a hurry," he said casually.

Jacob rubbed the back of his neck. "If he's the one, he's sure taken his sweet time about it. I looked through those files you brought up, but the only one I remember who left madder than hell was Josh Carmichael. Remember him?"

"Yeah," Gil said. "We caught him trying to steal a cylinder of semen and learned he'd been fixing to sell it to ranchers up north."

"That's the fellow," Jacob acknowledged. "Do you know where he is?"

"No, but we'll sure look into it," Zeke assured him. "Damn, Jacob, I'm sorry about all this. I should have been on top of the count awhile back. I should have..."

Jacob waved aside his apology. "No rustling is just one man's fault." He eyed his son, then returned his gaze to Zeke.

Luke looked at Zeke, too, wondering at his sudden contriteness when he'd been the one to drag his feet getting the count. The man seemed a bit two-faced.

"You've only been with us a few years, Zeke. Others have been here longer." Again he glanced over at Gil.

Gil had had about enough. He checked his watch. "I've got to run. I've got an appointment at the Whitney ranch."

Jacob's scowl returned. "Whatever for?"

"I'm having my mare, Beauty, bred to Max's stallion, Ulysses." He sounded pleased with himself.

Shay felt a tightening of her stomach muscles as she watched her father's face turn stormy.

"We don't have enough stallions here that you got to go over to the enemy camp?" Jacob asked, his voice angry again.

Gil tried to explain. "Ulysses has an impressive bloodline. He's prime stuff and . . ."

Jacob's eyes narrowed. "And what kind of a price you paying?"

Gil swallowed hard. "First foal. But I know Beauty'll give us a great colt and . . ."

"You crazy, boy?" Jacob roared. "Damn, haven't you learned anything working this ranch?"

Luke hadn't realized that the problems between father and son hadn't eased much in the years he'd been away. For the first time, he wondered if perhaps Gil could be selling off some Circle M cows and pocketing the money, either to build a nest egg and leave, or simply to get even with his father for years of unfair treatment.

"Jacob," Luke said, wondering if his opinion would lessen the tension, "most stallion owners get first foal down Texas way. I don't think it's such a bad deal. No money out of pocket and Beauty's young and strong, able to drop plenty yet. I think Gil did the right thing."

"The hell you say," Jacob muttered, not so easily swayed.

"I do, too," Shay chimed in, hating to see her brother humiliated. "Ulysses is a magnificent animal."

"Never mind," Gil said, noticing his father's unforgiving face. "It's just like always," he told Jacob. "Nothing I ever do around here is good enough for you." His face flushed, he turned and left the room, slamming the door after him. In the silence, Gil's footsteps on the stairs echoed loudly through the quiet house.

Zeke cleared his throat. "I'd better get back to work." He removed his ever-present toothpick. "See you later."

After he left, Shay stood and crossed her arms over her chest. "Dad, was it really necessary to chastise Gil in front of all of us?"

Jacob bunched the pillows behind his bed, still angry. "That boy's got the judgment of a ten-year-old kid," he grumbled.

"At times, we all do," Shay couldn't help adding as she moved toward the door.

"We'll let you get some rest, Jacob," Luke added, and left with her.

Shay waited until they were downstairs in the deserted kitchen before she spoke again. "It was nice of you to speak up for Gil." Most especially since she knew that Luke still wasn't sure he hadn't taken Luke's notes way back when.

"I meant what I said about the Texas ranchers. Jacob's a bit behind the times." The sunshine pouring in through the window turned her hair to flame and he lost his train of thought. She was wearing a blue T-shirt today with a vee

PLAY "LUCKY HEARTS" AND GET . . .

★ **Exciting Silhouette Special Edition® novels—FREE**
★ **"Key to Your Heart" pendant necklace—FREE**
★ **Surprise mystery gift that will delight you—FREE**

THEN CONTINUE YOUR LUCKY STREAK WITH A SWEETHEART OF A DEAL

When you return the postcard on the opposite page, we'll send you the books and gifts you qualify for, absolutely free! Then, you'll get 6 new Silhouette Special Edition® novels every month, delivered right to your door months before they're available in stores. If you decide to keep them, you'll pay only $2.71* each plus 25¢ delivery and applicable sales tax, if any*. That's the complete price and—compared to cover prices of $3.39 each in stores—quite a bargain!

Free Newsletter!

You'll get our subscribers-only newsletter—an insider's look at our most popular authors and their upcoming novels.

Special Extras—Free!

When you join the Silhouette Reader Service™, you'll also get additional free gifts from time to time as a token of our appreciation for being a home subscriber.

neck, its softness clinging to her deliciously. He stepped closer, backing her up to the counter.

Since their encounter at the pond last Sunday, Shay hadn't been alone with him. She tried to keep it light. "You smell like lemons."

His arms went around her. "You smell better." His hands caressed her back, then he pulled away and raised an eyebrow. "Hey, lady, you're not wearing anything under this shirt."

She blushed furiously. "Only in the house." She nodded toward the chair. "Outdoors, I wear that blouse over it."

"Mmm-hmm." Slowly he ran the backs of his fingers down into the vee of her shirt and hungrily watched her nipples harden.

Shay felt a shiver overtake her. "Luke, please don't get me all worked up again. I'm tired of taking cold showers."

He released a ragged breath and stepped back. He hadn't intended to touch her, yet always when around Shay, he found his control weakening. All he had to do was look at her to want her. "I understand perfectly. Maybe we should take a day and go into town. Find some quiet country inn with a restaurant. Have a leisurely lunch and..."

Just hearing the words had her blood heating. "And?"

"And we can be alone." The desire to be alone with her had been churning inside him since the first day he'd returned. He pulled her close again. "I need to be alone with you." Dipping his head, he took her mouth.

Shay had not considered herself a particularly sexual being, thinking that time by the stream with Luke had been adolescent fervor. She'd had trouble responding to Max, and it had infuriated her husband to the point where their bedroom had become a battleground.

But this, this madness she felt with Luke, was so intense that the need to finish what they kept starting burned in her. Winding her arms around him, Shay lost herself in his kiss. She didn't even hear the quiet opening of the back door.

Letting the screen close silently behind her, Liz stood in shadow. Thirty-some years slipped away, and she remembered kissing a man with that kind of fire, the man who lay upstairs in their marriage bed.

She remembered also being at Shay's wedding to Max, seeing the hint of sadness in her daughter's eyes instead of the joy she should have been feeling. Liz had seen no passionate kiss between bride and groom, no affectionate touches, no lingering looks. She'd known then that something was missing in Shay's marriage, and had wondered since if perhaps Shay, too, hadn't known.

Unwilling to intrude further on their private moment, Liz slipped soundlessly out the door. As she walked toward the corral, she sent up a fervent prayer that, whatever was developing between Shay and Luke, neither of them would get hurt.

Finding the rustlers was not a simple matter, Luke realized. He'd been foolishly optimistic thinking the problem would be solved in a month. Already it had been two weeks since he'd returned, and they were no nearer the truth than before. Driving the Jeep along the fence line, he wondered how much longer he could delay his departure.

Bouncing along as he swung down a gully then straightened, he frowned into the morning sun. Thoughtfully he considered all they'd done up to the present. He had men riding fence daily, hoping to thwart another attempt. He'd painstakingly checked out all of the men he'd had questions about and those who'd left rather suddenly, and come up with nothing concrete. He'd even tracked down Aaron Huxley and learned he'd been killed in a rodeo accident two years ago. Daily he mingled with the hands, working alongside them, eating with them, chatting with them, hoping someone with a loose tongue would betray something. So far, nothing.

Luke waved at a cowboy on horseback as he came to the stream and followed it along. Absently he rubbed his right knee, the old injury inexplicably aching today. He'd tried to keep an eye on Gil's activities and had even been monitoring Zeke's comings and goings, but both seemed legitimately busy with ranch duties. He'd driven into town, dropped in at the café for lunch and made the acquaintance of several nearby ranchers, even a couple who remembered him. He'd learned absolutely nothing helpful.

Damn, but two hundred and twenty cows didn't just vanish into thin air. Where were they, and who had taken them? He needed to find out so he could be gone, so he could start on his own dream. For too long, he'd been at the beck and call of owners, some honest and fair, some not so decent. He'd been a loner all his life, despite the lack of privacy involved in living in bunkhouses, in eating in crowded mess halls, in working with others every day of his life.

He longed for something of his own besides his truck and his stallion, something solid and permanent that no one could take away. Until recently, he'd thought if he could manage that, he'd ask for no more. Now that his dream seemed possible, he realized something else that he hadn't admitted before. He longed for *someone* of his own.

Shay.

She was free, and so was he. She wanted him, cared for him, he believed, as much as he did for her. But there were other hurdles that wouldn't easily be overcome.

She would one day inherit one-third of a hugely successful cattle ranch; the best he could offer her would be a small spread that he would have to work hard to build up. He didn't mind hard work, or waiting for stock to grow, to produce. But she might resent starting over.

Shay loved the Circle M, had been unhappy during her brief stay away from here and undoubtedly wouldn't want to leave again. Luke wasn't certain he would be a good father figure for Beth. Though he'd begun to care for the likable little girl, he felt that his parenting skills were practically nonexistent.

So many negatives, Luke thought. Could he just ignore them and go after Shay, hoping for the best? She'd been hurt once, badly. He had no intention of causing her more pain.

What, then, was the answer? To find the rustlers, say goodbye and move along? To leave the only family he'd ever known, the only woman he'd ever cared for? In the long run, it seemed either he'd hurt Shay, or himself. No contest there.

A huge explosion suddenly shattered the peaceful morning stillness, followed by several smaller ones that sounded like discharges. Slamming on the brakes, Luke scanned the area. He saw a black cloud of smoke rising in the sky off to his right, then smaller dark puffs trailing upward. The crackling noise continued, coming from the area upstream.

As Luke rushed in that direction, he saw several Circle M cowboys on horseback hurrying toward the reverberating sound. It seemed to have originated near the boundary line of the Circle M and the Whitney spread, or damn close.

Downshifting, he stepped on the gas, wondering what in hell had happened.

"Dynamite," Luke told Jacob. "Some Whitney men set off dynamite blasts at the fork of the stream to divert the mountain flow more toward their land, and all but closing off our supply."

"Damn, but they're not going to get away with that." Jacob's face was set and angry.

Seated at his side, Liz looked worried. "Jacob, please don't get worked up."

"Worked up? You think I should let that damn fool Morgan steal our water while we sit back and do nothing?" He narrowed his eyes at Luke. "Could be they've been grabbing our cows, too."

Luke had considered that at one time, then had dismissed the thought. "I doubt that. Shay and I flew over their spread. The cows we saw looked thin and scruffy. That's why they need our water."

"After Shay left the Whitney ranch, I stopped being a good neighbor. A man has to look after his own first. This is the first summer we've had it so dry, which is why Morgan ran out of options." He struck the bed with an impotent fist. "The nerve of the bastard." Then another thought hit him. "Where the hell were our ditch riders?"

"I don't know." Luke glanced at Liz's concerned expression. He'd been hesitant about telling Jacob, so he'd conferred with her. She'd thought a long moment, then decided the two of them should tell him together. Being kept in the dark, then later finding out would make him even angrier, Liz had said. Yet Luke hated seeing Jacob fighting mad, knowing it couldn't possibly be good for his recovery.

"How would you like this handled, Jacob?" Luke asked, knowing they had to take quick action.

"I want you to go over to the Whitney ranch and tell Morgan he's pushed me too far. Then I want you to send our men to repair the damage and reroute the water exactly the way it was. And you might mention that if he pulls another crazy stunt, I'll turn him over to the sheriff." He almost smiled at that thought.

But Luke was uncomfortable with parts of his suggestion. "A good plan, but I think Gil ought to deliver your message. After all, he's your son and..."

Jacob brushed the suggestion aside. "I can't trust that boy, Luke, and you damn well know it."

"Now, Jacob," Liz injected, "that isn't so." Had she brought Luke back only to have Jacob turn on his own son?

Luke saw the anxiety in her face and hurried to come up with an alternative plan. "All right then, Zeke should go, as co-manager." After he'd reached the explosion site, he'd tried to find both Zeke and Gil and hadn't been able to. Not wanting to delay, he'd hurried to the big house.

Jacob was insistent. "Why can't you go?"

Actually he'd love to be the one, especially if Maxwell Whitney was around. The opportunity to rearrange that man's face would give him great pleasure. But he hadn't the right. "Because I'm not on the payroll here and..."

"We can fix that. You're hired." Jacob looked satisfied.

Luke shook his head. "I don't want to be hired. I came to do a favor, to repay a debt—"

"Don't you know," Jacob interrupted, "you're just like a son in this house, Lucas Turner? There is no debt."

That stopped him. He'd longed to hear Jacob speak those words years ago. Even coming now, they warmed him. "I...thank you. But please, I need to do this without payment."

Jacob nodded, understanding. "Just don't forget what I said." He felt his wife's hand squeeze his and knew he'd pleased her. "All right, we'll do it your way this time. Send Zeke over to Whitney."

Since Jacob had calmed, Luke decided to push a little. "Maybe the best thing would be if Gil and Zeke went together, presenting a united front, laying it all out. You know what I mean?" He saw Liz nod approval.

Jacob's shrewd eyes studied the man who stood in front of him. He remembered how well Luke had managed the ranch hands at an early age, how fair he'd tried to be, how good his judgment calls had been. He'd missed Luke. He only hoped that he'd be staying on or at least settling nearby.

Rubbing the back of his neck, Jacob glanced at Liz and saw the hope in her eyes. Maybe he'd been a little harsh. He looked back at Luke. "I know exactly what you mean. Go do it." He made a shooing gesture. "Go on, get out of here." His arm circled his wife's waist as she sat on the edge of the bed. "I got a beautiful woman here. Think I want you hanging around?"

Luke grinned. "Yes, sir." With a wink at Liz, he left the room.

Liz moved closer and smiled at her husband. "I'm proud of you, Mr. McKenzie."

"Thank you, darlin'." He reached to touch his mouth to hers.

"But he's a stray. He's liable to bite you." Seated some distance from Luke on the grass alongside his cabin, Beth watched Luke hold out his hand toward the dog.

"I doubt it," Luke answered, his voice low so as not to scare the animal away. "He's been coming around for a couple of days now, and I've been leaving food out for him. But today, I decided to see if he's learned to trust me yet."

Coming around the corner of the house at twilight, Shay stopped. Odd how every time she went hunting for her daughter these days, she looked first at Luke's, for that's where Beth usually could be found. There they sat, man and child, dark head and fair, involved in a conversation. She took a moment to wonder why that was, just what drew Beth to this man who admittedly knew very little about children.

"But he's all dirty, and he smells bad," Beth insisted.

Luke tore off a piece of meat from the plate of beef and gravy he'd finagled from the cook and placed it on the tips of his fingers, then held his hand out again. "So would you be if you had to sleep out in the wilderness with no one to bathe you or take care of you."

"How'd he get lost?" the child wondered aloud.

"Oh, he could have wandered too far from home or somebody might have brought him out into the country and shoved him from the car, not wanting another mouth to feed in his house." A harsh reality, but true. He glanced at Beth to see if he'd shocked her, but her face registered only interest. The dog inched closer, his black nose sniffing.

"Why would you want a dirty old dog when we've got Beechie?" Beth wanted to know.

"Because we have enough food for him, too." He reached with his other hand to touch Beth's braid. "Don't you think we have enough room around here for two dogs?"

"Yeah, probably, if he was cleaner."

"As soon as he lets us, we'll clean him up." The dog was medium sized with mottled brown fur that probably would look healthy with a little attention. His eyes were bright and intelligent. There was a small cut nearly healed on the top of his head, as if he'd been in a fight. No doubt he had, Luke thought, for coyotes, elk and mule deer wandered freely in the open spaces and wooded areas.

"He doesn't look like any dogs around here," Beth added.

"You're right," Luke told her, "he's different. He's possibly been mistreated and abandoned. He's hurt and afraid to trust, afraid we'll treat him badly, too."

"But we won't," she protested.

"Of course not, but he doesn't know that. It takes time and patience to get a stray to trust you."

Finally the dog crept closer and his tongue shot out to grab the food, his eyes remaining wary. Chewing, he got up, circled around, then came back. Luke offered him another piece, which he took more readily this time. "See, he's hungry enough to take a chance on us."

Beth wiggled closer. "What about Beechie? What if my dog doesn't want this dog around?"

Luke set the plate on the ground and watched the dog quickly devour the food. "It'll be up to you to teach Beechie to accept this dog, to not feel threatened by him. Do you think you can learn to care for this stray the way you love Beechie?"

Beth wasn't convinced. "I don't know."

Luke slipped his arm around her. "I think you can. When your mom was just a little older than you, a stray showed up here one day. And most everyone had trouble accepting him. Like this dog, he was afraid and shy and kind of beat-up looking. But your mom always stuck up for him, making that stray feel like he was as good as anyone else. Your grandma helped, too, by cleaning him up and feeding him.''

At the side of the house, Shay leaned closer, recognizing the scenario.

Beth loved stories. ''What happened to him?''

''He stayed a long time and he grew very fond of your grandma. But most of all, he loved your mom.''

Beth's dark eyes, so like her mother's, gazed up at him. ''There's no dog here except Beechie. Where'd he go?''

Luke gave out a heavy sigh. ''He made a mistake one day and wandered off. He shouldn't have, but it took him awhile to figure that out. By then, it was too late.''

''Why doesn't he come back? My mom would forgive him, I know. When I do something wrong, she always forgives me. And she says she'll never stop loving me.''

Luke nodded. ''I believe you. You're lucky to have a mom like that.''

''Where's your mom, Luke?''

''She died a long time ago.''

''Did she love you?''

''I like to think so.''

Beth looked suddenly sad. ''My dad doesn't love me. He doesn't act like it, anyhow. Are you a dad?''

''No.''

''You should try it. Kids are nice to have around.''

Luke grinned, helping her up. ''They are, are they? I'll take that under advisement.''

Beth turned to the dog sitting half a dozen feet away from them, his head cocked as he watched them. ''Can I pet him?''

''Not yet. Promise me you'll only go near him if I'm around, until we're sure he accepts us as friends.''

''I promise.'' They watched the dog wander off into the pine trees around back.

Luke got up. "Let's go inside. Cora left a pitcher of my favorite lemonade and a plate of cookies on my back porch earlier. I could go for some. How about you?"

Nodding enthusiastically, Beth hopped up and skipped on ahead of him.

Needing a moment, Shay pulled back out of sight as she heard them go into Luke's house. She blinked back the moisture from her eyes, deeply moved by Luke's story of the stray. Had Luke felt like a stray her family had taken in, wanting badly to be accepted but afraid to trust? Her heart that was already his turned over.

But most of all, he loved your mom.

Did Luke still love her? she wondered.

Chapter Seven

Luke parked the Jeep in back of the barn, got out and stretched his aching muscles. It had been a long day. He was hot, dirty and tired. Walking to his cabin, he removed his hat and ran his hand through his damp hair.

He'd been riding fence early in the morning and had stopped awhile to watch the men reroute the stream's flow, which Zeke was overseeing. Then he'd come upon a mess.

Two head of elk had tried to get through the fence, probably after a nearby salt lick, and gotten tangled in the barbed wire. It had taken him and two other men several hours to free the one, but the second had to be shot as he'd been badly hurt. Then they'd repaired the fence.

Luke waved at Hollis as he came out of the barn, leading one of the young colts to the corral. He probably should stop at the mess hall and see if there was any food left, but he needed a shower first. The heat had just gotten worse. One of the men had said he'd heard they'd hit a hundred two degrees at midday. For a while there, stripped to the waist and dripping wet, Luke had thought it felt more like two hundred two.

He climbed onto his porch, his boots thudding heavily, and turned the doorknob. He'd forgotten that since the note had been left, he'd been locking the door. He dug into his pocket for the keys as he heard a voice coming from the side of the house.

"Just the man I'm looking for." Rhea appeared, walking between his parked truck and the porch. "I've brought you some of Cora's chocolate chip cookies." She held out the plate as she stepped up.

"Thanks." He slid the key into the lock, thinking that Cora seemed intent on fattening him up.

Rhea brushed back a lock of her brown hair. "I was going to leave them in your kitchen. I didn't know you locked your door. I even went around back, but that door's locked, too. You didn't used to be so distrusting, Luke."

That was before he'd had one too many uninvited guests in his house. "It's a habit I acquired recently." He went in and held the door open for her to follow. He tossed his hat and keys on the coffee table, then walked to the kitchen and opened the refrigerator. Liz had stocked it with a few essentials. He pulled out a can of beer. "Can I offer you one of these or some lemonade?"

She leaned against the archway. "No, thanks. You look beat."

"I am." Luke popped the can open, bent his head back and swallowed thirstily. He didn't stop till half the can was empty. "We've been wrestling a couple of stray elk out of barbed wire for hours. Don't come too close. I'm hot and sweaty." He pulled out a kitchen chair and dropped into it.

Ignoring his warning, Rhea put the plate of cookies on the table and took the chair opposite him. "Did you have dinner? I could bring you some stew that I made this morning."

The kitchen was small and her closeness a little cloying in the dim shadows of approaching evening. He hadn't spoken alone with Rhea since his return and had wanted to, but this didn't seem the best time. "I don't get very hungry in this heat. What I need is a shower." He hoisted the can again, hoping she'd take the hint and leave.

"So I guess you've decided to stay on, then," Rhea said, squirming uneasily on her seat.

Luke took his time setting down the can. It occurred to him that she appeared oddly jumpy. Probably because they hadn't talked together in so many years. Where was the fun-loving Rhea he remembered? He sent her a lazy smile, hoping to recapture some of the camaraderie they used to have. "You trying to get rid of me, Rhea?"

She seemed to relax a fraction. "I thought you were the one always trying to get rid of me, or don't you remember?"

"Back when you were a pesky kid, you mean?"

Rhea drew nervous figure eights on the tabletop with her finger, then suddenly buried her hands in her lap. "I wasn't such a kid. You just never noticed. All you could see was Shay."

Why would she sound resentful of something that happened so many years ago? "Yet both of you married other guys. Are you happy with Zeke, Rhea?"

For a long moment, she studied her hands clasped together in her lap. Then she brightened and put on a smile, looking more like the Rhea he had known. "Of course. Do you like Zeke?"

A tough question. "He seems like a regular guy," Luke answered carefully.

"He works awfully hard. He's a lot like you, you know." When Luke sent her a questioning look, she rushed on to explain. "I mean he came from a mixed-up background. His father abandoned the family and I guess his mother wasn't very maternal, moving his brother and him around from place to place. I just wish I could get pregnant. I think Zeke needs to feel he's part of a real family, you know?"

Luke knew the feeling well. "I imagine guys like us aren't all that easy to live with."

"Not always," she admitted reluctantly. "He gets so restless, and I don't know what to say or do to make him feel better. He's got this streak of jealousy...."

He turned the can on the tabletop thoughtfully as he watched her face from under lowered lashes. Rhea wasn't bad looking. If she lost about twenty pounds, she could even be called pretty. "Do you give him reason to be jealous?"

She made a sound that was intended to be a laugh but didn't quite make it. "Not jealous of me. Of people who have more than he does. Especially Gil. Zeke thinks Gil has it made as the only son of the owner of the Circle M." Absently she took a cookie from the plate and nibbled on it.

"One third will belong to you one day. As your husband, he'll be in on that. Not too shabby."

Her eyes met his, her look oddly speculative. "Not one third. One fourth. You're in Dad's will, too."

Luke straightened in his chair as shock registered on his face, followed by disbelief. "Come on, Rhea. That can't be."

Nodding, she swallowed the rest of the cookie. "They added you years ago. Of course, after you left, they may have changed it back again. But now, if you stay..." She let the thought hang in the suddenly tense air between them.

You're just like a son in this house, Jacob had told him recently. But to bequeath one fourth of his vast holdings to him? No, that couldn't be. He couldn't accept anything from the McKenzies when they'd rescued him. "I'm not entitled, and I won't take it."

"You'd turn down something worth a million bucks?"

Luke rubbed at a spot above his eyes, feeling a headache coming on. "Who else knows about this?"

She shrugged. "Zeke and I and Gil. I've never discussed it with Shay, but she probably knows."

He leaned forward, still suspicious. "Jacob told you this?"

"No, no. I... I got it from someone else. But it's true. Of course, the way you left so suddenly, Dad may have changed his mind, though he always favored you." Her smile had a bittersweet edge to it. "You were the golden boy, the one who could do no wrong. I wanted to hate you, but somehow I couldn't."

Luke was feeling confused. "Your memory of those years is a lot different than mine. I was the outsider, the drunk's son, the orphan kid."

Rhea shook her head slowly. "You were the kind of son Dad had always wanted, not someone sickly like Gil. Mom thought you were handsome and wonderful, Shay loved you and so did... everyone."

"Gil sure didn't."

"He couldn't help envying your looks, your strength. I think that's why he left after you did, because he felt he couldn't take your place."

"That's ridiculous. I never meant to compete with anyone. I just wanted..." *A family to love, one that would love me.* Luke cleared his throat. "To be accepted."

"Like Zeke wants."

Talking about Zeke had led to this startling revelation. "Does Zeke resent me, too?" Or was he getting paranoid?

She gave him a measuring look, as if wondering how much to tell him. "A little. He and Gil were getting along fairly well until you showed up. Now, Gil's all tense again. And Dad asked you to go over to talk with the Whitneys about the dynamite."

Luke sighed impatiently. "But I suggested that Zeke and Gil go together. And they did."

"But *you* were Dad's first choice."

There didn't seem to be a way to win. "Look, Rhea, I came back because your mother asked me to help out, not to stir up trouble. I'm only here temporarily."

"Are you? I saw you with Shay. The two of you seem to be getting close again."

Luke felt his jaw tighten. Was everyone on the ranch hiding in the shrubs watching him and Shay?

Before he could answer, Rhea stood. "None of my business, I know." She flashed him a quick smile. "I'm being that pesky kid again, it seems. You bring out the worst in me, Luke." She stared at him a long moment, then reached a hand to lightly stroke his cheek. Looking embarrassed at her own gesture, she turned to leave. "See you later."

Watching her walk away, then skip down the porch steps, Luke rubbed his chin. Rhea had given him a lot to think about. Rising, he went in to take a shower.

"I don't see how this could have happened," Luke said quietly. He reined in his skittish stallion and looked at Zeke who sat calmly in the Jeep. "I thought you told me you increased the number of men on horseback in this pasture?"

"I did."

They'd met in the far pasture near the road where the count had first been noticed to be short. Zeke had just told him that another twenty cows had turned up missing. Luke swore under his breath. "Who was in charge out here last night?"

Zeke glanced down at his clipboard on the seat beside him. "Charley Brice, and he had another good man with him."

"What the hell were they doing, playing poker all night or sleeping under a tree?" Annoyed, Luke rearranged his hat.

Zeke's full lips thinned. "Are you accusing my men of not doing their job?"

My men. Interesting that he felt that way. "I'm not accusing any one person. But someone sure as hell wasn't doing his job, or we wouldn't have another twenty cows missing. Have you told anyone else about this yet?"

Slouching back in the seat, Zeke shook his head. "You said you're in charge of the rustling problem, so I told you as soon as I heard."

The man wasn't even trying to hide his animosity while they were alone out here. But in front of Jacob, he was a humble cowboy. Gil wasn't pleased about Luke's involvement in finding the rustlers, either. Swell. The two managers were surly and resentful. Small wonder they were getting nowhere. "All right." Luke turned Maverick around.

Curious, Zeke looked up. "What are you going to do?"

"Talk this over with Jacob. It seems to me we need to make some changes around here."

Zeke's eyes turned cold as he sat up and stuck a toothpick into the corner of his mouth. Without another word, he shoved the Jeep into gear and roared off.

It would appear that behind that seemingly relaxed facade, Rhea's husband had a short fuse, Luke thought, as the man drove down the incline. If Zeke wasn't to blame for the laxity of his men, why would he get so angry? Nudging Maverick, he started back toward the ranch house. He needed to ask a couple of cowboys a couple of questions.

Luke left the corral where he'd turned his stallion loose and walked toward the big house. Charley Brice and the men he wanted to question were still out on the range, not due back till near sundown. He decided to talk with Jacob first, not wanting to overstep his authority.

As he turned the corner, he noticed the afternoon sun glinting off the windshield of a shiny white limousine parked by the foaling barn, and wondered who it belonged to. At the back porch, he paused and turned in time to see a uniformed chauffeur step out from behind the wheel and casually lean against the door. A stray cat wandered by, and the chauffeur leaned down to pet it. Stepping inside, Luke saw Liz standing at the kitchen window, also watching the limo.

"Somebody important visiting?" he asked, joining her. Few people in this part of Montana rode in limos, and why would the silly thing be parked at the barn and not the house?

"He thinks he is," Liz answered cryptically. "Maxwell Whitney." Her voice was filled with derision.

So that was it. Luke stepped behind her so he could watch over her shoulder. "I take it Shay's in the barn?"

"Yes." She stood hugging her arms.

"Do you want me to go out there?" He'd love to meet Shay's ex-husband.

Liz glanced at his set face and shook her head. "We'd best let Shay handle it." The last thing they needed was for those two to get into a fight.

Luke stuck his hands into his pockets, his concern making him restless. "How'd he know she's in there?"

"He came here first and spoke with Beth ever so briefly. Then he asked me where Shay was and had his chauffeur drive him to the barn." She picked up the dish towel and pulled it through her fingers nervously. "Can you imagine? He couldn't walk a couple hundred feet?"

The picture he'd formed of Max was worsening by the minute. As he watched, Shay came out through the open barn doors walking fast. Close behind her was a tall man with a burly chest. Max was wearing sunglasses and his thin blond hair blew about in a light breeze. The chauffeur got back behind the wheel. Shay was shaking her head. Suddenly Max grabbed her arm and pulled her around to face him. Luke felt himself stiffen.

Liz touched his arm. "Stay calm."

"Does he do this often?" Luke asked, not taking his eyes off the outdoor scene. "Come over like this and harass Shay."

"Too often to suit me."

Through the open screen door, they could hear Max's voice, angry and loud, but couldn't make out his words. He shook his pointed finger at Shay, who wasn't even looking at him. But he must have said something that riled her for she balled her fists at her side and answered back. Apparently it wasn't what he wanted to hear. He took a menacing step closer.

"That's it." Luke made for the door. "I'm going out there."

"Luke," Liz called after him, "she won't like interference."

"I don't give a damn." He slammed the screen door and started down the stairs. Taking long strides, he saw Max glance over his shoulder, then drop his hand from Shay and duck into the waiting limo. The driver started off before Max had closed the door completely. Luke glared at the tinted windows of the big car as it zoomed past him. Then he turned to look at Shay.

She was crying. Her eyes collided with his, and she gave a quick shake of her head, then turned and headed for the woods.

"Shay, wait!" Luke yelled after her as he began to run. He watched her disappear into a clump of trees and slowed his pace, finally stopping.

If she needed to be alone, he would allow her her privacy. Now that he knew she was physically safe from Max, he would wait until she felt composed enough to come back on her own. He returned to the kitchen.

"Thank you for being perceptive enough not to follow her," Liz said. "Shay's a very private person."

"I remember." Luke realized his hands were tightly clenched into fists and forced himself to relax.

"She often goes off for a while after one of his visits, just to be alone and collect her thoughts." To cry and get it out of her system in privacy, Liz thought.

"I'd like a few minutes alone with that bastard."

"Wouldn't we all. Beth's probably in her room crying as well. He always upsets her badly, and she tries so hard to hide it."

My daddy doesn't love me, Beth had told him several days ago, almost matter-of-factly. But she felt the loss all the same, he knew. "Do you think she'd mind if I went up and talked with her?"

Liz registered surprise. "I think she'd like that very much." She'd often tried to comfort her granddaughter after one of her scenes with her father, but it was a man's attention she craved. Beth had somehow gotten the notion that men didn't love children. Liz knew Luke was new to coping with a child, yet the fact that he wanted to try was to his credit. "Her room is next to Shay's. Do you remember the way?"

He smiled at her. "I won't get lost. I need to talk with Jacob, too. We've lost another twenty cows."

"Oh, no. Listen, Jacob overdid today. He insisted on coming downstairs and going over the books with Shay in his den. He looked worn-out and fell asleep right after lunch. Could you put off telling him till later, possibly tomorrow?"

"Sure, no problem." He'd catch Charley Brice after dinner and maybe Gil would show up here.

"Luke," Liz added, following him out of the kitchen, "come for supper tonight. It might be good for Shay if you're with us."

"All right." Moving quietly, he went upstairs. At Beth's closed door, he knocked gently. "It's Luke. Could I come in?"

He heard nothing for several moments, then a very quiet, "Yes." Luke walked in and found Beth sitting on her window seat with Beechie curled up beside her. The room was all in pink and ivory with a canopy bed, and on top of the dresser was Beth's collection of carved horses. He pulled out her desk chair and sat down facing her.

Beth sat stroking her dozing dog. "Is he gone?" Her room faced the back of the house overlooking a horse corral, and she couldn't have seen Max leave.

"Yes." He'd have to fly by the seat of his pants on this one, Luke thought, for he'd never tried to talk with an upset child before. He searched his mind, hoping he'd say the right thing. "I'm sorry he upset you."

"Why does he yell so much? I hate yelling."

Luke's father had been a yeller, especially after one of his drinking bouts. He remembered how, as a boy, he'd hated that, hated the attention the old man had attracted by his loud rantings. "Some people seem to think that being loud in what they say makes them right."

"He's ugly and awful." There was a catch in her voice, a little like a dry sob. "My mom says I don't have to listen to him, that he can't hurt us. But he said..." She turned to him now and her eyes were ready to overflow. "He said I *had* to go to Billings with him."

Acting on instinct, Luke opened his arms and she leaned forward to hug him, laying her cheek against his chest as a surprised Beechie looked up. "No, you don't have to go with him. I promise you." He would see to it if it was the last thing he did, he thought as he held her small, trembling body close.

Beth blinked away the tears as she angled to look up at him. "Do you mean it?"

"Absolutely." He smoothed her hair back from her flushed face, realizing that Beth evoked in him the same need to protect that he'd always felt for her mother.

She drew in another shaky breath, then swiped at her face. "I don't mean to be such a baby." Beth moved back onto the seat and patted Beechie's head reassuringly.

"You're not a baby at all. Nobody should be forced to do something they don't want to do, unless it's something necessary, like visit the doctor or go to school."

"My mom told me last night that you once saved her from some bullies on the way home from school. Did you?"

Luke handed her a tissue from the box on the desk, then sat back, hoping the story would distract her. "Yeah, I guess I did. She was about ten, and the school bus had dropped her off at the road, probably like yours does, right?" He saw her nod, the sadness leaving her eyes as she listened with interest. "I don't know where your Uncle Gil and Aunt Rhea were. Maybe they'd run on ahead. Anyhow, a couple of boys older than your mom were teasing her. She began to run, and they chased her."

"And she said she climbed up a tree."

"That's right. Way up. The boys were climbing up after her when I got off a different school bus. I was older and already in high school."

Beth was smiling now. "And the boys took one look at you and ran off."

Luke nodded. "Right. Then I told your mom to come down. Only she had a problem. She was wearing this jumperlike dress and it had gotten snagged in one of the tree's branches. She couldn't free it, couldn't come down."

"So you climbed up and rescued her, only you were mad."

He laughed, remembering. "Oh, she told you that, did she? I was mad because I'd just gotten these new pants. They were gray, and I really liked them. I tore them getting her out of that tree."

"I know what happened then."

"All right, tell me."

"You both came home to Grandma, and she wasn't mad at all. She said you'd done the right thing, that people were more important than things." Beth screwed up her little face thoughtfully. "I think Mom was trying to teach me a lesson with that story. But it really happened, right?"

"Yes, it did. And I think your grandma was trying to teach us a lesson with what she said, too. People *are* more important than things."

"And dogs are important, too. I saw Sebastian sleeping on your back porch today."

Luke frowned. "Sebastian?"

Beth brightened. "That's what I named the brown dog. Sebastian's the crab in the movie, *The Little Mermaid*. He used to be kind of crabby, but he isn't anymore. I talked to Beechie about him, and I think they'll become friends." She stroked the Labrador's sleek head.

"Good. You didn't get too close to Sebastian, right?"

She shook her head, her braid shifting with her movements. "I was waiting for you."

"We'll feed him together tonight after supper." Luke stood and replaced the chair. "You going to be all right now?"

Beth slid off her seat, nodding.

Luke reached into his pocket and handed her a pack of the gum he'd begun carrying. "Here, for you and Beechie."

Beth smiled. "Thanks. Do you know where my mom is?"

"She went for a walk," Luke told her. "She'll be back soon." At least he hoped it would be soon.

But as Luke stepped into the big house that evening for dinner, the first thing he noticed was that the one person he wanted to see wasn't around. "Shay hasn't come back yet?" he asked Liz in the kitchen.

Liz placed warm rolls in a basket. "She was here earlier. She went up and talked with Beth for a while, then she took a shower and told me she was going for a walk and not to hold dinner for her."

"Did she talk with you, tell you what Max wanted?"

Liz dropped a napkin over the warm rolls, her jerky movements revealing her emotional state. "The same thing he always wants—the privileges of fatherhood without any of the responsibilities."

Luke ran a frustrated hand through his hair, still damp from his shower. "But why does he want to parade Beth around? You said he's engaged to some socialite and about to start another family. Isn't that enough?"

"Apparently not." Liz sighed as she handed the rolls to Cora to take into the dining room. "You see, everyone around here knows Max has a daughter. Folks aren't going to look too kindly on a man who simply walks away from his child. I'm sure his political advisors have told him he'd better flash Beth in front of the voters before election day so they can see that, though he's divorced from her mother, he's still a loving father to his little girl."

Luke swore under his breath. "I promised Beth she wouldn't have to go with him since she doesn't want to."

That caught Liz off guard. "Did you?"

"Yes. There must be something Shay can do about Max. He doesn't even pay child support."

"I don't know. Today, the courts consider father's rights, as well. They don't just automatically favor the mother."

Luke found himself pacing the kitchen. "Shay needs to look into her options, to force Max to leave them alone once and for all."

Liz watched him striding back and forth, his steps angry, his voice agitated. Luke seemed to have more than a passing interest in Shay's problem, though he said he'd be leaving soon. Interesting. "I agree. But it's Shay's decision."

Luke stopped to look out the kitchen window. The sky was darkening early and in the distance, he heard loud rumblings. They badly needed rain, but tonight wasn't the night. Shay was out there somewhere, walking around and hurting.

Listening to the thunder, Liz frowned. "I wish she'd come back. I don't know where she goes when she disappears like this."

But he did, Luke thought, with sudden insight. Her favorite rock down by the stream. He turned to Liz. "I need to go find her, Liz."

She thought of the quiet supper she'd hoped they'd have, of disappointing Beth again when she learned that Luke wouldn't be eating with them. But Shay needed him more. "Yes, go."

"I'll see that she's safe, but I may take her to my cabin. I want to talk with her." Luke leaned to place a kiss on Liz's forehead, grateful for her understanding, then rushed out the back door.

She was sitting exactly where he'd thought she'd be, on the smooth, flat surface of the large rock on the edge of the stream. Tall pine trees surrounded the peaceful spot, the silence broken by the musical sound of the water splashing over stones. It was a bit gloomy, but not yet dark. The oppressive heat of the day had been replaced by a pervasive mugginess. Occasional spurts of thunder seemed to be coming closer, and periodic flashes of lightning streaked through a gray sky.

Luke stopped near a tree to observe her a minute. She wasn't crying. He almost wished she was. Soul-wrenching tears could cleanse away pain, he knew. Instead, she looked sad, so sad he felt his heart turn over at the sight. Her hair hung down her back in burnished copper waves.

She wore a light blue, long-sleeved blouse over jeans and she'd slipped off her shoes. Her knees were drawn up and she hugged them with her arms, her chin resting there as she gazed into the gurgling water.

He moved forward, deliberately stepping on a twig so she'd hear his approach, so he wouldn't frighten her.

At the sound, Shay turned and her eyes met his. She hadn't really been expecting Luke, yet oddly she wasn't surprised to see him. Once, when this ranch had been home to both of them, he'd been so attuned to her feelings that he'd often shown up at the exact moment she'd needed him.

And, though she hadn't admitted it even to herself until just now, she needed him again.

There was plenty of room, and he sat down alongside her on the rock. He badly wanted to touch her, to take her in his arms and tell her everything would be all right, but she looked so fragile, so vulnerable, that he was afraid she'd shatter if he reached out before she was ready. "Are you all right?"

Luke had always been so gentle, Shay thought. He'd been reticent with many, seemingly arrogant to a few, and tough when he had to be. But with her, he'd been achingly tender. Strength cloaked in gentleness—a difficult combination to resist.

She ignored his question because there was no good answer. "I understand you've been telling my daughter tall tales about me." When she'd talked with Beth earlier, she'd been pleased to discover that her daughter wasn't as upset over her father's visit as usual. Instead, she'd rambled on about Luke's visit, Luke's stories, Luke's promise. Like Shay, Beth was falling for Luke's gentleness, and it worried Shay. How would Beth cope with the loss when Luke moved on? No better than she would, most likely.

He would play it her way, Luke decided, and skirt the real issue for now. "A few. She's already heard some of them. I didn't know you'd been reminiscing about us with Beth."

She hadn't spoken of him to her daughter until he'd returned and now found it impossible not to since Beth brought Luke's name up constantly. But perhaps it wouldn't be wise to tell him that. "So far, I've only told her the good things. Maybe I should mention some of the stunts you pulled back then."

She was trying to drag her spirits up and he would help her. "Oh, yeah? What stunts? I was a model teenager."

Shay stretched out her legs. "Really? How about the time you and Gil put the field mouse in my bed, only Mom found it first."

"Circumstantial evidence. You don't *know* we put the mouse there. It could have wandered in."

"Sure, wandered in the house, climbed the stairs, opened my bedroom door and decided to take a nap in my bed." She almost smiled, remembering how the two boys had tried to look blameless while she'd been horrified at the sight. "And then there's the case of the traveling broccoli. Do you recall?"

Luke stroked his chin, hiding a smile. He'd always hated that particular vegetable, and Liz had insisted he taste a small serving at least. So he'd often as not managed to cause a commotion at the table to distract everyone—spilling his milk or whipping Shay's napkin from her lap onto the floor so she'd have to retrieve it—then slip his broccoli onto her plate and proceed to look innocent.

"I believe I was a pioneer in the study of broccoli. At an early age, I discovered that if a female child ate lots of it, she'd turn out to be exceedingly beautiful. But if a male ate it, he'd grow warts on the end of his nose. I was only helping you out by making sure you had lots of broccoli." He smiled at her. "And it worked. Look how beautiful you are."

Shay stared into his eyes, such a deep blue. She saw a hint of humor there and something else. Tenderness. She felt her chest tighten with emotion. "I can see why Beth is so taken with your stories." Unable to resist, she reached to touch his face with a trembling hand. "You're so very special."

Luke felt the first raindrops sprinkle down, but he ignored them. He took her hand and laced his fingers through hers as he slipped off the rock and drew her up with him. She'd been upset and shaken, her eyes looking empty when he'd found her. She needed to be reassured, to be consoled. She needed to be loved. "You are everything beautiful in this world, Shay. Everything fine and good and honest. I wish we could erase the last ten years and start over. I wish I could keep you from ever being hurt again."

She let out a shaky breath. "I don't think it's possible for one person to do that for another."

The rainfall was picking up. They were moving from damp to soaking wet in moments. Still, neither seemed to notice.

"I'd like to try," Luke said, his voice husky.

In the fading light, Shay searched his eyes, then made her decision. There were at least a hundred reasons she should walk away from him and only one reason she should stay. Because she loved him. "Make love to me, Luke. It seems I've wanted you to all my life."

Without another word, he picked her up, cradled her in his arms and set out through the woods toward his back door.

Chapter Eight

By the time Luke unlocked the door and got them inside the kitchen, they were both drenched. He set Shay down, flipped on the light, then relocked the door. From the adjacent laundry area, he grabbed two terry-cloth towels, handed her one and used the other to dry his hair. She hadn't said a word since they'd left the rock, and he wondered what she was thinking.

He'd dreamed of this happening for so many years, of having her alone in a quiet place, yet now that the time was at hand, he struggled with a case of nerves. He wanted so badly to make their time together good for her.

She stood by the counter and he saw that her hands, as she dabbed the moisture from her face, were trembling. He went over, took the towel from her and framed her lovely face with his hands. Tenderly he kissed her eyes closed. When she opened them again, he saw that they were huge and vulnerable, but some of the wariness had disappeared. "If you've changed your mind..."

Finally she smiled. "No, have you?"

By way of answer, he touched his mouth to hers with infinite care. He found her lips wet and cool and not in the least hesitant. She went up on tiptoe, her arms circling him. She tasted sweet, like expensive brandy, like that first taste of honey, like everything he'd ever wanted.

Unhurriedly they relearned the shape and texture of each other's faces with slow, lingering kisses, with long, searching touches. He kissed the corners of her waiting mouth, then she angled around and breathed warmly in his ear, feeling the deep shudder that went through him.

Lightning flashed outside the window. Luke reached up to pull down the blind, shutting out the world. He searched her face and decided she was waiting for him to take the lead. Almost lazily, he unbuttoned her blouse while her fumbling fingers freed him of his shirt. His hands paused at the front clasp of her bra. "I've waited so long to look at you."

Shay's shyness melted away under his intense gaze. She gave an imperceptible nod of permission and felt him unfasten the lacy garment and ease it open. His eyes admired, devoured. The heat rose in her, coloring her cheeks, staining her flesh. Her breathing grew ragged as she closed her eyes with a sigh.

Luke's hands, those wonderful hands, moved under her blouse, up her back, sliding over damp skin, warming her. He drew her closer, and she gasped at the shocked pleasure of her sensitive flesh rubbing against his chest. He buried his face in her hair, his hot breath sending shivers up and down her spine. She felt her knees weaken and her fingers closed around his arms for support.

"Let's find a better place," Luke said, leading her into his bedroom.

It was a small room compared to sleeping accommodations in the big house, but invitingly cozy and intimate. A grandfather clock ticked softly in a corner, and the bed was rough-hewn pine with four big posts. She watched Luke close the wooden shutters and turn on a low lamp. The scent of lemons and Cora's furniture polish lingered in the air.

Her nerves making her jumpy, Shay sat down on the edge of the bed and held the ends of her blouse together in front of her. She didn't look up when Luke came to stand in front of her, not until he took her hand and pulled her up to face him.

"Don't hide from me. Not ever from me. By the time this night is over, I want to have seen and touched and tasted every part of you." He saw her lower her gaze, but he wouldn't let her look away as he tilted up her chin. "Shay, I want to know everything there is to know about you. How you take your coffee, whether you like hot showers or warm, which side of the bed you prefer to sleep on. All the little things, as well as the big, everything I've missed out on the last ten years."

She looked embarrassed, apologetic. "I'm sorry. I'm not used to being so open about things."

"But we always have been open with each other."

"Yes, you and I. It...it wasn't always that way for me." But she didn't want to talk about her marriage or think about Max. She badly wanted things between Luke and her to be different, better. Swallowing her fears, she decided to set aside the past and go with her instincts. Her fingers only shook a little as they settled at the snap of his jeans. "All right, if I'm exposed, then you should be, too."

He smiled, knowing how much the effort at nonchalance cost her. She was all the more dear to him for her reluctance. "Go ahead. Take them off me."

She looked down at the swollen bulge beneath his zipper and her eyes grew wide. "Maybe you'd better do it, this time." She took a step back and sat down on the bed.

Luke laughed. "Coward." He sat down to remove his boots, wondering just what kind of a marriage she'd had that she was so hesitant. When he was down to just his briefs, he knelt on the bed and drew her up to face him.

He was so beautiful, Shay thought as she let her eyes roam his broad chest and his muscular thighs. "I like you like this," she told him.

"Turned on by a man's underwear, are you?"

"Not just *any* man." She watched the lamplight turn his blond hair gold. She couldn't resist reaching up and twining her fingers in the curls at the nape of his neck. To be free to touch him like this, to look her fill, seemed like a dream come true. The way his deep blue eyes caressed her made her forget everything.

Almost everything. Shay pulled back, frowning. "My mother doesn't know where I am. I left the house before the rain, and I know she'll worry."

"It's okay. I told her I was going after you. She'll figure it out." Gently he slipped her blouse from her, then tossed aside her bra.

Shay fought a shiver. "Are you sure? Beth..."

"Will be fine. Will you relax?" But he could still detect a residue of tension in her. Or was it merely nerves? "Close your eyes, Shay, and I will, too. Let's just touch each other." To demonstrate, he thrust his hands into her hair and massaged her scalp. Slowly her eyelids lowered.

On her knees, she leaned closer to him, their bodies aligning. The pleasure seeped through her like fine wine.

Her hands skimmed along his back, appreciating the corded muscles, the smooth skin. She could feel herself growing aroused inch by slow inch.

Now his hands moved lower down her back, lifting her and pressing her against his throbbing hardness. Open and hungry, her mouth sought his as her body quivered in reaction. Shay found herself squirming, trying to get closer to the heat.

"I want..." she murmured restlessly against his mouth.

"If you had only one wish, Shay, what would it be?" Luke asked, swaying with her, supporting her weight and his own.

Her hesitation vanished at the familiar question. She drew back, meeting his eyes. "You. I would wish for you. Only you."

"Whatever you want to do, do it. Anything goes."

"To touch you. I want to touch you."

Luke took hold of her hand and guided it down until her fingers cupped him.

"Oh, Luke," she whispered as her fingers closed around him for the first time. A hunger rose inside her so strong that she nearly toppled with the force of it. A hunger to know him completely, to love him absolutely, to feel that pulsating strength inside her. "Please, I need to know..."

"Too soon, sweetheart," Luke said, and lowered himself onto the mattress, taking her down with him. He shifted so her hand left him, knowing if she kept that up, he wouldn't be able to wait. Pulling off her jeans and panties, he tossed them aside. With his eyes only, he examined the elegant line of her hip, the sweet curve of her breasts, the shadowy secrets he wanted to explore more fully.

Outside, the storm had escalated and the wind whipped the slanting rain against the window. Thunder rumbled and groaned, lightning flashed in jagged streaks. But inside, two lovers neither saw nor heard any of it. They were lost in a storm of their own making.

With tiny, teasing kisses, he trailed his lips over every inch of her skin, lingering at her breasts, pausing to taste the sensitive skin inside her elbow, exploring the softness behind her knees. She was moving restively beneath his hands now, twisting and turning, unable to lie still. He heard her murmur his name, then thrilled to the soft sounds she made as she strained to keep up.

Shay had never experienced such an onslaught on her senses. With lips and teeth and tongue, he was driving her mindless, removing all her lifelong barriers. She could feel no shame, for he would have none of it. She could have no secrets, for he would ferret out each and every one. She could deny him nothing even as she struggled to believe he could make her so helpless so quickly.

Before she could catch her breath, he returned to kiss her deeply, drawing a response from her she'd thought herself incapable of at this point. His teeth nipped along her shoulder, his tongue swirled around her nipples, his hands left a trail of fire wherever they touched. Then his mouth slipped lower and in moments, he had her writhing in shocked surprise. Pleasure shot through her from so many points that she could only tremble in reaction. He would drive her up and up still further, then skitter away and leave her wanting, needing.

"Luke, I . . ."

"I know." He'd pushed himself as far as humanly possible. With some difficulty, he removed his briefs and hovered over her, swollen and aching. "Do I need protection?" he asked her, his good sense returning for that split second.

Shay closed her eyes as her hands reached for him. "No. Just hurry."

He let her guide him inside her, then heard her gasp as her body struggled to accommodate him. The tightness made him realize it must have been a long time for her. He slid forward, waiting for her to adjust.

But she needed too badly to pause too long. Her hips arched forward and her hands urged him closer. With her softness surrounding him, Luke began to move. Her hunger was as great as his, her need perhaps greater. But he wanted to savor, not to rush.

Deliberately slowing, he touched his mouth to hers, kissing her passionately, his tongue matching his body's thrusts. And he was lost, lost in a wonder he'd waited for half his life. She fit him like the proverbial glove, as if made for him and him alone. He'd loved her from the first day he'd met her, had dreamed of her nearly every night since. Never had he forgotten her. Never could he.

Shay felt as if she were reaching, reaching. She'd come further than ever before toward the shattering release she craved so desperately. Yet she was afraid she wouldn't make it again, wouldn't reach that pinnacle that Luke had managed to give her so effortlessly the night of her nineteenth birthday. Her breathing shallow, she strained with him, her hands curled tightly around his shoulders.

And then suddenly she was flying, hurtling through space, her face flushing, bathed in a feeling so intense it was almost frightening. As she hit the peak, she felt Luke finally let go and join her.

Long minutes later, her hands resting on his damp back, her heart still beating rapidly, she lay there pondering the most staggering sensations she'd ever experienced. And the man who'd shown them to her.

"Are you all right?" Luke asked after a while, wondering why she was so quiet. He'd shifted alongside her some time ago and settled her on his chest where she lay snuggled into him. He could tell she was awake, but she had yet to speak.

"All right? Pretty tame words for what I'm feeling." Shay lifted her head, brushed back her hair, then crossed her arms on his chest and leaned her chin on top of her hands. "What would you say if I told you that that's never happened to me before, except that one time with you?"

She couldn't have said anything that pleased him more. "I'd say that Maxwell Whitney's an even bigger fool than I thought he was." He stroked her hair, a teasing light in his eyes. "Want to try it again?"

She smiled even as she blushed. "Yes."

He laughed. "Give me a minute or two. But I could use a kiss." He put his hands on her forearms to draw her up, then saw her wince at this touch. Frowning, he loosened his fingers and examined her arms. Four dark bruises on one, three on the other. "What the hell is this?"

Shay studied the spots, then sat up. Silently she touched the blackened circles obviously made by strong fingers.

Luke's face darkened. "Max, today in the barn. Damn it, Shay, why didn't you tell me? That son of a..." No wonder she'd run off to be alone. He sat up, wishing he had a cigarette.

"I honestly didn't realize his grip had been that hard. But if I had, what would have been the point in telling you?"

He scooted back to face her. "The point is if I'd known he'd hurt you, I'd have smashed in his smug face."

She bunched the pillow against the headboard and leaned back, drawing up the sheet. "Lower yourself to his level?"

Something in the way she asked the question had him wondering if there had been more than just today's incident. "To his level? You mean this has happened before?"

She hesitated but a moment. "Only once."

Luke struggled with his rising temper. "He hit you?"

"I told you, once. He does a lot of yelling, a lot of threatening. But that once..."

"Why did he do it?"

She watched her fingers pleat a corner of the sheet. She hadn't thought to go into all this and probably wouldn't have had to if Max hadn't bruised her arms today, if Luke hadn't noticed. She'd never told a soul, but she knew Luke wouldn't let it alone until he found out. Maybe it was time.

"Beth was fourteen months old when I lost our second child. The doctor said the baby would have been a little girl. I had a rough time, developed an infection, and I just couldn't seem to bounce back."

"Liz told me you went into a depression."

She nodded, still not looking at him. "That was only part of it. They tried one antibiotic after another. By the time they hit on something that worked, the doctor said there'd been some damage. He told Max the chances of my having another child were slim to none. He'd wanted a son, a male heir, and so did his father. Carry on the bloodline and all that."

So that was why she'd said they didn't need protection. Had he been thinking straight, he would have realized that it was unlikely that she was on the pill. And that was probably why she'd gone into such a long depression, learning she couldn't have more children. But she still hadn't answered his question. "Go on."

"Max had been angry with me when Beth turned out to be a girl. The baby I lost was also female. He flew into a rage, telling me I was useless, that I'd only produced girls so far, and now there'd be no more. Then he...he hit me."

Luke hadn't realized he'd grasped her hand somewhere in the telling and was now clutching it in impotent rage. He eased his hold on her. "If I ever see him again..."

She shook her head. "Let it go. I have. That same afternoon, I packed all of our things, and Beth and I came back home."

"And you didn't tell anyone?"

"I didn't want it to continue. Dad would have gone over there with his gun, and Mom would have just felt worse knowing everything. Gil was gone, and so were you. What options did I have? I just wanted Max out of my life. I still do."

Yes, he'd been gone. Guilt washed over Luke. "I'm sorry I wasn't there for you."

She touched his face, so dear to her. "You couldn't have known."

Luke moved to lean against the headboard, drawing her back with him so he could hold her. "There are things you can do to make sure Max doesn't bother you or Beth ever again. You need to look into it, Shay." When she didn't answer, he knew he hadn't convinced her. "Why is it you're afraid to go after Max? If you told a judge that he'd hit you, that he had a violent nature..."

"It's not a matter of fear. I'd hoped to keep Beth from learning just how rotten her father is, for one thing. And there's a matter of money. Lawsuits are expensive. The divorce dragged on for two years because Max kept delaying things, and he'd do it again. He had a friend represent him, but my attorney cost plenty. I can't—I *won't*—ask my parents to pay for my problems. They have enough of their own to contend with. One day, if I sell a book and I have my own money, I can do something about Max."

Thoughtfully Luke wondered about offering her another way, of asking Shay to share his dream, of letting him take her and Beth away from Max's long reach. Until recently, he'd thought he'd prefer going it alone. What he hadn't considered until seeing Shay again was that being alone was different from being lonely. Over the past ten years, he'd gotten used to being without her. But now, having loved her, the thought of being without her filled him with loneliness. Yet what kind of husband would he make? What kind of father? And what if he failed?

So much at risk, but he had to try. "I want to help. You must know how I feel about you."

A sudden gust of wind slammed a sheet of rain against the window and Shay shivered. No, she didn't. She didn't know much about love and very little about sex. He wanted honesty and openness. She'd give him both and let the chips fall where they may. "I'm not good at this, Luke, fencing about issues. I haven't had many relationships, and I've only been with one other man. He was a great disappointment in every way. I don't know how to act, what to say."

"Just tell me what you feel."

"I've already told you that making love with you was everything I'd ever hoped it would be. But I don't know what men want, except probably that they like experienced women in bed."

Luke scowled. "Who told you that?"

You're a cold fish, a woman who doesn't know the first thing about satisfying a man. The words Max had flung at her often echoed in her memory, and she closed her eyes.

Luke read the message there as surely as if she'd spoken aloud. Max had made her feel inadequate. "Look at me, Shay." Slowly she raised her head. "I've wanted you forever, it seems, and tonight I found you to be passionate, exciting and wonderfully responsive. In bed and out, you are everything I've ever wanted in a woman."

She wanted so badly to believe him. But the past still held her in its fierce grip. "But you've lived all over. There must have been other women who..."

"Nobody else counts. No one ever has. It's always been you, only you. Don't you know how much I love you?"

The sheet slipped to her waist as she shifted to move into his arms. "Oh, Luke," she whispered. She'd waited so long to hear those words again, had wondered if she ever would. Yet she'd counted on him once before, only to be badly hurt when he'd left.

"I want you with me always." As soon as the words were out, he realized how true they were.

She spoke into his neck, not looking at him. She had to know. "You'd stay here, settle down?"

There it was again, as he'd known it would be, her desire to remain on her father's ranch. How could he compete with the Circle M? How could he ask her to settle for half a loaf?

He badly wanted to tell her about his Wyoming ranch, but this revival of their feelings for each other was so new, so tenuous. He couldn't take a chance just yet of asking her to give up all she had here to start over with him so far from everyone she loved, from everything familiar. When the love between them was stronger, when he was more sure of her.

He'd waited so long to answer that he'd felt her tense up, preparing for his refusal. "On the Circle M? No, I can't stay here. But we have other choices."

Other choices. Luke was good at what he did, she knew. He would have offers from other ranches, to manage, to oversee. But his restless nature would have him moving on often. Married to him, she would have no choice but to go along, dragging Beth with them. No, she couldn't do that to her daughter, no matter how much she cared for Luke. "Let's not either of us make promises we might not be able to live up to. Let's see how things go."

It wasn't all he'd wanted from her, but it would have to do for now. "All right, but answer one question for me. Do you still care for me the way you did ten years ago?"

Shay could feel his anxiety, the tautness in the arms that held her. She wasn't the only one who needed reassurance. "More. You're the *only* man I've ever cared for."

Luke released a deep groan and buried his face in her neck as the tension drained from him. His lips trailed along her throat, finally settling on her mouth in a deep, open-mouthed kiss that left them both out of breath. He reached to smooth back her hair, to caress her beautiful face. "I find I want more from you than I've ever wanted before from any woman, Shay. Good as it is having you here in my bed at last, that isn't all by far."

She would be equally honest with him. "And I want to give more to you. But we have some things we need to work out." Like his wanderlust and her need to put her child's welfare above her own desire to be with Luke.

"Then we'll work on getting rid of the obstacles, of overcoming our problems. We can do anything together, if there's enough love."

Because she wanted to believe that, she nodded, then pressed her mouth to his. For now, she had this, Luke here in her arms. Luke loving her and making love with her. It was more than she'd had before he'd returned, and if he would again choose to leave, at least she would have this much to remember.

The hot, earthy kiss stole her concentration, emptied her mind of disturbing thoughts, as she'd known it would. Half of her struggled against relinquishing control while the other more powerful half sought more of the mindless oblivion he offered her. Each time he touched her, each time those strong hands stroked her, her overwhelming need for him took over. This freedom to explore him was liberating, yet her love for him imprisoned her.

Shay needed to forget, to escape, if only temporarily, Luke decided. This he could do for her. He could teach her the beauty of physical love possible between a man and a woman perfectly in tune. She would trust her body to his care, and he would not abuse that trust as her ex-husband had. One day perhaps, she would trust him completely, with her mind and heart, as well.

His mouth fused to hers, he shifted her onto her back and let the raging passion take possession of them both. She needed to be cherished, and he would show her that he cherished her. He'd not had a chance to romance her—to gift her with flowers, to share a glass of wine with her, to lie with her in candlelight—but that, too, he would give her one day. For now, he would treasure her, revere her, make the harsh world go away for her.

His lips skimmed down her body, so patient, so reassuring. He was seducing her as if he didn't know the seduction had taken place years ago, charming her when she was already under his spell. He slid back up her, waited for her eyes to focus on his, then touched his tongue to her lips, tracing from corner to corner and back again. His tongue slipped inside her mouth then, the tip tangling with hers, then he leaned in to deepen the kiss, drawing a response from her that left her limp.

She wanted to give back to him, to match him pleasure for pleasure, yet her body felt heavy, drugged with sensations she'd only discovered tonight. She tasted his dark flavors on her tongue, inhaled the clean, masculine scent of him, and heard his breathing become ragged. Had she made his hand less than steady? Had she made his blood heat, his skin hum? Heady stuff, the thought that she could make this powerful man tremble.

Now he rolled to his side and pulled her close, worshiping her suddenly aching breasts with his mouth. Lower, she felt him pulse against her, hard and persistent, seeking her heat. The sensuous suckling caused a contraction deep inside her and she cried out in stunned pleasure.

Luke lifted his head. "Am I hurting you?"

"No," she murmured, "you never could. Not you." Her hands roamed his back restlessly as her body arched into him. "How do you know so much, all the right things to do?"

He smiled into the hazy passion in her eyes. "Because I love you, because I want to please you."

"You do please me." Again her mouth sought his, not having had enough of him. Never would she have enough of him.

"And because you make me want you every time I see you." He punctuated his words with a soft kiss on her brow, then on her stubborn chin. "Even when I don't see you. Sometimes when I'm out riding, something reminds me of you. When I first wake up, I think of you. No matter how I tried to forget you, you were always with me. And I want you so much."

She was floating from the impact of his words. No man had ever said things like that to her, no man had ever needed her so fiercely. "I want you just as much."

"Show me."

Made bold by his words, Shay brought his mouth back to hers as she insinuated her hand between them, touching him intimately. She felt rather than heard his gasp as she made her desire known to him.

The mists closed in on Luke, and he knew he'd run out of time. She moved beneath him as he tried to keep control of his pacing, but she was quickly taking over. Ruled by her own needs, her busy hands were arousing him to the breaking point.

He took over, entering her slowly. This time there was no need to wait for her to get used to him. She was as eager, as ready as he. Her lips at his ear whispered soft words of love, snapping his control.

In seconds, they were catapulting over the edge, clinging to each other, two hearts beating as one.

Chapter Nine

It seemed as if the dry ground had sucked up the previous night's rainfall like a thirsty sponge, Luke thought, as he stepped off his porch the next morning. There was scarcely a trace of the downpour to be seen except that the bed of purple and yellow pansies and red geraniums Liz had planted alongside her porch appeared less droopy. Automatically Luke's eyes drifted to Shay's bedroom window in the big house, and he noticed that her blind had been raised. He'd walked her back a mere two hours ago at five, hating to let her go but knowing it was best she not spend the entire night with him. She hadn't had much time to sleep in her own bed, but she'd apparently gotten up at her usual hour to keep questions to a minimum.

He wondered if she felt as good as he did this morning, despite the lack of sleep. He felt wonderful, eager to face the day. He'd lost count of how often they'd made love last night, and yet just thinking of Shay made him want her again. That kind of focused need for one woman had never happened to him before.

There was no sign of activity at the big house as he passed on his way to the barns, but inside he imagined that Cora had already served breakfast, Shay was likely in her father's study working on the books and Liz was undoubtedly sharing a private hour with Jacob in their bedroom.

Luke recalled knocking on their door one morning last week and being invited to enter by Jacob. The older man had been sitting in his big, comfortable chair by the window, and Liz had been shaving him. The picture they'd presented had put a lump in his throat—of shared intimacy, of marital affection, of loving tenderness. Moments to cherish, the likes of which he longed to experience with Shay one day.

Walking on, Luke waved at the bunkhouse cook having a smoke in the doorway. The man yelled out an invitation to join some stragglers for breakfast, but Luke declined. He'd already had an early breakfast. Very early.

About two in the morning, temporarily sated from lovemaking, he and Shay had both realized they hadn't eaten dinner. Suddenly starved, they'd gone into the kitchen, she wearing only his denim shirt and he in his jeans. He'd made scrambled eggs and fried slices of ham while she'd fixed toast and perked coffee. They'd talked and eaten and laughed.

Then, hearing a scratching at the back door, they'd let in the wet, muddy brown dog. Shay had insisted on bathing Sebastian in the laundry tub and drying him with a big, fluffy towel. They'd fed him then and settled him on a soft rug in the corner of the kitchen. Afterward, they'd gone back to Luke's big four-poster bed and made love again.

Luke sighed. No, he wasn't hungry, not for food. But just the thought of what it had felt like to have Shay in his arms at long last could make him hunger for a different kind of satisfaction.

She loved him. He was certain of it. Perhaps, like him, she always had. The fact that he'd introduced her to the sensual side of her nature had helped. He'd watched her change, seen her open to him like a delicate rose reaching toward the morning sun. But he wasn't fool enough to believe that just because they'd been compatible in bed, all their troubles were over.

He needed to find a few answers. About the rustlers, about who had taken his letters years ago, and who had recently left him that warning note. He needed time to do all that, and time to win Shay's trust.

When he'd arrived, he'd told Liz that he'd give her a month and then he'd have to leave, to get on with his life. But he'd come to realize that in order to accomplish all he wanted to, it might take longer. So this morning, he'd called Gray Fielding, his old friend and fellow cowboy who'd already gone on ahead to Luke's Wyoming ranch, and told him he'd be arriving later than he'd planned. Gray was in his early forties and he'd recently lost his wife to cancer. He and Luke had worked well together at Royce Ranch, and when Luke had asked him to sign on with him, Gray had welcomed the opportunity for a change of scene.

He was anxious to get started on his own place, Luke thought, as he rounded the bend and walked into the breeding barn, but he'd be patient. Working things out between him and Shay was important enough to warrant the delay.

"Hey, Hollis, how's it going?" Luke approached the old cowboy, who was bent over the freezer unit.

"Can't complain, Luke," Hollis said, straightening. "How about you?"

"I'm managing." He watched Hollis lift half a dozen small glass tubes from the aluminum cylinder. "Inseminating some cows today?"

"Yup. Gil said he wants to aim for six every day for a week. I think they're trying to make up for some of the pregnant cows that have been stolen." The older man pushed back his hat as he put the frozen semen straws into the refrigerator to thaw before the process could begin.

"Makes sense. Got to replenish the herd somehow." Luke glanced around the near-empty barn, knowing most of the men were out on the range by now except the regulars assigned to fertilization, to newborns or those who worked with the milking. "Do you know where I can find Charley Brice?" He'd never been able to corner the man since learning yesterday that he'd been in charge of the section where the last batch of twenty cows had disappeared. Of course, last night when he probably could have located Charley, Luke had had other things on his mind.

"He left early. Took the Jeep and went out on the range."

"Do you know where he was headed?"

Hollis scratched his head, then adjusted his hat. "West pasture, I think he said." He squinted up at Luke. "Why? Is something wrong?"

"Just want to talk to him, that's all. Have you seen Zeke yet this morning?"

"Can't say I have."

"Okay, thanks." Luke turned and headed back toward his house. He'd passed the parking area on the way over and seen that all the rough-terrain vehicles were out. He'd have to go get his pickup, which would do nicely since it had four-wheel drive, as well. He wondered if Charley had heard from Zeke that Luke was looking for him. And he wondered just what Zeke had told him about their less-than-cordial conversation out by the fence yesterday.

Deep in thought, Luke didn't notice someone walking toward him from the big house until he was almost at his own cabin. Turning, he was surprised to see Gil approaching, looking hesitant and uncertain.

"Luke, you got a minute?" Gil asked, stopping six feet away.

"Sure. What's on your mind?"

"I wanted to thank you."

That took him by surprise. "For what?" Luke asked.

Gil stepped closer, removed his hat and brushed minute specks of lint from it, obviously having trouble finding the right words. "Twice now since you've been back, you've stuck up for me. In Dad's bedroom about the Whitney stallion... and Mom told me it was your idea that I be the one to go over and discuss the dynamite with Morgan Whitney. It was damn decent of you, and I wanted you to know I appreciate what you said."

Taken aback, knowing that this sort of thing didn't come easily to Gil, Luke tried to keep his expression bland. "I did what I thought was right, Gil."

"I know that." He gave a sorry little shrug. "Probably won't change Dad's opinion of me—we just can't seem to get along—but it was good of you to try. Especially... especially after what I did to you."

Luke angled a step or two so the sun wasn't in his eyes. "Just what is it you did to me?"

Gil sucked in a deep breath, as if for courage. "That evening before you left, the night of Shay's birthday, I told you I overheard Dad making a deal with Max Whitney to marry Shay and... and well, I said a lot of other rotten things to you."

Luke waited silently for him to continue.

Gil cleared his throat noisily. "That wasn't what I overheard at all. I heard Mom and Dad planning to redo their will, leaving one-fourth of everything to you. I'd seen you with Shay, and I knew you wanted to marry her. That would have meant, with her share and your own, the two of you would control half of the Circle M. I felt betrayed." He looked over Luke's left shoulder, his dark eyes anguished.

"I know it was wrong of me," he went on, "but I was jealous. After all, I'm his son and...oh, hell!" He made a dismissing sound. "I didn't think you'd understand."

Luke laid a hand on his shoulder. "You're wrong. I do understand. Rhea, Shay and you are blood heirs. I have no right to one fourth of the Circle M, and I'd turn it down if it were offered. If you'd have just come to me, I'd have told you that."

Gil's brown eyes studied him long and hard. "You really mean that, don't you?"

"Yes."

For a moment, Gil looked relieved, then the worried look returned. "I'm going to have to tell Shay, too. I don't know if the two of you can ever forgive me."

Without hesitation, Luke stuck out his hand. "She can, and so can I."

Struggling with an emotional reaction, Gil shook hands warmly. "I hope we can be friends again."

"Yeah, me, too." Luke was curious about something. "What made you decide to tell me? Just because I stuck up for you a couple of times with Jacob?"

"That...and because I see how crazy you and Shay are about each other. I messed that up once. I really want to make it up to you both."

In light of Gil's changed attitude, he'd ask one more time. "And you're sure you didn't take those envelopes off the vestibule table?"

"No. Like I told you, I never saw them, honest."

"Okay, I believe you."

"I'd like to help you find whoever took those letters and the person who left the warning note in your cabin. To kind of make up for things."

He sounded sincere. Luke would take him at his word and see what developed, he decided. "I appreciate that."

Gil wiped his sweaty hands on his pant legs. "There's something else. I thought that maybe if I really worked hard to solve this rustling matter, that Dad would...well, you know. Be a little more open-minded."

"Have you come across something?"

"I think so. I spent two long days riding fence, and I was out again at five this morning. I tell you, I stopped to examine every post, every gate, all of it. And there's something mighty odd in the northwest section. There's a post that's split in half and held together with new wire, but not anchored in the ground. If someone were to snip those wires, the two halves of that post would swing free, opening a whole section of fence. That someone could lead a whole mess of cows through there in no time, then quickly wind more new wire around that post and prop it back in place."

"Rigged sort of like a gate made to look like a solid post?"

Gil nodded. "That's right. And it's about a hundred yards from that old dirt road that eventually leads to Highway 310."

"And winds down into Wyoming."

"That's it. I didn't take the time to check that road, but after last night's rain, I'd be willing to bet we'd find trailer rig tracks and maybe tire marks from the truck that hauled them away. Had to be at least a three-quarter ton.''

"I'll be damned. Did you tell anyone else?"

"No, I wanted to see if maybe you'd work with me on this. Zeke's a good man, but he's got a loose tongue, and I figure the fewer who know about this, the better."

Luke remembered that first Jeep ride he'd taken with Zeke, the way the man had talked about everyone, prodding Luke to do the same. Gil was right. Zeke was a curious gossip at best, a rumormonger at worst. "Let's take my truck out there so we can check out that road."

"Right." Walking over to Luke's truck, Gil felt better than he had in a long while. Maybe, after all this time, he'd have back the man he could regard as a brother.

Climbing behind the wheel, Luke glanced toward the manager's cabin. Zeke's voice, loud and argumentative, could be heard coming from inside. He frowned at Gil. "Those two seem to fight a lot."

Gil shrugged, having become accustomed to his sister's yelling matches with her husband. "I warned Rhea not to marry Zeke—we all did—but she seemed to think if she didn't grab him, she'd never get another chance."

Luke started the truck, shifted into gear and took off. "Sure doesn't seem like the great love match of the century."

Stretching out, Gil crossed one booted foot over the other. "I thought for a while there that all the McKenzies had really rotten luck when it comes to choosing a mate. Shay with Max, Rhea with Zeke, and I didn't do so hot, either."

Luke had been wondering why Gil didn't have someone special in his life. "Did you get involved with someone while you were gone?"

"Yeah, in Billings. Her name was Megan, and we got along pretty good. Might even have married if it hadn't been for one thing. She wanted us to live in town. I tried—got a good job, nice clothes, an apartment, shiny new car. Problem is that ranching gets in your blood, you know?"

Luke took the truck down the embankment and eased closer to the fence line. "It sure does. So you left her and came back."

"I asked Megan to marry me and come live on the Circle M. But she wouldn't even come out and take a look around." He shook his head. "Women. Now, Rhea, she'd live in town in a minute, but Zeke's a cowman through and through. Maybe that's why they fight so much. Maybe she wants to leave, and he doesn't." He sent Luke a lazy smile. "Or maybe they just fight 'cause it's a lot of fun making up. I notice Shay's more friendly than when you first got here. You two make up?"

"You could say that."

"You going to ask her to go off with you?"

"Do you think she'd consider leaving the Circle M?"

"Don't know. She left once and sure was unhappy. But maybe that was on account of who she left with. And now, she's got Beth to worry about." Staring straight ahead, Gil frowned. "Maybe I can grease the way for you. When I tell Shay all I've told you about the night you left, she'll come around."

Guiding the truck through a cluster of trees that bordered the fence, Luke wished he felt as sure as Gil sounded.

"I'd say those tracks were made by at least a twenty-four-foot gooseneck trailer rig, wouldn't you?" Gil asked as he stooped down to examine the muddy marks in the road.

"I think you're right." Luke walked a ways along the infrequently used path. They'd left the truck at the fence line, and Gil had pointed out the split post. This whole section was dotted with trees and shrubs except for a zigzagging path made by trucks driven by the men checking the fence. A man would have to look closely to see something amiss here, but the one post was exactly as Gil had described it, split in two and not anchored in the ground. In contrast with the older rusty wire, this post was twined with shiny new stuff.

They both stepped carefully between the barbed wiring and followed the obvious trail of hoof prints. If it hadn't been for last night's rain, the evidence wouldn't be as clear. There surely had been some cows marched along this path, and very recently. "I think we need to get another head count quick."

Gil shoved back his hat disgustedly. "I can't believe that someone was out here last night in that rain stealing our cows."

Luke swung around and walked back. "What better night than a rainy one when the few men on pasture patrol would be under cover and not many others would be out." Returning to the truck, he grew thoughtful.

"What do you think we should do?"

"Keep this between us for now, but get that head count. If it comes up short—which I think it will—then we're on the right track. Let's not bring Zeke in on this yet, either, not because of anything other than the man talks too much."

"Agreed." Gil climbed up into the truck's cab.

"Something else has occurred to me. If this rustler is not selling off the cows for butchering, but instead stocking his own ranch somewhere, it seems likely that one of these nights, he's going after one of our bulls."

"I've thought of that, too. If he's stealing pregnant cows, he's not apt to be selling them for slaughter, but to build his own herd. We'd better post a guard on Bullseye and Demon. They're the only two we use regularly. There are a few others we're grooming, but they're too young yet."

"To be safe, let's confine all the bulls in the barns overnight and set up a watch." Luke started the engine. "You know, I've passed by here several times and missed this. Good job, Gil."

The younger man tried not to look pleased but missed by a mile. "Probably we should talk to Dad if there are more missing, so he knows what we're up to. He gets bent out of shape if he's left out."

Luke nodded, moving the truck down the hilly terrain. "I've thought from the beginning that this has to be an inside job, so we'll have to be careful. Together, we can determine who we can trust—men like Hollis and Ray and Jim. You probably know some others—good men who've been with the Circle M a long time. We'll set a trap and see if we can snare us a rustler or two."

Gil slid back on his spine. "Yeah, that'd sure make Dad feel better." The truck rumbled down the incline, bouncing both of them enough to touch their heads to the ceiling. "Hey, man, slow down. Why are we in such a hurry?"

But Luke had touched the brakes, and they'd failed to respond. Sitting up straighter, he steered the truck through the trees and pumped the brake pedal. Nothing. "I think we've got a problem," Luke told him.

"What the hell!" Gil held on as the truck, having picked up momentum, was racing wildly. "Hey!" he yelled out his open window, hoping to catch the attention of a nearby cowboy on horseback. "Runaway truck over here!"

Luke gripped the wheel, his lips a thin line. He always kept his vehicles in top condition. This giving out of the brakes was no accident, of that he was sure. Now he was having difficulty steering. He spotted a clearing through the trees and headed for it.

But as he turned the wheel to avoid hitting a tree stump, the truck swayed and bounced. Suddenly Luke lost control and they shot forward. He saw the tree looming ahead and braced himself. "Hold tight, we're going to hit," he yelled to Gil.

And they did, the sound of crunching metal ringing loud in the hot, still air.

The tree hadn't been too thick, for which Gil had reason to be grateful as he brought down the arms he'd raised to protect his face. The windshield hadn't shattered, but the front end was pretty messed up, he saw as the dust settled. Amazingly, he was in one piece and only mildly bruised.

He turned to look at Luke. "You all right?"

Luke's face was pale as he struggled with the jolt of pain that shot through him as he tried to straighten. "My knee," he said slowly. "Damn, not my knee."

"I should have gotten out here earlier," Liz said as she brushed a lock of hair from her forehead. Kneeling by her flower beds, she yanked at a particularly stubborn weed until it finally gave way and she threw it onto the growing pile. "With last night's rain, the soil was soft this morning, but the sun's already dried things up."

"We could sprinkle them if you like," Shay suggested as she hammered a stick in the ground next to a droopy rosebush.

"Oh, they're coming. They're just reluctant."

Shay reached for the roll of string. "I didn't get a chance to visit with Dad yet today. How's he feeling?"

"Good. He plans to ask Dr. Emmett if he can come downstairs more frequently and even if he can start taking drives."

"I'm sure he's anxious to check out the ranch for himself. He's never been one to enjoy taking someone else's word for things." Finished attaching the rosebush to the stick, Shay sat back on her haunches, yawning. She'd give a lot to be able to curl up and take a long nap, but that would really shock her mother. "Want me to stake those geraniums, as well? A couple are so large they're nearly bent double."

"Mmm, fine." Liz let her eyes slide over her daughter's features before returning her attention to her weeding. "You seem a little tired today. Late night?"

She might have guessed that her shrewd mother would put two and two together. Liz had known Luke had gone after her and had seen to Beth for the evening. A restless sleeper, Liz often wandered the house at night, unable to sleep. Shay glanced over, met her mother's eyes and felt the heat rise. "You saw me come home." It wasn't a question.

"You're a grown woman, Shay. I'm not criticizing or condemning."

She faltered, reaching for the right words. "I was upset. Luke and I talked. He took me to his house out of the rain. We made something to eat and . . ." Why did she feel this compulsion to reveal something so personal?

"You owe me no explanations. I know you love him. You always have." Liz sighed and removed her gardening gloves. "Perhaps if I hadn't interfered years ago, you two would have been together much sooner, and you wouldn't have had to go through that unhappy marriage to Max."

Shay sat down in the grass. "How did you interfere?"

They should have had this conversation a long time ago, Liz thought. But until Luke returned, there'd seemed no point in dredging up the hurtful past. Yet now, she had to tell Shay. "Shortly before Luke left, he came to me and told me he wanted to marry you. He was worried about how your father would feel about his intentions. Luke's always felt that he had to apologize for his troubled background, that he wasn't quite good enough."

"I wish he'd get over that. We can't be held accountable for how our parents were or weren't."

"I agree, but Luke has a lot of pride. At any rate, I told him I'd talk to Jacob and smooth the way, if he'd not rush things. Your father badly wanted you to finish college since Gil had already quit and Rhea wasn't interested in going."

"And what did Luke say?"

"That he'd try to wait. But then, he must have thought things over and decided he wanted to make some quick money so he'd have more to offer you."

Shay brushed back a strand of hair from her face. "I can't imagine why he thought money was the answer. Max had money. I would have climbed on a horse and ridden off with Luke if he hadn't had a dime to his name."

"Ah, yes, but you see, he was trying to be practical. And so was I." She reached to touch her daughter's face. "We both should have realized that love is rarely practical. Do you think that this time, things will work out for the two of you?"

Shay considered the question a moment. "The three of us, Mom. I'm not sure how he feels about Beth. And there are other problems. As much as I want to be with him, I can't—I *won't*—wander all over, moving from ranch to ranch, as Luke seems to like to do."

"You could live here," Liz suggested, which was her fondest hope.

"But I don't think Luke would be happy staying in any one place for long." She shook her head, as if she were weary of struggling with the problem. "We have a lot to work out."

"I know you'll try because I—"

"Mom! Grandma! Come quick." Beth was running toward them from the area of the barns, her young voice shrill in her anxiety. "Luke's been hurt."

Shay's heart skipped a beat, then began racing as she rose quickly to her feet and hurried to meet her daughter. "What happened?"

"Uncle Gil and Luke had an accident with a truck. Some of the guys brought them in on horseback." Beth was nearly out of breath. "Uncle Gil's all right, but they're putting Luke into the station wagon to take him to the hospital."

Shay was running now, racing toward the back where she saw men gathered in a cluster. She was scarcely aware that Beth and her mother were close on her heels. Her thoughts were totally focused on Luke. Dear God, he had to be all right. She couldn't lose him now when she'd just found him again.

Accidents on a ranch were common, and most weren't fatal. She would count on that. At last, she reached the station wagon and caught her breath as she saw Gil and Jim carefully maneuvering Luke into the back seat. "What happened?" she demanded of her brother.

"Brakes gave out," Gil told her. "We hit a tree."

Luke was grim faced and pale as he looked at Shay. "I'm all right. It's just my knee."

"I'm driving him to the hospital," Gil said. "The injury's probably minor, but he needs to have that knee X-rayed."

She saw that it was his bad knee. "I'm going with you." Shay scooted onto the backseat, taking Luke's head in her lap.

Luke grimaced. "Shay, I've had worse. It isn't necessary for you to come."

"It is, for me." She turned to Liz, who was standing by the open door. "Mom, keep an eye on Beth for me, please."

"Of course." Liz touched Luke's shoulder affectionately.

Looking into Beth's worried little face, Luke managed a smile. "I'll be back soon. Sebastian's on my back porch. Take care of him for me, but be careful, okay?"

Beth brightened and nodded.

Shay saw that Gil was already behind the wheel. "Let's go, all right?" The doors were slammed shut and they moved toward the arches. Finally she looked down into Luke's eyes as he lay in her lap. Her face was sober, frightened. "How is it that those brakes gave out?"

Luke knew she was bright enough to have figured it out after reading the warning note left in his kitchen. "Someone tampered with them."

It was early evening before they returned and settled Luke in the downstairs back bedroom of the big house, at Liz's insistence. Setting aside his crutches, Luke sat down on the big bed, then eased his legs up. His damaged knee was wrapped in a knee brace, and the pills he'd been given took the edge off the sharp pain.

Thank goodness the X rays had revealed that there were no breaks or cracks, Luke thought, just a severe bruising.

Still the doctor had warned him to stay off that leg for several days and had put him on anti-inflammatory medication to reduce the swelling. He watched Liz put the ice pack in place and smiled. "Looks like you've got two of us to fuss over now."

Liz ignored his teasing. "Jacob has been asking about you, and Cora's made your favorite chili for dinner. I'll bring you some whenever you like." She looked at Shay. "Meantime, I leave you in good hands."

Grateful for her mother's perception, Shay waited until Liz had closed the door behind her before sitting down on the bed alongside Luke. They hadn't been alone all day. "Are you hurting? Do you need another pain pill?"

He shook his head. "They make me light-headed. I don't want any more." He'd been through worse, bone surgery twice, and knew the pain could be quite severe. But the fuzzy way the pills made him feel was harder to handle.

Her eyes warm and concerned, Shay brushed a lock of hair from his forehead. "You gave me quite a scare for a moment there." Which was a vast understatement. For desperate minutes, her fear had been huge, devastating. The fear that he would be taken from her. Ever since that realization, she'd been struggling to adjust to feelings that intense, that overwhelming.

How could she let him go when she cared this much?

Luke watched the play of emotions move across her face. He was male enough to be somewhat pleased she was a little worried about him, even though he knew there was no need. "Shay, no one dies from a bump on the knee."

How like him to trivialize his injury. It wasn't life threatening, of course, but she knew it was hardly a mere bump. But there was more. "Luke, it isn't your injury that concerns me. It's the way you got it. First, the menacing note left in your cabin. Now, your truck's brakes have been tampered with. It's screamingly obvious that someone wants you gone, or perhaps worse. Perhaps..." She couldn't complete the thought.

He took her hand, laced his fingers through hers. Naturally he'd come to the same conclusion. On the drive to the hospital, they'd avoided the subject, talking instead of the post and prints in the mud that he and Gil had discovered before the accident, about the trap they planned to set to catch the rustlers. On the way back, medicated, he'd dozed. But the mists were clearing and he knew he had to face a burning question.

Was someone trying to kill him?

"Do you think it's the same person who's involved in the rustling?" Shay asked.

"Not likely. Some two hundred cows were missing before I ever arrived on the scene. At first, I thought it was Gil who wanted me gone." He told her then of the conversation he and Gil had had before they'd driven out to the northwest pasture, of her brother's confession.

Shay shook her head. "I can't believe this. Today, my mother tells me she tried to interfere with us by telling you to back off until I'd completed college to please my father. And now I learn that Gil told you an outrageous lie about my father plotting to marry me off to Max when, in fact, my own brother was worried he'd lose control of the Circle M. What a family! Why couldn't they have left us alone?"

Luke squeezed her hand. "Remember how you told me to let it go when I got so hot about Max? I think you should let this go. Your mother meant well, and she's trying to make up for her mistake. And Gil, well, I might have felt the same, in his shoes."

Shay frowned at him. "You would not have. I'd be willing to bet you wouldn't have taken your share of this ranch if Dad had offered it to you."

Luke raised a surprised eyebrow. "I didn't think you knew me that well. Look, Shay, what's done is done. We go on from here."

"Do you believe Gil, that he's really sorry?"

Did he? A good question. Luke was certain he wanted to, but he was a man who weighed things as a rule, who made up his mind slowly. "Time will tell, but I lean toward believing him. He sure as hell didn't mess with those brakes, then climb in the truck and take a chance at getting injured himself."

He had a point there. "Luke, we need to report this, to get the sheriff in on it. A warning note is one thing, but causing an accident . . ."

"Not yet, Shay." He didn't want to go into his reasons, that the guilty party might still be someone related to her. "We need to ask around, to see if anyone saw someone hanging around my truck."

"But we're not detectives. What if whoever it is grows impatient and tries something else?" Finally she'd blurted out her greatest fear.

Though he moved slowly, his arms feeling weighted, he pulled her up closer. "Maybe you'd better stay with me, not let me out of your sight."

Despite her concern, Shay smiled. "That was going to be my next suggestion." Her cool hands opened his shirt, then moved inside to tangle in the crisp hairs of his chest.

"That probably means you'll have to stay by my side, to sleep with me. What will your mother say?"

Her mouth was a breath away from his. "My mother will understand because she knows that I love you."

His fingers that had been threading through her thick hair stopped in mid-motion. "Say that again."

She brushed her lips lazily along his. "I love you. I can't remember a time when I didn't."

"It was worth getting my knee bashed to hear you tell me." Then he closed his eyes so she couldn't see how deeply her words had affected him. Three little words, yet Luke had so seldom heard them. Not from the mother who'd died too soon, not from the father who'd saved his feelings for the bottle. Only from Liz, a couple of times.

But it was Shay he needed to hear it from, Shay he wanted with him, Shay he loved. Touching his mouth to hers, Luke kissed her.

There was an edge of desperation to the kiss, Shay thought, due to the emotional afternoon, she was certain. Things had shifted again between them, at least for her. She wanted a lifetime with this man, she knew. How were they going to get past all their obstacles?

She took over, needing the oblivion of feelings and not disturbing thoughts. Mindful of his injury, still she deepened the kiss, slipping her tongue inside his mouth, teasing, coaxing, exciting them both. Dormant desire awakened, sprang to life and had the sound of her own racing blood roaring in her ears.

And then the door burst open.

Startled, they pulled apart, looking up. Standing there, out of breath as if she'd run all the way, Rhea rushed over. "Luke, are you all right? Are you *really* all right?"

Chapter Ten

"I'm fine, Rhea," Luke said.

Shifting to sit at the foot of the bed, Shay studied her sister's agitated face. She'd never seen Rhea in such a state.

Winding a lock of hair nervously around her finger, Rhea dropped into the chair by the nightstand. "I've been out riding most of the day. I had some things to think over and . . . and when I got back just now, I heard about your accident. I'm so sorry."

Luke bent his good knee. "Yeah, so am I."

"Are you in pain? Can I get you something?" When Luke shook his head, she swung her eyes to Shay. "Mom said he's just badly bruised. No permanent damage, right?"

Puzzled at her overreaction, Shay nodded. "Right. Rhea, is everything okay? You look upset."

"Upset. Of course I'm upset." She rose to her feet and restlessly paced to the window, pulling back the curtains to peer out. "A truck out of control. You could have been badly hurt, even killed. And Gil, too," she added belatedly.

Her voice sounded odd, Luke thought, and wondered what was going on in Rhea's life. There certainly was more here than met the eye. He glanced at Shay and saw that she was as baffled as he.

Abruptly Rhea let the curtain drop back and swung around. "I have to go." She sent a jittery smile Luke's way. "I'm glad you're all right. I'll see you both later." She hurried out the door, leaving them alone.

"What do you make of all that?" Luke asked, tugging Shay back closer.

She was thoughtful, her face serious. "I don't know, unless Rhea's finally pregnant. I used to have these off-the-wall emotional outbursts both times I was pregnant. Afterward, I'd be so embarrassed."

"I hope for Rhea's sake that's what it is, though I'm not sure how good an idea it is to bring a baby into a shaky marriage." He'd been a baby such as that, and he had the scars to prove it.

Shay's eyes had turned sad. "It seems that the people who want children so desperately are the ones who wind up unable to have them."

Luke wondered if she was thinking of Rhea or herself. He let his eyes drift to her flat stomach and wondered how it would feel to know she carried his child. Could he manage fathering Beth, much less another? A moot question, since Shay couldn't have any more. He lifted his eyes and saw that she was watching him.

"You were thinking about a baby, one we could have together." Her voice was scarcely a whisper.

It bothered him, that he'd lost his poker face with this woman. Looking at her, he realized how badly she wanted another child. "Yes, for a minute."

"Do you believe in miracles? That's what the doctor said it would take." She swallowed hard as her eyes filled with tears.

Luke pulled her down so that she was half reclining on his chest. "You're here, aren't you? Here in my arms where I never thought you'd be. Yes, I believe in miracles." He saw how deeply his words affected her and felt himself respond to her need. Perhaps he couldn't give her a child, but he could give her his love. "Go lock the door."

A slow smile spread across Shay's face, but she shook her head. "There are too many people wandering around the house just yet."

As she finished speaking, they heard a knock on the door. "Luke, it's Beth. Can I come in?"

"See what I mean?" Shay asked, rising.

He kept hold of her hand. "All right, but will you come back later?"

Shay leaned down. "Wild horses wouldn't keep me away." She gave him a brief kiss, then went to open the door for Beth.

Gleefully Beth took hold of her red king and jumped over the last of Luke's black men. She shot him a triumphant look. "I won again. Are you sure you used to play checkers a lot?"

A hard kid to fool. Lying on his good side in the bed, Luke smiled at her and touched her braid, delighted with her as always. "Yeah, I did." Raised in any number of bunkhouses across the country, he'd often played checkers with the older cowboys while his father had worked the ranch. "But it was a long time ago, and you're simply too good for me."

Beth glanced toward the open bedroom door. "Grandma said I shouldn't tire you out. But maybe one more game?"

"How about tomorrow?" He helped her gather the checkers and return the board to its box. "I asked your mom to help you feed Sebastian."

"I can do it alone."

The dog had tamed considerably, but when it came to feeding time, Luke was wary of allowing Beth to approach the animal alone. "You can give him fresh water and play with him on my porch. But I want someone with you when he eats."

Looking chagrined, she nodded. "Okay." Suddenly she threw herself at him in a big bear hug. "I'm so glad you're all right, Luke."

Surprised and enormously pleased, Luke kissed her silken hair. "Thanks, sweetheart."

"She is a little sweetheart, isn't she?" Jacob asked from the doorway. He raised the cane he'd brought Luke. "Thought you might be able to use this, after you're off your crutches. Liz thinks I should lean on it, but she's not going to get her way on that one."

Beth hopped up and pulled the desk chair nearer the bed. "Here you go, Grandpa."

"Thanks, darlin'." Jacob sat down, his movements still a bit stiff. "Would you do me a favor and find your Uncle Gil for me? I think he's in the kitchen. Ask him to come here, please." He watched her leave. "She's getting mighty fond of you, Luke."

"The feeling's mutual." Unused to being in bed, Luke shoved back until he was resting against the headboard, hating even a short confinement. "How'd you stand it, all those weeks in bed? One afternoon, and I'm about nuts."

Jacob nodded. "I know how you feel. Only thing that kept me from getting up sooner was knowing that if I didn't listen this time, they'd be nailing the lid down on me."

A sobering thought. "Yeah, well, this is only a knee."

"A man who runs a ranch has a hell of a time getting around if his knees don't work. You listen to Liz and to Shay and mend that joint before you go climbing back on that stallion."

"It's not the stallion that gave him trouble. It was the truck." Gil walked in. "Glad to see you looking better, Luke."

"Close the door, Gil," Jacob said. "I mean to have a talk with you two."

Gil sat down at the foot of the bed. He felt no apprehension at his father's request this time. He knew he'd done the right thing today and that Jacob just might even admit it, if only to himself.

Jacob looked at both his son and the man who'd been like a son. "All right, we're all alone in here. I want to know what the hell happened today, and don't leave anything out."

So Gil told him, with Luke jumping in with an occasional comment. "Then, after we got back from the hospital, Zeke and I went out and hauled Luke's truck back and went over it thoroughly. I'm not a master mechanic, but I sure as hell had no trouble finding the problem. There's a hole in the brake line and another in the line to the steering column."

"Smart bastard," Jacob commented. "Starts a slow leak and the driver doesn't realize he's in trouble till he's on his way."

"The truck was steering hard on the way out," Luke added, "but on rough ground, I didn't think too much of it."

Jacob again looked at both men. "You were lucky to escape without serious injury, both of you." His expression told them he was grateful for that, even though he was unused to verbalizing his feelings.

"I think it's me this guy's after," Luke said, then told him about the note that had been left in his kitchen.

Jacob's fists curled in a rush of anger. Deliberately he made himself relax, as they'd taught him in the hospital. Curbing his temper was vital to regaining his health. "Who the hell would want to harm you and why?" He looked at Gil. "You have any ideas?"

"Could be the rustler, I suppose. He's learned that Mom asked Luke to come back to help ferret him out and that Luke's spending a lot of time working on that. First, the guy threatens Luke in writing, then he tries to get him hurt and out of commission."

Jacob shook his head. "He sure doesn't know Luke very well if he thinks he scares easily."

"At least we think we know how he's getting the cows out." Luke nodded toward Gil. "Tell him what you discovered." He could have just as easily described the split post, but it had been Gil's find and Gil who needed to be elevated in Jacob's estimation.

Gil watched his father's face as he told him about the rewired post, the trailer-rig tire tracks and the cow prints in the mud. Slowly Jacob's expression changed, a solid look of respect replacing his skeptical frown. Hard as this rustling had been on their profit picture, perhaps some good would come of it if he and his father reevaluated their relationship.

"We also think that he's not finished with his plan," Gil went on, "whatever that is. He's trying to buy time and divert our attention with this accident. Luke and I believe he might be stocking his own ranch somewhere and that his final goal is to grab one of our bulls as his last haul before he disappears for good."

The older man thought that over. "Then you've checked with the slaughterhouses already?"

Gil nodded. "We called the men you suggested. No suspicious sales there and no piecemeal sell-offs we can detect."

"We don't feel he's selling off the stolen herd," Luke interjected. "Too many pregnant cows in the missing number."

Jacob leaned forward. "So, have you come up with a plan to catch him?"

Luke and Gil exchanged a look, and Gil got the nod. "We're stepping up the watch on the northwest pasture where the swing post is. We're housing all the bulls at night *and* posting a guard as well."

"You're going to need some help on this," Jacob interrupted. "Luke shouldn't be up on the leg for several days and, Gil, you certainly can't be everywhere at once."

Gil acknowledged that. "We've come up with a list of men we feel reasonably certain wouldn't be involved. Old-timers we can trust. Those are the only ones we're going to share this information with for now."

"Besides Zeke, who have you got?" Jacob asked.

Luke readjusted the ice bag on his knee before answering. "We decided not to include Zeke on the rustling matter, Jacob."

He looked shocked. "You certainly don't think my own son-in-law would be stealing from me, do you? Damn, after the way we've treated that boy like a member of the family. Why, I..."

Gil hurried to explain. "No, Dad, we don't suspect Zeke. It's just that Zeke's buddies with most of the guys who work for us. He's awfully friendly and..."

"And far too talkative," Luke took over. "A loose tongue right now would tip our hand."

"I didn't want him with me when I examined Luke's truck, but he was hovering around when we got back, asking what he could do to help. I warned him not to discuss our findings just yet." Gil ran a hand through his short hair. "He means well, but..."

"I see what you mean," Jacob conceded. "Well, it sounds like you've done all you can for now. However, about this other thing, the brake tampering and the note. Maybe we should call the sheriff in on it." He hated doing that, hated to ask for help on his ranch and hated letting outsiders in on his problems. "They have handwriting analysts these days who can work wonders, I hear."

Gil shook his head. "It's an ordinary piece of white paper, printed block letters made by a common blue ballpoint pen. Like looking for a needle in a haystack. As to the truck, even harder to pinpoint. Luke's kept it parked next to the guest cabin for weeks now where any one of fifty guys would have had access."

"When'd you last drive your truck, Luke?" Jacob wanted to know.

"At least a week ago. I've been using the Jeep. Matter of fact, I was going to grab the Jeep this morning, but Hollis told me Charley Brice had taken it out early."

Gil frowned thoughtfully. "You know, speaking of Charley, he bothers me. In checking back on some of the men's references, the last place Charley put down said they'd never heard of him."

Jacob leaned back. "Hell, that probably applies to half the men we got here. You know how transient some of these cowboys are. They have a falling out with a trail boss or the owner and they lie as to where they last worked so you won't think they're a troublemaker if you check."

Gil looked unconvinced. "All the same, I think I'm going to keep digging into his past. The man's always got more money than any ordinary cowpoke I've ever met."

"He's a poker player," Luke threw in. "Maybe he wins big."

Gil was ready for that, too. "I've been checking on that with the boys. He doesn't always win, yet he's back the next weekend with more cash, looking to set up a game."

Jacob had been thoughtfully watching the two men and finally had to ask. "I'm curious about something. Since Luke's return, you two been glaring at each other most of the time, from what I've heard. Suddenly today, I notice that you're not only cooperating but seem to be friends again. What happened?"

Another necessary confession and apology, Gil thought, bracing himself. "We had a long overdue talk this morning and..."

"And decided to bury the hatchet," Luke chimed in. He sent a silent message to Gil that explaining further was unnecessary. Gil had been wrong years ago, had admitted his mistake like a man and was now trying to make up for it. There was no need to shout it from the rooftops. "We've had our problems, but we've worked them out."

Gil's expression changed from surprised to hesitantly grateful. "Yeah, that's right."

"I see." There was more to it, Jacob knew, but he wouldn't push. As long as things were better, that was all he needed to know. Slowly he rose. "I think it's time for me to wander back to my room before my lady comes looking for me." He'd been a little surprised Liz hadn't already interrupted them.

Gil stood, too. "I think I'll head on down toward the bunkhouse, see if I can overhear anything."

His hand on the knob, Jacob turned back. "I got to tell you nothing lately's made me feel as good as seeing you two friends again." With that, he left the room.

Gil's eyes met Luke's. "I find myself needing to thank you again."

"No thanks necessary."

Gil held out his hand and Luke shook it warmly. "See you tomorrow."

Somewhat awkwardly, Luke scooted down until he was lying flat, then raised his arms and crossed his hands under his head. It had been quite a day. Thoughts, possibilities, suspicions ran around in his head like mice in a maze. His knee was throbbing, but he wasn't about to take a pain pill and get all fuzzy.

Shay had said she'd come. He wished she'd hurry.

"You're still dressed." Shay stood just inside Luke's bedroom, closing the door at her back. The hall clock had chimed the midnight hour some minutes ago. The house had been quiet for a while, but she'd waited, wanting to make sure no one was around when she came to her lover.

Her lover. In a shaft of moonlight coming in through the open window, she could see that Luke was awake, his blue eyes watching her. A fat candle in a brass holder across the room sent slanting ribbons of light skittering along the wood-paneled walls, propelled by the night breezes. A sheet was draped across his middle and he wore an unbuttoned shirt.

Luke held out a hand to her, bidding her come closer. He felt as if he'd been waiting for her forever. He hadn't been able to sleep or to think clearly. Now that she was here, he felt his world was finally right again. When she stepped to the bed, he saw she wore pale peach silk, a long gown and an open robe. "I was beginning to think you weren't coming."

"I probably shouldn't have, with my daughter and my parents sleeping just overhead." She slipped the robe off and dropped it onto the nearby chair. "But my head is so full of you that I had to come." The bed dipped slightly as she sat down.

"My head is full of you, too." She'd left her hair down and it flowed along her back and skimmed her pale shoulders where the gown's thin straps rested. He reached to comb her hair back, thrusting his fingers deeply into the thick waves. "So beautiful."

Shay closed her eyes, his touch causing the simmering heat to begin. She breathed deeply of the scent that was his alone, clean and masculine, already achingly familiar. She heard the rustle of leaves on the tree just outside his window and a night bird's song sounding very near.

Luke pulled her close and captured her mouth. The kiss was deep, totally consuming him in seconds. Carefully he angled her fully onto the mattress beside him until the sweet flesh of her breasts caressed his chest where his shirt fell open. Gently he sprinkled kisses along the satin line of her throat, then kissed the curve of her shoulder as he slipped the straps of her gown down. His searching mouth trailed lower, nuzzling then suckling. He felt her draw in a quivery breath.

"I've been thinking about this all day," he whispered. "While they were X-raying my knee, I thought of you to keep my mind off what they were doing. I almost embarrassed myself in front of the technician."

She chuckled low. "I had no idea you entertained such sexy thoughts in broad daylight."

"Only of you." His fingers slid the gown to her waist, and he covered her breasts with his hands, tracing the hard peaks in soft circles.

His tongue replaced his hands, and she sighed deeply. "I feel as though I've been waiting all my life to know you like this. Always before, I wanted more, but I didn't know there *was* so much more."

Luke shifted then flinched as a jolt of pain shot through his knee.

"I don't think this is the night to get too athletic," she told him. "Are you in pain?"

"Only because of this need to be with you."

Shay felt a slow blush stain her cheeks, still unused to hearing such a bold admission.

With a soft moan, he kissed her again, then sat up.

With trembling hands, she slid his shirt from him and tossed it aside. As she threw back the sheet, she saw he wore only dark briefs and his white padded knee brace. "I don't want to hurt you."

"Don't worry, you won't." His powerful hands lifted her as he removed her gown and eased her onto her back. Bracing himself on one elbow, he gazed at her. "Do you know how incredibly beautiful you are, with your hair spread out on the pillow and the candlelight turning your skin golden?"

Her color deepened. "I'm not. I'm very average and..."

His finger touched her lips, shutting off the rest. "Your eyes are so wonderful," Luke went on. "They can turn so frosty, like the day I arrived. And yet, when you're with me like this, they're dark brown and shimmering with heat." Lingeringly he kissed each of her eyes in turn.

Shay floated with the languid pleasure of his words, his touch, her breath unraveling with a shaky sigh.

"And your mouth. Such lovely lips, full and delicious. You were maybe only twelve, and already I was fantasizing about kissing your mouth."

She smiled. "Cradle snatcher."

"Ah, but I held off for four more years and, believe me, it wasn't easy." He kissed her now, slowly, thoroughly. Her eyes, smoky with passion, fluttered open. "Your breasts are enough to make a strong man weak." Lowering his head, he tasted her again and felt her grow fuller.

Adrift on a sea of sensations, Shay felt her breathing become tremulous.

His hands circled her slim waist, then parted her thighs and moved to touch her intimately. Her welcoming warmth embraced him. "I think your body's missed me, Shay."

Her pulse racing, she had to agree. He was sweet, unbearably sweet. Never had she been more aware of her body than just now as he explored it patiently, utterly absorbed. Never had she felt more desirable, more appreciated. "Perhaps yours has missed my hands, as well."

"Why don't you see?" he said as he probed still further, feeling her tighten around him.

After the many ways he'd taught her to touch him last night, Shay was no longer hesitant. But she would go slowly, drawing out the pleasure for both of them. Her fingers scraped along his chest then down his rib cage, losing themselves in his male textures. She felt his stomach muscles jump as she trailed lower. Inching inside the band of his briefs, she found him hot and eager for her touch.

But in moments, the hours he'd spent waiting were making him desperate to be joined with her. "I want very badly to be deep inside you, so deep that there's no room for anyone else."

"You've always been deep inside me, in my heart."

Shifting, he slipped out of his briefs, then lifted her until she straddled him. Angling his injured knee aside, he pulled her down to him, filling her. "You may have to do most of the work," he whispered close to her ear, "but I'll make it up to you next time."

She was certain he would. At last, she was flesh to flesh with him, this strong, hard body that hers had begun to hunger for. Moving her hips, Shay found the rhythm. In this position, she could watch his face, his shining face as he climbed with her. Rising, then falling, and rising again, she raced them along down an endless, echoing tunnel where ecstasy awaited them.

When it was over, they lay entwined together in the tangled sheets. "Stay the night with me, Shay. I don't want you to leave." In his entire life, he'd never spent a whole night lying in the embrace of a woman he loved. His defenses down, Luke waited for her answer.

She would risk it, risk the censure that being seen might bring to her. Because today, for that split second, she'd been so frightened that she might have lost him.

She would stay also because he needed her, and she needed him no less.

Easing her weight from him, she cradled his head on her breast. "I'm here, Luke."

At last, he was able to fall asleep.

The following week crawled by for Luke. Dr. Emmett, on one of his usual visits to check on Jacob, had stopped to see him, as well, and said that the rest and anti-inflammatory pills were working. After the third day, he'd graduated from crutches to the cane Jacob had given him and had begun to go on short walks.

He'd read, played checkers endlessly with Beth, read to her and ate most of the food Cora kept shoving at him. He felt much stronger in five days and moved back to his cabin, but spent a large part of his day at the big house, enjoying the unfamiliar spoiling.

And each evening, after Beth was asleep, Shay would come to him and spend the night in his bed, in his arms.

He'd talked again to Gray in Wyoming and told him to hang tight, that another complication had come up delaying him even further. Fortunately, Gray wasn't a man who questioned much.

All in all, Luke had to admit his sudden incapacitation had its pluses, besides the loving warmth of Shay. He had time to sit with Jacob, reminiscing about when Luke had been a youth on the Circle M, time to listen to stories the older man liked to tell of when he was a boy on this very ranch, and time to just plain shoot the bull. Man-to-man talk, and no women invited. Often Gil had joined them.

Gil. Luke thought of Gil as a bit of a paradox. Filled with anger and bitterness in his early years due to the restrictions from his illness, he'd grown into a surly, jealous young man. But seemingly, he'd overcome his youthful resentments, making it possible for people to see his intelligence, his wit and his sensitivity.

When they were alone, just he and Gil, Gil would talk more freely—about some of his ideas on how to improve things on the Circle M, about tentative plans he had, about a few of his dreams. Since the evening the three of them had talked in Luke's bedroom, Gil now spoke more freely in front of his father, too. Perhaps it was because finally, after seeking approval from both Jacob and Luke, he had it and it gave him a confidence, a trust he'd not had before. Whatever it was, Luke was grateful for it.

Through the years, he'd made a lot of acquaintances living in half a dozen states the way he had. But Luke realized he'd made few lasting friends. Either the men he'd thought to form a friendship with had moved on, or he had. From the first, he'd liked Gil, yet Luke admitted that he'd had his resentments, too. Maybe they'd started off on the wrong foot and had never been able to get past that bad beginning. Now, it seemed, neither felt the other offered a threat, and a tenuous friendship had begun.

Each morning, Gil would stop to talk with Luke before going out early to set up his watches, to surreptitiously keep an eye on some of the men, as well as the cattle. And each evening, he'd return to update both Luke and Jacob. It appeared by the end of the week that the rustler was lying low.

"Nobody's quit," Gil said as he sat in the kitchen of the big house drinking a tall glass of iced tea. "So he's still got to be around."

"He and his accomplice," Luke agreed. They both doubted that the rustler was acting alone. Seated across from Gil, he stretched out his leg, then bent it at the knee. He'd been using the exercise weights the doctor had brought out and could tell his knee was nearly back to full strength.

"We know he needs that bull. I'd bet he's biding his time." They were alone in the kitchen at mid-morning, Cora having gone into town for groceries with Liz driving the station wagon.

"He's had to have noticed how certain men seem always to be around, watching, counting cows, no pasture ever without at least two men on horseback patrolling day and night." Luke crossed his knee, testing the flexibility.

Thirsty from having been outdoors for over four hours already, Gil drained his tea and wiped his mouth. "He's waiting for us to make a mistake, to drop our guard. Then, bingo! He'll grab that bull, probably throw another couple dozen cows on a separate rig and he'll be out of here. Or so he thinks.''

Luke frowned. "And still no one's seen anything suspicious, anyone out and about where they shouldn't be?''

"So I'm told. And I've been patrolling a lot myself.''

"How's Zeke acting?''

Gil shrugged. "Like he knows something's going on, and he can't figure out why he's not in on it. Yesterday, he plain came out and asked me. I told him the truth, or some of it, that we're looking to prevent more cows from being taken.''

"I was sitting out in the side yard yesterday, getting some sun on this knee, and I heard Rhea and Zeke quarreling again. So after he left, I went over to her. She was sitting on the porch listening to this country-western station and quietly crying.''

Gil frowned. "What do you suppose is wrong over there?''

Luke shook his head. "I asked Rhea if I could help, and she just looked at me, and said, 'No, no one can.' ''

"I guess she means about not being able to have a baby. She's going to make herself sick over that.''

"Why don't they adopt a child?''

"If you ask me, Zeke's not all that fired up to be a daddy. It's Rhea who thinks he'll be happier if they have one.'' Gil crammed his hat back on his head. "Women. I'll never understand them.''

The swinging door between the kitchen and vestibule opened, and Shay came hurrying in as both men turned.

"I'm so glad you're both here," she said. "Beth's been throwing up all morning, and she's cold and clammy. I've called the doctor, and he said to get her to the hospital quick."

Chapter Eleven

"It'll be quicker if we fly her there," Luke said, rising and grabbing his hat. He put his arm around Shay and gave her a reassuring hug. "Get her ready, and I'll prepare the plane."

"Beth's *never* sick, Luke. Never." Shay heard her voice tremble and knew she'd have to be strong so her daughter wouldn't pick up on her fear.

"She's going to be all right," Luke told her, and prayed he was right.

"I'll go, too," Gil said.

Luke shook his head. "No, we need you to stay here. This might be just the opening our rustlers are waiting for. I can handle Beth and Shay."

Gil saw the wisdom of that. "You're right. Come on, Shay. You wrap her up, and I'll carry her down."

Luke kissed the top of her head, then hurried out the back door, relieved that his knee felt good.

* * *

Luke touched the brakes on the Land Rover lightly, slowing the heavy vehicle as they bounced along the bumpy stretch of road, his face grim. "We'll be to the highway in a few minutes and past all these potholes."

Shay sat in the passenger seat, her daughter cradled on her lap. "Where do you suppose Zeke took the plane without telling anyone?"

A muscle in Luke's jaw tightened. "I don't know, but I mean to find out." He'd gone to the landing strip where the ranch plane was housed and found it was gone. Rushing into the barns, he'd found Hollis, who said he'd seen Zeke take the plane out hours ago. Quickly Luke had asked around, but no one seemed to know where the co-manager was headed.

Having little choice left since his truck was undrivable and Liz had taken the station wagon, he'd jumped into the Land Rover. He couldn't spare the time to question Rhea to see if she knew where her husband was. Considering their explosive marriage, she would probably know nothing. And Gil had been out on the range early and hadn't realized Zeke had left, either. Gil had talked with Zeke the night before, and there'd been no mention of a planned flight today.

"I'm cold, Mom," Beth said, her small body shaking.

Shay tucked the blanket more closely around the child, aware that Beth was bathed in sweat, yet shivering. Her temperature had been erratic the last time she'd taken it. The aspirin she'd given her had come back up, and the cooling bath hadn't done much good, either. "We'll be there soon, sweetheart," she murmured, kissing Beth's damp head.

Memorial Hospital in Red Lodge was about thirty miles away, Luke knew, which would have taken them minutes to reach by plane. As it was, winding along this rough mountainous road en route to the highway in the Land Rover would slow them down considerably. Beth was nauseated so he couldn't pick up speed and jostle her around too much. He glanced over at her small form huddled into her mother, her eyes closed against the bright sun.

"Hold on, sweetheart," he said. He heard her moan as she curled into a tighter ball. Luke gripped the wheel, directing his frustrated anger to visions of what he'd like to do to Zeke Crawford.

Luke hated hospitals. He'd been confined several times during his rodeo days, the last stay a rather lengthy one when he'd had his final knee surgery. Inhaling the antiseptic smells brought back memories of those dispirited weeks. He'd been alone, with no one sitting alongside his bed or in one of the small waiting-room alcoves worrying about his recovery.

The difference this time was that Beth had him and Shay waiting in just such an alcove near the nurses' station across from the elevators. Luke watched Shay pace the small room, then turn to walk over and stare out the window awhile before resuming her worried strides. She paused to look out and he got up, slipping his arms around her, feeling her concern, her agitation.

She leaned into him a long moment, trying to absorb his strength, his warmth. In her entire life, she'd never been so frightened as when she'd had to watch the hospital personnel wheel Beth, looking pale and listless, into the examining room and close the door. "What's taking so long?"

"The tests take time. She's only been in there twenty minutes." He shifted his hands to rub the tension from her shoulders.

"It seems like much longer."

"I know." He kept at it, his strong fingers massaging under her heavy hair, on up into her neck, working out the knots. At last, her head drifted forward and he could feel her forcing herself to relax. Then abruptly, she twisted free and began to pace again, as if to relax was to abandon her watch over her daughter.

Luke leaned against the wall, knowing he could do little to help her through this except be here with her. He'd never known what it was like to worry over someone like this, to have another life mean more to him than his own. But now, loving Shay the way he did, he could relate. He knew how desperate he'd feel if Shay was the one in there with some unknown illness weakening her.

Beth was a small extension of Shay, yet very much her own person already. He thought of the little jokes she made when they played checkers, of her gentleness with the stray dog, of the day he'd found her dry-eyed and upset on her window seat with Beechie, of the spontaneous hug she'd given him after his accident. She'd moved into his thoughts and then into his heart so effortlessly that he'd scarcely noticed.

It startled Luke to discover he loved the child so fiercely. But could he be a good father to her? Could loving Beth mean that he'd know the right things to do and say to guide her through life? He fervently hoped so because he was coming to realize that he wanted both of them with him.

"I hate this helpless feeling," Shay said, coming alongside him. "Dr. Emmett and all those nurses. They just take her away and shut the door, not letting you in on what's going on until you're half-crazy."

Her anxiety was making her unreasonable. Luke pulled her close. "Let's go sit down." He urged her toward the orange vinyl couch, surprised when she didn't resist. She sat with his arm around her, the only visible signs of nerves were her hands restlessly twisting in her lap.

The hospital was small, only eighty beds, but often filled to capacity as the facility served several nearby communities. Luke watched the change of shifts, nurses leaving and coming, doctors bustling by, their lab coats flapping behind as they hurried on. He heard the spongy sound of crepe soles on clean tile floors and the muted announcements paging people for phone calls and a variety of emergencies. Taking in a deep breath, he acknowledged that he hated this waiting as much as Shay.

It was a full hour later that Dr. Emmett came toward them wearing a long white hospital coat over his buttoned vest. He was missing his usual smile.

Shay leaped to her feet. "How is she, Doctor?"

"She's a very sick little girl, Shay."

"Did you find out what she has?" Luke asked, also rising.

"At first, we thought it was food poisoning, so we pumped her stomach. Then she started convulsing and slipped into a mild coma."

"Oh, God," Shay whispered.

Luke slipped a steadying arm around her. "Go on, Doctor."

Dr. Emmett stroked his gray beard a moment, as if wondering how much to tell them. "She's apparently ingested poison somehow. Arsenic, according to our findings."

Shay gripped Luke's hand. "How could she have gotten ahold of arsenic? Beth's bright. She wouldn't eat something unfamiliar."

"It's hard to say," the doctor went on. "Accidental poisonings are very common in children. You probably have a variety of poisons around the ranch."

Luke was frowning thoughtfully. "Arsenic is the basis of rat poison. We keep it in the barn, use it in sprays. I don't see how any of that would have gotten into her food. Cora's so careful."

"She's going to be all right, isn't she?" Shay insisted, because to think otherwise was impossible.

"Most probably." Silas Emmett held up a hand sporting a large pinkie ring before she could say more. "I don't want to mislead you. Beth is very ill, but she's basically a healthy child. I don't think it was in her long enough to cause liver damage. She's fighting, and we have every reason to believe she'll win."

"But . . . something could still go wrong and . . ." Shay put her hand to her lips, unable to complete the thought.

Dr. Emmett had delivered Shay and her daughter after her. He'd been with her when she'd lost her second child. He was fond of all the McKenzies and now reached to touch Shay's hand in reassurance. "We both know there are no absolutes in medicine. But you have my word, Shay, that I will do everything humanly possible for Beth."

Shay nodded as she blinked back tears that had been threatening to fall for some time. "I know you will, Doctor."

"How long before you can tell she's out of the woods?" Luke asked.

"The next twenty-four to forty-eight hours are crucial."

"Can we see her?" Shay wanted to know.

"In a bit. We're transferring her to a room where she can be monitored more closely." At the sound of the page, he paused to listen. Taking note of the message, he stepped back. "I have to go. Leave word where I can reach you, and I'll keep you informed."

"I'll be right here, Doctor," Shay said. How could he think otherwise? she wondered vaguely.

Luke watched him walk away, then eased Shay back to the couch before her legs gave out from under her.

"Where would she have gotten arsenic?"

"We'll have to question her gently once she's out of danger," Luke said.

Shay raised brimming eyes to his. "She's just got to be all right, Luke. Nothing can happen to my baby."

"She *will* be all right," he told her, pressing her head to his shoulder, his thoughts whirling. Arsenic. Poison. A freak accident, or something else? Was he automatically overreacting since the warning note and the truck incident? Or had Beth eaten tainted food meant for him?

It was the longest night Luke had ever spent. Because Beth was in intensive care, they weren't allowed to see her except for ten minutes every hour. Each visit to the child's bedside, he felt his heart twist as Shay stood alongside her daughter, touching her hand, adjusting the sheet over the frail form, brushing back Beth's hair. She would pat dry her damp face, murmuring words of love and hope to her all the while. More than once, Luke had to turn away, swallowing around a lump in his throat that threatened to choke him.

And then they'd go back to the tiny alcove and huddle together there. He'd tried to coax Shay to the cafeteria to eat, but she wouldn't leave. Several times, he'd gone down to bring back two cups of steaming coffee which they drank without tasting. The only time she'd left the floor was to visit the small chapel off the lobby. Luke had never considered himself a particularly prayerful man, but he found himself praying alongside her.

He'd called the ranch and updated Liz on Beth's condition, but when Liz had said she'd be right there, he'd talked her out of making the trip just yet. He knew that eventually Shay would be so exhausted he'd have to take her somewhere to rest. Liz could take up the vigil then.

And he'd talked with Gil, who'd told him that Zeke and the plane were still gone. It was particularly odd since he'd never stayed away overnight before. Rhea couldn't seem to shed any light on her husband's whereabouts, either. Luke wondered if Zeke was hiding something, but other than this unexpected flight, he'd never done anything to cast suspicion on himself.

Nevertheless, Luke had confided his suspicions about the possibility of the arsenic being meant for him to Gil and told him to be extra careful and very watchful. Luke also told Gil to allow no one into the big house except family. Returning to Shay, he'd sat holding her, his mind too troubled to doze off.

Mid-morning of the next day marked the end of the first twenty-four hours. Dr. Emmett stopped to update them, saying that Beth still wasn't out of danger, but that her vital signs were stable.

"Medical people," Shay grumbled after he left, "they talk in a language all their own. Stock phrases. Meaningless. Vital signs stable. What does that mean?" She felt as if her nerves were raw and bleeding, her temper moving quickly to the edge of no return.

"It means she's holding her own and hasn't gotten worse." Luke ran a hand over his unshaven face and longed for a shower. His eyes felt grainy, and his stomach was queasy from far too many cups of hospital coffee. Rising from the bench, he stretched his stiff muscles and bent his knee several times, working out the kinks. "I think we need to freshen up a bit in the rest rooms, then go down and have some breakfast."

Shay shook her head. "I couldn't eat. You go ahead."

He felt a wave of exasperation. "Look, it's not going to do Beth any good if you fall apart."

She ground her teeth, trying to keep from snapping at him. She was well aware he was right, but the very thought of food had her stomach roiling. "Please, Luke. I can't." She walked to the window and stared out unseeingly.

He didn't want to argue. "All right. I'm going down for coffee. I'll be back shortly." She didn't acknowledge she heard, but he knew she had. Perhaps she needed to be alone with her thoughts for a bit. Luke pushed the elevator button.

Shay stood looking down at the hospital parking lot two floors below, but seeing another day years ago. She'd been rushed here hemorrhaging badly, so weak she could scarcely lift her head. She'd promised God all manner of things if only her baby wouldn't die. Things hadn't worked out.

Nevertheless, she found herself doing the same thing again. He had to hear her this time, to save Beth. She would do anything, *anything,* if only her little girl would be well again. Trembling, with fear and fatigue, she pressed her hand to her mouth, pressing back a sob that wanted to break free.

She wasn't sure how long she stood there like that. Suddenly she became aware of the elevator doors behind her opening and she blinked rapidly, not wanting Luke to see her upset. He'd been so good, so supportive. Slowly she turned.

Three men stepped into the hallway, but she recognized only one. The tall man with thinning blond hair spotted her at the same moment and came forward. How had Max gotten wind of Beth's illness? Shay wondered as she hugged herself, her fingers gripping her upper arms almost painfully.

"Shay," Max began, "how is my daughter?"

It took every last bit of self-control Shay had not to reach out and strike him. She wouldn't, *couldn't* answer him.

"Shay," he said again, "did you hear me? I want to know what's happening to my daughter." Exasperated, he turned to the short man with the thick glasses standing to his left. "She's evidently in shock. I'll ask at the desk."

She watched Max stride to the nurses' station, the other two following closely behind. When the third man turned, she saw that he held a camera in front of him, the strap dangling down in a leather loop. Then she noticed that the shorter one was carrying a notebook and pen. *No!* Not even Max would stoop so low as to bring the press to his sick daughter's bedside, to exploit Beth for the sake of publicity, would he?

Her shoulders slumping, she realized that of course he would. Max would stoop as low as the snake she knew him to be. If she rushed over, she'd only cause a worse scene. Chewing on her lip, she watched him give the charge nurse his public smile while he politely demanded to see the doctor and his daughter, in that order. Shay was relieved to see the nurse shake her head, saying he'd have to wait for the allotted time period to visit Beth, and that Dr. Emmett wasn't in the building at the moment.

Annoyed but trying to camouflage it, Max swung about and returned to where Shay stood watching him with haunted eyes. "I want to know what they've told you about her condition. I demand that you answer me, Shay. After all, I *am* Beth's father."

Peripherally, Shay saw the nearsighted man scribble on his notepad. She was suddenly too tired to care what she said. "You've never been a father to Beth. Get out of here."

Max took a step closer, his pale eyes narrowing. "Now you listen here," he snarled.

The elevator doors slid open and Luke stepped out, holding in each hand a plastic cup of coffee. He saw Shay backed against the window, her eyes blazing. He didn't know two of the men, but he recognized Maxwell Whitney even from the back. As he set down the coffee, he heard Max say something to Shay, something he shouldn't have by the look on her face. Luke moved closer.

"Shay, is this man bothering you?" he asked, his voice low and menacing.

Max didn't wait for her answer but instead swung about. He remembered Luke Turner's face, had glimpsed him at the Circle M the day he'd visited. A shiftless cowpoke trying to be a hero. He squared his shoulders. "Stay out of this, Turner. This is between me and my wife."

Luke stood balanced on the balls of his feet, his hands loose at his sides. "She's no longer your wife. Leave her alone." His eyes flicked to Shay. The blood had drained from her face. "Are you all right?" He saw her nod.

Max straightened to his full height, which still left him several inches shorter than Luke and a good thirty pounds lighter. For a moment, he regarded the nuisance in front of him, very aware of the press watching.

Luke couldn't help noticing that Max wore the same kind of silk shirts he remembered Morgan preferred. A natty twosome, the Whitney men.

"Who asked you to interfere in a family matter? That's my child in there, my little girl. You haven't any rights here." Max's voice was filled with righteous indignation.

Luke saw red, literally. Moving faster than Max could possibly have predicted, Luke shifted, grabbing a handful of Max's silk shirtfront and backing him against the wall. His head snapped back, hitting the plaster, with a sharp crack that caught Max off guard. Shay moved aside, and the two men stepped back. Within inches of Max's startled, slack-jawed face, Luke spoke so quietly that the people at the desk weren't even aware of an altercation in the alcove.

"Shay asked me here, not that it's any of your business. But it's you who haven't any rights here, you who don't deserve that little girl in there. You don't pay a dime for her support, or visit except to upset her. You don't even remember her birthday. The last time you came by, you left marks on her mother's arms. You've touched Shay for the last time, Whitney."

"You can't threaten me. I . . ." But his words sounded weak in the small, quiet room, even to his own ears.

"I just did. And if you *ever* go near Shay *or* Beth again, I'll not only call a press conference of my own and spread the details of the real reason behind your divorce all over the papers, but I'm going to take great pleasure in smashing in your face." Abruptly he let go and watched Max slump against the wall, then regain his footing.

Red faced, adjusting his clothes, Max turned to glower at Shay. "You haven't heard the last of me. I'll be back and—"

Grabbing Max's arm, Luke whirled him around. "Apparently, I didn't make myself clear." Behind them, he saw a flashbulb go off. His fury rising, he let go of Max and reached the photographer in three angry strides. "Or you, either." Yanking the camera from the startled man, he turned it over, flipped open the back slot and pulled out the film, exposing it in a long, wiggling strip.

"All right, all right," the photographer whined. "Just give me back my camera."

Luke thrust it at him as the shorter man shoved his note pad into his pocket and hurried to the elevators. Luke's hard eyes took in all three of them. "Get out of here, all of you, *now*." His voice was low, calm and all the more lethal because he hadn't had to raise it.

Wisely Max didn't say another word, just sent Shay a scathing look before following the newsmen onto the waiting elevator.

As the doors closed, Shay sagged against the wall.

Luke took her into his arms, his hands gentle as they smoothed her hair. "He's gone. It's all right."

"I can't believe what he wanted to do."

"Believe it."

"Do you think he'll stay away?"

"Yeah, I do."

Her arms circling his solid waist, she looked up at him. "Thank you."

About to kiss her, Luke saw from the corner of his eye a man in a white coat hurrying toward them. Turning Shay, he waited for Dr. Emmett, bracing himself.

The doctor smiled. "I have good news. Beth's out of danger."

Shay burst into tears of relief.

"I don't know what you mean. A flight plan?" Zeke chewed lazily on his toothpick as he leaned against the barn door where Luke had intercepted him.

"Sure you do," Luke went on, noticing that Zeke's eyes were alert despite his casual appearance. "It's a little logbook kept in the plane. You copy down the date, your destination, the time you left and returned, the mileage. I used it the day I took the plane up. Gil tells me it's standard operating procedure around here to log your flights.''

''I have no idea what he's talking about. Nobody ever showed me no logbook.'' Teeth clamping down on the pick, he stared outside past Luke's head.

He's lying, Luke thought, and wondered why. ''At the very least, isn't it customary to let someone know where you're going when you leave the ranch?''

''I already told you. I flew across the border into Wyoming. You know that Jacob isn't keen on having our mares bred to the Whitney stallions, so I went to see Vern Smith at his ranch near Powell. Heard tell he's got quite a stallion. The weather got bad, and I had to stay overnight. You can call Vern and check it out.''

''Why didn't you at least call your wife?''

Zeke lost his lethargic look, his eyes narrowing. ''Because I didn't, that's why. I told Charley Brice where I was going that morning. Guess he forgot to tell you all.''

''Yeah, I guess he did.''

In the morning sun, Zeke squinted up at Luke. ''I don't much like your questions, Turner. I happen to be a son-in-law around here. Just what are you?''

Several comebacks occurred to Luke, but he let them all go. ''Just an old friend of the family.''

''I'd watch who I interrogate, *old friend.*'' Zeke shoved away from the wooden door and strolled off.

Watching him go, Luke stuck his hands in his pockets. There sure as hell was something funny about the guy, but he couldn't put his finger on what. He'd wanted badly to ask about the man's rocky relationship with his wife, but decided that would really rile him. Maybe he'd go have a talk with Rhea. But first, he wanted to climb up into the cockpit of the plane and see if he could discover anything. It sure would help if he knew what he was looking for.

An hour later, he was back in his small cabin, packing a bag. He'd already picked up the suitcase Liz had given him for Shay.

The stubborn woman refused to leave the area of the hospital. So he'd taken a room for them at a highway motel and driven back to the ranch for clean clothes. He didn't know how long they'd be staying, but he did know he wasn't about to leave either Shay or Beth. He wouldn't truly be able to relax until he could bring them both back home.

Beth was still quite ill, but improving daily. If she kept it up, she'd be out of intensive care and into a private room in a couple of days, Dr. Emmett had said. Shay was anxious for that, so she could sit beside Beth longer than ten minutes at a stretch. And Luke was anxious for the child to be well enough to answer a few questions.

Luke zipped his bag closed, then shoved the checkers box into a side pocket. Hopefully, Beth would feel like playing soon.

He stopped for a minute to see if he'd forgotten anything. He'd talked to both Jacob and Liz, who were naturally both worried about their granddaughter. Liz had driven in several times, but with Shay away, she was needed at the big house.

Hearing a footstep on the porch, he turned to see Gil entering, his face angry. "What's up?" Luke asked.

"You're not going to like it." Gil dropped into a chair and pushed back his hat. "You know that stray dog you've been feeding?"

"Yeah. Beth named him Sebastian."

"Well, he almost died the same day Beth took sick. Hollis found him on your back porch too weak to walk and carried him to our vet. You won't believe what was wrong with him. Rat poison."

Luke frowned. "But what did the dog eat that Beth might have tasted? And I warned her never to feed him unless someone else was around."

Gil rubbed a hand over his unshaven face wearily. The long hours of vigil were taking its toll on him. "That's what I wondered, so I did some poking around. You know how Cora often leaves a thermos of lemonade on your back porch?"

Luke nodded. At first, Cora had put the pitcher in his kitchen, but since he'd been locking his doors, she'd left the lemonade on the porch.

"It was still there alongside a plastic glass and the dog's dish."

Luke's hands curled into fists. "Damn, but he's gone too far this time. We can call the sheriff, have the remaining lemonade analyzed and..."

"The top wasn't put back and it's all evaporated. There're probably traces of arsenic left, but even so, that wouldn't prove who did it. He probably only put in a small amount, which would have made a big man like you pretty sick, but it wouldn't have killed you. However, a little girl and a dog—that's another story."

Luke paced the small room restlessly. "This has to be the rustler wanting me out of the way. You haven't seen anything suspicious, and there aren't any more cows missing?"

Gil shook his head. "I can't figure what he's waiting for. Of course, we've got the watches so tight that he'd have a tough time making a move right now."

Luke glanced at his watch. "I've got to get back to the hospital. Why don't you put the pitcher and stuff in a safe place in case we need them later? For now, let's keep this between us. Only watch your back. He might go after you next."

Gil stood and touched Luke's shoulder lightly. "You take care, too. And give my best to Shay and Beth."

Carrying his bag out to the Land Rover, Luke glanced over at Rhea's place. It was quiet, the blinds drawn against the sun. He'd give a lot to know what all went on in that house. Climbing behind the wheel, his mouth a grim line, he set off for the hospital.

It had undoubtedly been the longest two weeks of her life, Shay thought, but at last, she and her daughter were back home in the big house. Looking down at Beth sleeping safely in her own bed, she smiled.

Beechie was curled up at the foot of Beth's bed. The Labrador had all but stopped eating in the absence of his little mistress and had scarcely left her side since her return. And lying on the floor, his head resting on his crossed paws but his eyes watchful, was Sebastian, looking none the worse for all he'd been through.

Luke had told her how sick the stray had been, nearly dying as Beth almost had. When she was well enough, Luke had questioned Beth and learned that the morning she'd taken ill, she'd been on Luke's back porch with Sebastian. It had been hot, and she'd poured herself a glass of lemonade from Cora's pitcher standing by the door, and shared some with the dog. Shay shuddered at the thought as she touched Sebastian's head affectionately.

When she'd learned of the deliberate attempt at poisoning, Shay had wanted to call the sheriff immediately. But Luke and Gil had both talked to her, assuring her that they had a better chance of revealing the person responsible if they didn't tip his or her hand. Shay hadn't agreed, but she'd gone along with their plan, trusting them both. For now. But if another incident occurred, she'd decided she'd keep silent no longer. Her child had nearly died, and someone was trying to harm the man she loved. The whole thing was making her frightened and jittery.

She touched Beth's forehead and found it cool and normal. She'd been a little trooper, rarely complaining, doing all they asked of her, eating when she wasn't terribly hungry to regain her strength, taking naps again. She was still pale and had lost weight, but she was on the mend. Leaving the door ajar, Shay tiptoed out of the bedroom and went downstairs.

Wandering into her father's study, she glanced at his desk. She'd returned only yesterday and already her conscience was nagging her about the work that had piled up in her absence. Her mother had done the essential bookkeeping, but there remained a great deal of posting to be done and checks to be written.

Tomorrow, she told herself, then strolled over to the side table and lifted the large manila envelope. During the long hours while Beth had been sleeping through her illness, Shay had sat reading her revised manuscript, making minor changes. She had only to retype the corrected pages and it would be finished at last.

Soon she would send it off to the editor she hoped would buy it. A long shot, but a chance. Setting it aside, she picked up her yellow pad and pen and wandered to the kitchen.

She found Cora peeling potatoes. "Where is everyone?" she asked as she picked an apple out of the fruit bowl. She'd been upstairs with Beth for the past several hours and hadn't talked with anyone.

"Lots of excitement around here," Cora said, her eyes bright. "Luke and Gil were sitting here having lunch when that fellow, Jim, came running in. First, there'd been a dynamite blast in the east pasture that spooked the cattle. Then someone discovered that a whole mess of fence in the northwest pasture had been cut and cows were straggling out by the droves. All three of them jumped onto their horses and took off."

Shay frowned. "Cut? He said the fence had been cut?"

"That's what he said. Just about every available hand's gone out to help."

"Well, then, I guess they don't need me. I think I'll go out to the barn for a while." She had another idea that had been churning around in her brain for some time. The best way to keep herself from worrying about the manuscript she was about to mail off was to start another story. "Do you think you can check on Beth from time to time? I just left her, and she's asleep."

"Sure I will." Cora sent Shay a smile. "I made her favorite chocolate pudding for tonight. I hate to see my little angel so thin."

Shay gave Cora a hug. "I know you'll fatten her up in no time. By the way, where's Mom?"

"She took your daddy for a drive. Been doing that daily for the last week or so. Good for him to get out."

"Yes, I think so, too. Don't let anyone but family in the house, Cora," Shay said, hating the necessity for such reminders. Outside, she headed for the solitude of the barn. Despite the sun beating down, the interior was slightly cooler, the piped-in music calming. Walking down the cement aisle, she found an empty, clean stall at the far end and sat down in the fragrant hay.

Leaning back, Shay propped her pad against her bent knees and bit into her apple. If they bought her book, she'd have the money, the independence she wanted. But she'd come to want more.

Luke Turner.

After the turmoil of her failed marriage and the loss of her baby, she'd prayed she'd never be made to feel that vulnerable, that needy again. But after spending an emotional two weeks at her sick child's bedside, she'd come to realize she did need again. She needed Luke.

He'd been with her nearly every minute, never wavering, always there for her. She'd had fierce mood swings, countless tearful sessions and a couple of temper outbursts she wasn't proud of. Through it all, he'd been the epitome of understanding. He'd not only run off Max but he'd reminded her to eat, helped her to sleep and cheered her when she was down.

He'd been wonderful with Beth, also, patient and loving. His concern for her daughter was enough in itself to push him to find the person who'd poisoned Beth, she knew. In the few hours they'd spent in the nearby hotel room, he'd held her, loved her, been there for her, as no man ever had. She loved him, wanted to marry him, perhaps have him adopt Beth.

But she wanted more. She wanted to know Luke was capable of settling down, finished with wandering. And she wanted him to honestly *want* that, not just do it to please her. Ah, that was the fly in the ointment. He'd been back a total of six weeks, yet he'd said nothing recently about leaving. But then, he'd promised her mother he'd catch the rustler, and that hadn't happened yet. She almost wished the thief would make his move so things would come to a head. So she would know if Luke's feelings for her were strong enough to build a marriage on.

She'd had one rotten marriage. She didn't want another. She wanted to marry Luke only if they both wanted the same things from life, envisioned the same kind of future. She'd seen him watching her speculatively, too, and knew that soon they'd have to talk seriously.

The barn was peaceful and quiet, only a few calves dozing in adjacent stalls, the music a nice backdrop for imagination.

Finishing her apple, Shay set the core aside and picked up her pen, her mind already sorting through the characters for her next book. For long minutes, she wrote rapid notes, fleshing out the people, describing the setting she pictured, creating the drama she envisioned.

So involved was Shay in her own thoughts that at first, she was scarcely aware of the intrusion of voices. It wasn't until she recognized them that she paused, tilting her head to listen more closely. The one voice definitely belonged to Zeke, and she thought the other speaker was Charley Brice.

"Did you put all our stuff into the cargo compartment?" Zeke asked.

"Yeah, just like you said. You sure no one's around?" Charley sounded nervous.

"They're all out at the northwest pasture, I'm telling you."

Charley chuckled. "That was a touch of genius. First to divert them with a dynamite blast, then to cut the fence on the far range. Those cowboys are riding back and forth all over the place. It'll take them till nightfall to round up all those strays."

"We'll be long gone by then. Where's the cooler?"

"Right outside. Hey, what about your wife? She going to give us any trouble?"

"Not anymore," Zeke said, his voice turning hard. "I set her straight. She's too scared to say a word to anyone."

In the stall, Shay's heart picked up speed. Just how had he set her sister straight? Cautiously she shifted to her knees, then started easing upright, wondering if she could see them without being seen.

"Go get the cooler," Zeke instructed. "I'll get the tank."

Charley lugged in the cooler and set it down next to the freezer with a thud. "I have to laugh at the way they've been guarding those bulls. They didn't have a clue what we had in mind here."

Zeke hoisted the aluminum tank up, huffing as he did so. "Damn, this thing weighs a ton."

"Maybe so, but there's enough semen in there to keep those cows pregnant for the next two years."

Good Lord! Shay thought. Everyone was out rounding up cows, and the two rustlers were here stealing the fertilization straws. She couldn't let that happen. Looking around, she spotted a pitchfork leaning against the stall, grabbed it and crept forward. Surely Zeke wouldn't hurt her. She didn't know Charley that well, but her sister's husband had lived on the Circle M five or six years. Holding her weapon defensively, Shay stepped out into the aisle.

Hearing a sound behind him, Charley swiveled. "Shay!" he yelled.

"Put that tank back," she ordered Zeke, who had his back to her.

Slowly he turned and Shay's eyes grew huge. In Zeke's hand was a gun pointed right at her.

Chapter Twelve

She'd been crying a long time. Not just today, but every day for weeks now. Crying over her broken dreams, her childless marriage, her disappointing life. Crying because it seemed all she and Zeke did was fight. But this last quarrel had been the worst ever.

Sniffling, Rhea sat up and blew her nose. She looked around the bedroom she'd shared with Zeke for three years and wished she had more happy memories of their time together. Perhaps they would have helped her get through the bleak months ahead.

He was leaving. Correction: had left. Hadn't she known all along that one day he would? Even after she'd humiliated herself by begging him to stay, by practically throwing herself at him. Oh, but he'd said such cruel, such hurting things. Rhea dabbed at her eyes in a vain effort to stop the flow.

He'd said he'd never really loved her, that he'd married her for her share of the Circle M. Recalling that, she sobbed again, deep in her chest. She was certainly not the first woman a man had married for money, but she'd never really thought Zeke didn't care for her at all.

Oh, she'd known they didn't have a perfect marriage. He'd been her first and only lover and her inexperience in the bedroom hadn't exactly pleased him. After making love to her, he'd often gotten up without a word, dressed and gone out to the barns to be with the guys or the horses. Were all men like that? Rhea wondered.

She'd thought if they had a child, if they'd been a family like the one he'd never had, that he'd want to spend more time with her and the baby. But minutes ago, he'd told her he didn't want kids, he wanted a *real* woman and she'd never be that. Swallowing hard, Rhea rose and went to splash cold water on her face.

A real woman like Shay, she supposed. Shay had always been prettier, smarter. How she'd envied her sister years ago when Luke still lived here. Rhea had had such a crush on him, done everything she could to get him to notice her, but he'd had eyes only for Shay. Then Luke had left, and Rhea had been glad. She'd wanted Shay to pine for him the way she herself had.

But after Luke's departure, Shay changed. She seemed unhappy, yet she married Max Whitney. But her marriage hadn't turned out any better than Rhea's own. All her life, it seemed, she'd been jealous of Shay. Funny how she hadn't been able to relate to her sister until things started going wrong in Shay's life. But at least, Shay had Beth. Rhea felt her heart twist, knowing she'd give anything for a child of her own to love.

Perhaps if Luke hadn't returned, Zeke wouldn't have gotten so restless. They'd both noticed that Luke and Shay were still wildly attracted to each other. And Gil had set aside his differences and become friends with Luke. Zeke figured Luke would marry Shay and Luke and Gil would run the Circle M one day, leaving him out in the cold. He wasn't going to sit around and beg for crumbs. And he wasn't going to stay with his frigid wife, he'd told her. Drying her face, Rhea walked to the front of the house.

They'd been relatively happy such a short period of time—just for the few months Zeke had managed the Circle M alone, when neither Gil nor Luke were around. Then Gil had returned and soon after, Zeke had been demoted to co-manager. The final straw had been when Luke had come back and everyone seemed to accept him again.

Rhea sighed, deciding that she had to pull herself together, to stop Zeke from hurting her family further. At first she'd tried to help him, leaving a note in Luke's cabin warning him he'd better leave so Zeke wouldn't feel threatened by Luke's presence. But it hadn't worked. For some time, she'd suspected Zeke was up to something, but she'd never had proof. Until the day she'd seen him crawl out from under Luke's truck.

When she'd asked him about that, he'd claimed he'd been freeing a stray cat who'd crawled under the hood and gotten stuck. But she hadn't seen a cat around. She'd gone horseback riding then, trying to sort out her thoughts, only to return and learn that Luke had been hurt in his runaway truck. She'd confronted Zeke again, but his eyes had turned cold and hard and he'd warned her not to start rumors, that he hadn't done anything but rescue a cat. She'd been near hysterical that night.

Twisting a lock of hair around her finger, Rhea stood gazing out into the lazy summer afternoon. She suspected Zeke of something else, yet hadn't allowed herself to dwell on her hunch until today. The rustling. Had he been planning to leave for a long while, siphoning off a few cows at a time, taking them somewhere and starting his own herd without her? Had Luke's return and subsequent probings slowed him down, messed up his plans so much that he wanted Luke out of the way? Had Zeke's greed turned him not only into a thief, but a potential murderer? Rhea cringed at the thought.

Then yesterday when Shay and Luke had brought Beth home, Rhea had been in the big house and overheard someone mention that poisoned lemonade had nearly killed her niece. They all knew that Cora often left a thermal pitcher on Luke's back porch. But only one person Rhea knew would have been driven to put rat poison in it in still another attempt to sideline Luke. Except that little Beth had tasted it first.

She had to do something to stop him. She knew what he was probably doing right now. Loading one of the prime Circle M bulls onto a cattle truck and leaving for good. She'd heard Gil talking about posting extra guards on all the bulls. But today, a large section of fence had been cut and all the men had rushed to round up stray cows. Zeke had to have set that up so he'd have the opportunity to quietly steal the bull he needed for the cows he'd already taken.

She was aware that she was the only one who knew enough about his activities to put all the pieces together. Zeke had warned her to stay put until he was gone. It infuriated Rhea to think he thought her so cowardly, so stupid, that she wouldn't figure things out and do something to halt him. Perhaps she had had her head in the sand up to now. No more.

Charley Brice had been waiting for him on the porch when he'd grabbed his suitcase and left her, weeping and begging. Without a backward glance, Zeke had marched off with Charley. Squaring her shoulders, she decided she'd show Zeke Crawford that he couldn't dump her like so much excess baggage and ride off into the sunset.

Hurriedly Rhea left her house and ran into the corral. She'd ride out to where the men were and tell Luke and Gil. They'd stop Zeke. She was ashamed she'd not determined sooner what Zeke was really like. But she'd wanted so badly to have a good marriage like her parents had, to *really matter* to someone. Maybe it wasn't too late. She would make it up to her family somehow and hope for their forgiveness.

Opening the corral gate, she rushed to her horse.

The rope Charley had tied around her ankles and wrists wasn't nearly as uncomfortable as the cotton handkerchief he'd used to gag her, Shay thought, as she sat in the corner of the stall where the two men had literally dumped her. The cloth in her mouth was tight, pressing against her tongue, gagging her. Perhaps if she stopped struggling against it, she decided, forcing herself to push back the panic and breathe deeply through her nose.

It had been foolish of her to try to stop two strong men with a mere pitchfork, she now realized. But she truly hadn't dreamed that Zeke would pull a gun on her. Recalling that terrifying moment when she'd stared into that menacing barrel, Shay shivered. At least they hadn't knocked her out or shot her, something she wouldn't put past either man after looking into their cold, determined eyes.

Zeke had held the gun on her while Charley had grabbed the pitchfork, then methodically tied her up. They'd carried her into the stall and gone back to the freezer unit. Now, straining to listen to their conversation, she became aware that something was wrong.

Zeke pulled out another glass tube, held it up to the light and checked its contents. "Damn, another empty one."

"I had a feeling something like this might slow us down," Charley said. "Gil's had the men fertilizing cows left and right lately, trying to recoup their losses."

"Yeah, but they're not supposed to put the empty straws back into the cylinder." Annoyed, he lowered the cylinder into the tank filled with liquid nitrogen. He'd planned to take only one tank, since each held a thousand straws, and leave the other here, thinking that Jacob wouldn't get too angry if he left him the second batch. He knew the older man hated involving the law in his affairs. If he hadn't sought help from the sheriff when over two hundred cows were missing, Zeke didn't think he'd do so now and let everyone know he'd been bested by his own son-in-law. Not that the law would in all probability be able to trace him to the ranch he'd bought in the foothills of Wyoming's Absaroka Mountains. He even had a small hangar to house Jacob's plane.

But now, he had no choice, Zeke thought. He couldn't risk taking the time to sort through the straws, ferreting out the empty ones. They'd wasted precious minutes with Shay. He'd needed to get her out of the way, but he hadn't wanted to hurt her. He knew that if harm came to either of his daughters, Jacob wouldn't rest until he'd exacted revenge on Zeke. Which was the only reason he hadn't backhanded his whining wife before he'd walked away from her. He'd purposely frightened and humiliated Rhea, knowing it was her habit to stay put, sobbing her little heart out after one of their bouts. By the time she figured things out, he'd be miles from here.

"Seal them both up, and we'll shove them into the cargo hold," Zeke told Charley.

"You sure the plane can handle that much weight?" Each tank weighed close to a hundred pounds and they'd already loaded aboard their saddles and bags and all they both owned.

"Yeah, yeah, just get going." He was edgy, worried one of the men might decide to come back for some reason. Or that Jacob and Liz would return early from their daily drive.

"We don't have another cooler," Charley said, clamping down the tank's lid and securing it.

"We'll have to do without. It's not that long a flight, and I don't think the semen will thaw that quickly." Zeke closed the second tank and was about to hoist it when he heard a distant sound growing louder.

Peering around the corner of the barn door, Charley spoke over his shoulder. "We got trouble. Two men on horseback headed this way. I'd bet my last dollar it's Luke and Gil."

Zeke swore ripely, his mind racing.

Shoving the cooler nearer the door, Charley braced himself. "Give me your gun. I'm a better shot than you are."

Zeke knew Charley was right and slipped him the gun, then looked around for another weapon. Spotting a pair of long shears, he grabbed them and moved to the other side of the barn door. Chances were good that neither man had a pistol since Circle M men seldom carried guns except at night on the range. He'd seen Gil and Luke rush out to help round up the cows and knew they probably wouldn't have thought to arm themselves. "Don't shoot to kill, Charley," Zeke whispered. "Jacob will never stop looking for us if they die."

Crouched down in firing position, Charley waited.

Suddenly Zeke had a better idea. "Hold on," he said, and walked back to the stall where Shay sat hunched in the corner. Bending down, he pulled her upright. "Come on, sweetheart. I have a feeling you're our ticket to freedom."

Luke had never ridden so hard in his life. Rhea had intercepted them returning to the barn area from the pasture with the cut fence. Some time after arriving to assess the damage, it had occurred to both him and Gil that this deliberate act could well be a setup. So they'd turned around and were halfway back when they'd seen Rhea coming toward them. She'd barely finished telling them about Zeke before the two of them had left her there and ridden like the wind.

Nearing the compound, Luke saw the plane out and in takeoff position. Certainly Zeke couldn't load a bull on that small plane. Then it hit him. "They're going for the semen tanks," he shouted to Gil, who was close alongside him.

"We should have figured that," Gil yelled back.

The Jeep was parked with its back end facing the barn door where the fertilization tanks were stored. Luke aimed Maverick straight away, then reined him in as they approached. The big stallion had scarcely come to a halt before Luke slipped off, ignoring the twinge in his knee as he hit the ground hard. Gil was beside him in seconds.

Carefully Luke crept closer to the barn door, which was ajar but only slightly. He could see nothing except dust motes dancing in a ray of sunshine and the dim interior beyond. Signaling Gil with his hand to stay back he inched forward, listening. No sounds. They had to have heard the horses arriving. Wishing he had a weapon, he looked around for one. The only thing available was a three-foot length of board on the ground. Grabbing it, Luke took a

deep breath, then threw himself on the ground, rolled
through the doorway and leaped to his feet.

"Hold it right there, Turner, or I rip your lady's
throat," Zeke snarled.

Luke blinked, his eyes adjusting to the shadowy interior, and what he saw nearly stopped his heart. Standing
near the first stall, Shay's arms were tied behind her and
there was a gag in her mouth. Zeke had a tight arm around
her and was holding a pair of shears near her throat. Luke
felt sweat trickle down his spine as Shay's eyes met his. She
looked oddly more defiant than frightened.

"Drop that board, and call your buddy in here," Charley ordered, still holding the gun.

Luke dropped the board as he glanced at Charley, not-
ing he was to the left of him, about a dozen feet from the
door. Ignoring Charley's instructions and guessing that
Zeke was calling the shots, Luke fixed his gaze on Rhea's
husband. He assumed that all Zeke wanted was the tanks
and time to take off. Zeke undoubtedly knew Jacob well
enough that if serious harm came to Shay, he'd never rest
until Zeke was made to pay. "Let her go, Zeke, and we'll
step aside and let you fly out of here."

Tempted, Zeke narrowed his eyes thoughtfully. After a
moment, he shook his head, deciding he'd be a fool to trust
Luke. "Gil," he shouted. "Get in here with your hands up
or your sister dies."

Luke decided on another gamble. Perhaps Gil would get
the message. "Better do it, Gil. Charley's by the freezer,
with a gun pointed at me."

Zeke waited a moment, then lost his patience. Any
minute, other riders could return. "Don't push me or
I'll—"

The sound of a crash, of breaking glass was loud in the
still, hot air, surprising everyone but Luke. His body rolled

in a tight ball, Gil came hurtling through the window above the freezer chest, landing atop it, then pitching right into Charley. The gun went flying as Gil came up with fists pounding.

A startled Zeke saw Luke about to tackle him and tried to shield himself with Shay. But she gave a mighty kick at his shins, causing him to lose his grip on the shears as she dropped to the floor, rolling out of harm's way. Zeke felt a strong body hit, throwing him to the ground. Roaring mad, he tried to get in a punch, but Luke was too fast. A hard fist rammed into his jaw, followed by a second.

Shay scooted farther away and managed to get to her feet, wishing she could free her hands. She saw Charley and Gil pummeling each other, rolling over, reversing positions. Now Charlie was straddling her brother. Obviously larger and stronger, Charley was doing a fair amount of damage. With a groan of dismay, Shay watched blood trickle out of Gil's mouth.

She could stand it no longer. Walking nearer, she kicked Charley hard in the back. Like a pesky fly, he swatted her away, scarcely pausing. His backhand sent her flying into a pile of straw. Hitting her head on the side wall, she sat there dazed.

Luke had managed to stun Zeke long enough to get to his feet and search around for the gun. It was too far away, over by the door. Instead, he picked up the discarded board and moved to Charley, hitting him on the back of the head. Soundlessly Charley slumped to the floor alongside a very bloody, unconscious Gil.

Turning, Luke raced for the gun, but by then, Zeke was scrambling for it, too. The two struggled in the straw bed, grunting and swearing. At last, Zeke's fingers closed around the gun and he held it out at arm's length, pointing it at Luke. Breathing hard, Luke sat on the floor, measuring his options.

Getting to his feet, Zeke swiped a shaky hand across his swelling face. How had this happened after all these months of careful planning? "Stay put," he ordered Luke. Taking several steps backward, he kept the gun trained on Luke while he assessed the situation.

Shay sat in the pile of straw, her eyes on her brother-in-law. "Don't you move, either," Zeke snarled at her. Stepping back, he saw that neither Charley nor Gil was moving, though he could see both were breathing. Damn!

All right, he could still get away. He'd take one tank to the plane and take off. He could still make it work, Zeke decided. But first, he'd have to take care of the man who'd messed up all his plans.

Luke sat, watching him, coiled and ready to roll if Zeke took aim. He saw that Zeke's face was twitching with nerves and felt that he was desperate enough to do something even more stupid than that which he'd already accomplished. He was probably beyond reason, but Luke thought he'd give it a shot. "Put down the gun, Zeke. You don't want to add murder to your list, do you?"

His chest heaving, Zeke's eyes narrowed nastily. "Shut up."

"You're a son-in-law," Luke went on. "We can get Jacob to drop the charges, if nobody gets seriously hurt." He thought that unlikely, but he would use what he could in this tight spot. From the corner of his eye, he saw Shay sit up straighter, struggling against the rope that bound her. He made a quick staying motion with his hand, hoping she'd get his meaning and stay put.

Sweat dripped down Zeke's face as his eyes narrowed meanly. He'd made up his mind. Luke wasn't a blood son. Jacob would be mad, but he wouldn't go looking for revenge. His lips curled in a smile. "Say your prayers, Turner. I'm going to enjoy this." He cocked the gun and raised it.

A shot rang out, followed by a startled scream. Zeke dropped the gun and grabbed his arm. Turning slowly, he saw Rhea standing in a beam of sunlight from the open door, in her hand a smoking gun.

His face changed as he quickly switched tactics. "Rhea, honey, I'm glad you're here. We can go away together, just the two of us." Holding his bleeding arm, he took two unsteady steps toward her.

Luke leaped to his feet, found the gun and turned toward Zeke. "Forget it, chum."

"Get him, Rhea," Zeke ordered. "Help me, and we'll get out of here."

Unwilling to take any more chances, Luke grabbed Zeke's arm, swung him around and hit him hard on the chin. He watched his face go slack as he fell to the floor with a groan. Turning to Rhea, he held out his hand, but it was as if she didn't see him. Her face devoid of expression, she dropped the gun, turned and walked away.

He would deal with her later, Luke decided. Hurriedly he untied Shay's hands and removed her gag. "Are you hurt?"

Shay coughed, then gathered him close. "No. Thank God you're all right."

"But they're not." Luke knelt alongside Gil and felt his pulse. "Strong. Get some water to pour on him and I think he'll come around." Reaching for the rope, he then pulled Charley's arms behind him and began tying his wrists together before doing the same with Zeke.

Shay heard the sound of approaching horses as she picked up the bucket. "Do you think it's over?" she asked Luke.

"Yeah, I think it's finally over."

A light breeze drifted in through the slanted blinds on Luke's bedroom window along with a liberal sprinkling of moonlight. Walking to the bed, Shay gazed down at the man lying there. "Are you asleep?"

"No. I'm waiting for you—again."

Sitting down at the foot of the bed, Shay slipped off her sandals. "It took Beth a while to fall asleep. Everyone's been so keyed up with all the excitement around here."

"How's Rhea?" Luke asked, watching her undress.

Shay sighed. "Better, I think. Mom and I talked with her for a long while. Some of the things she told me, I can hardly believe."

Slowly she unbuttoned her blouse, angling one leg up and facing him. "Did you know she'd had this terrible crush on you when she was growing up and how jealous she'd been of me, thinking I had everything she didn't?" She touched his arm. "She's the one who took your notes that morning, Luke."

He took her hand, needing the contact. "I'd about figured that out. She was the only suspect left."

"She said she'd only intended to read them, then put them back. But after reading them, she decided that if Mom and I turned against you, then you wouldn't come back and she wouldn't have to be tortured by watching us together." Shay shook her head. "If only I'd have known she was in all that pain."

He'd guessed that Rhea's feelings for him were more than his for her. "Didn't she relax when you left to marry Max?"

"Not until I came back with this failed marriage under my belt. Then she realized that perhaps everything didn't always go well for me."

"But I came back and she saw it starting all over again, is that it?"

"Well, she did leave that note in your kitchen trying to get you to leave, but it was because Zeke had become more restless with you here. She wanted Zeke's attention, his devotion and his love—all of which he denied her." Shay sighed and slipped off her blouse. "She's got a lot of buried feelings to work through. I feel sorry for Rhea."

"So do I."

"What do you think will happen to Zeke?"

Luke trailed his fingertips along her arm and up over her shoulder. "Prison for cattle rustling and attempted murder. Charley, too. I assume Rhea wants to divorce Zeke?"

"Yes, as quickly as possible. He said some terribly cruel things to her. That he married her for her future inheritance, that he never loved her."

"Was that why she finally blew the whistle on him?"

"Partially. She'd seen him under your truck the morning of your accident."

"So that's why she was so upset when I got back from the hospital."

Shay nodded. "And she'd come across the plane's missing logbook where Zeke had hidden it in his dresser. I guess he figured that someone might notice that the plane's actual mileage didn't coincide with the numbers written in the logbook, because of all the secret flights he'd made over the border to this ranch he was setting up. Then yesterday, Rhea heard that it was rat poison intended for you that nearly killed Beth. That finally did it." Shay released a trembling sigh. "I feel so bad for Rhea. All she wanted was for him to love her."

It's what we all want, Luke thought, to be loved.

Shay sighed. "I think I've got her talked into going back to school. She doesn't really like ranching. She needs to find something she does like to do."

"Like you did, with your writing."

She met his eyes. "I should have my manuscript ready to mail off soon."

He'd been expecting that. "I wish you the best of luck in selling it. And one day, when you're rich and famous, we'll all be able to say we knew you when."

The bedside lamp glowed softly, but his face was in shadow, his expression unreadable. "Is that what you think I want?"

Time to tell it like it is, Luke thought. After the commotion at the barn, the men had returned from mending the fence and rounding up the strays. And the sheriff's men had arrived, taking both Charley and Zeke to the hospital under police custody.

Luke and Shay had taken Gil to the big house where Cora had fussed as she tended to his cuts, just as Liz and Jacob returned from their ride. Despite the fact that his face was badly bruised and swollen, Gil would be all right. There'd been much to talk over, then Shay and Liz had walked over to Rhea's while Luke had gone to his cabin to clean up.

Later, all except Rhea had gathered in the dining room for one of Cora's wonderful dinners, but by mutual consent, they'd avoided discussing the events of the day during mealtime. It was best that Beth not know all the gory details. Afterward, Luke had come back here again, telling Shay he'd wait for her. They, too, had much to talk over.

Now she sat beside him, waiting for an answer. But Luke had some questions, too. "What is it you want, Shay?"

She wanted this man. Oh, how she wanted this man. But she would not settle for less than a hundred percent, as her sister had. "I want you, a marriage, Beth, a home of our own."

So far, so good. "I want all that, too. What else?"

"I want to write, to see if I'm good enough to sell. All along, I've wanted to sell for financial independence, not for fame and glory. And..." she dropped her eyes, folding her blouse neatly in her lap, suddenly nervous "...I want to stay in one place."

Luke waited a moment before asking. "You mean in this place, at the Circle M?"

"Not necessarily. I'd go somewhere else. What I mean is, that I want to settle down in *one* spot, not drift around from ranch to ranch. Luke, did you know that Dad really did change his will years ago, that you're to inherit one-fourth of the Circle M?"

Where was this leading? he wondered. "So I've heard. What about it?"

"We could get a loan against that money, use it as collateral perhaps. So we could buy a ranch of our own. Or maybe build one." Speaking from the heart now, she leaned closer down to him. "Oh, Luke, I don't care where it is. I just want it to be ours, and I want us to stay put."

He kissed her nose. "That's exactly what I want, sweetheart." Then he kissed her surprised mouth. Pulling back, Luke laughed. "But we don't need to borrow, and I don't want your father's money. I've already bought a place down in Wyoming." Smiling at her shocked expression, he took a few moments to describe it to her.

"Why didn't you tell me this sooner?"

"Because I thought you would never leave the Circle M." Again he took her hand. "Shay, the place is small. Really nice, but small. And I've only got a few cows so far.

I have to build up a herd. There'd be a lot of work ahead. I . . . well, I'll understand if you don't want to leave all you have here to start over practically from scratch."

She squeezed his hand, her eyes radiant. "I don't care about the Circle M, only the people on it. I want to be with you and Beth."

That brought up another question. "How do you feel about me as a father?"

Her face registered surprise that he needed to ask. "Wonderful, of course. Why do you ask? Look at you with Beth. Already, she adores you."

If Shay had faith in him, then maybe he should believe, also. Believe he'd be good for both Shay and Beth. And believe he would succeed in his ranch. Pride, as Liz had said, can be a lonely bedfellow. "Then I feel good about it."

Shay looked regretful. "But I won't be able to give you children of your own."

Luke's hand slipped down to caress her stomach, remembering she'd told him that the doctor said it would take a minor miracle. "Maybe one day, we'll have that small miracle. When a man loves a woman the way I love you, anything's possible."

Shay felt her eyes fill. "Are you absolutely sure you want all of us, Mr. Turner? A seven-year-old girl, assorted dogs and a woman who's crazy about you?"

Luke raised both hands to frame her face. "I've wanted you to be mine since I was fourteen."

"Then maybe you should ask me."

"Down on one knee, or will this do?"

Her lips twitched. "Since you have a problem knee, this will do."

"All right. If you had only one wish, Shay, what would it be?"

She blinked back the tears. "To be your wife."

"Then, will you marry me?"

"I thought you'd never ask."

"How do you think your mother and father will feel about our getting married?" he asked, his lips nuzzling her neck.

"Like it's a celebration long overdue." With that, she slipped beneath the sheet, wrapped her arms around him and reached to meet his kiss.

* * * * *

**Silhouette Books
is proud to present
our best authors,
their best books…
and the best in
<u>your reading pleasure!</u>**

Throughout 1993, look for exciting books
by these top names in contemporary
romance:

CATHERINE COULTER—
Aftershocks in February

FERN MICHAELS—
Whisper My Name in March

DIANA PALMER—
Heather's Song in March

ELIZABETH LOWELL—
Love Song for a Raven in April

SANDRA BROWN
(previously published under
the pseudonym Erin St. Claire)—
Led Astray in April

LINDA HOWARD—
All That Glitters in May

When it comes to passion,
we wrote the book.

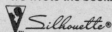

BOBT1R

Take 4 bestselling love stories FREE

Plus get a FREE surprise gift!

Special Limited-time Offer

Mail to Silhouette Reader Service™

3010 Walden Avenue
P.O. Box 1867
Buffalo, N.Y. 14269-1867

YES! Please send me 4 free Silhouette Special Edition® novels and my free surprise gift. Then send me 6 brand-new novels every month, which I will receive months before they appear in bookstores. Bill me at the low price of $2.71* each plus 25¢ delivery and applicable sales tax, if any.* I understand that accepting the books and gift places me under no obligation ever to buy any books. I can always return a shipment and cancel at any time. Even if I never buy another book from Silhouette, the 4 free books and the surprise gift are mine to keep forever.

235 BPA AJCH

Name _____ (PLEASE PRINT)

Address _____ Apt No. _____

City _____ State _____ Zip _____

This offer is limited to one order per household and not valid to present Silhouette Special Edition® subscribers. *Terms and prices are subject to change without notice. Sales tax applicable in N.Y.

USPED-93   ©1990 Harlequin Enterprises Limited

It takes a very special man to win

She's friend, wife, mother—she's you! And beside each Special Woman stands a wonderfully *special* man. It's a celebration of our heroines—and the men who become part of their lives.

Look for these exciting titles from Silhouette Special Edition:

January   **BUILDING DREAMS** by Ginna Gray

February   **HASTY WEDDING** by Debbie Macomber

March   **THE AWAKENING** by Patricia Coughlin

April   **FALLING FOR RACHEL** by Nora Roberts

Dont miss THAT SPECIAL WOMAN! each month—from your special authors.

AND

For the most special woman of all—you, our loyal reader—we have a wonderful gift: a beautiful journal to record all of your special moments. See this month's THAT SPECIAL WOMAN! title for details.

TSW1